★THE LEGEND OF JUAN MIGUEL

ANNA K. SARGENT

Publisher's Note

The Legend of Juan Miguel was published in Austin, Texas, the United States of America, in 2013. All rights reserved by the author. No part of these pages, either text or image, may be used for any purpose without the consent of the author. Reproduction, modification, storage in retrieval systems or retransmission in any form or by any means for reasons other than personal use, is strictly prohibited without written permission.

This is a work of fiction. Names, characters, places, and incidents are either the product of the author's imagination or are used fictitiously. Any resemblance to actual persons, living or dead, business establishments, events, or locales is entirely coincidental.

Cover and interior design by Kathryn Sargent

Marketing by Violet Crown Publishers

Printed and published in the United States of America

ISBN: 978-1-938749-06-3
978-1-938749-07-0

Anna K. Sargent

The Legend of Juan Miguel

By Anna K. Sargent

A Tale Told in Four Parts

Prologue
South Texas, 1882   Page 5

Part One
Texas Six Years Earlier   Page 9

Part Two
Mexico and Texas 1879   Page 153

Part Three
Mexico and Texas 1880   Page 239

Part Four
Mexico and Texas 1881-1882   Page 295

Prologue

A blast of wind like the breath of hell blew up from the coast on the day the infamous outlaw Primo was laid to rest. It roared across the barren land, at times shrieking like a wild beastly phantom, blistering the faces and stinging the eyes of the thousands who came to mourn.

People who were there swore they could smell the ocean even though the del Valle Rancho was more than a hundred miles from the Gulf of Mexico. It was much too early in the year for such intense heat, and any hint of salt air that far inland was unheard of. A full moon, risen at midday and shining as bright as the sun, wove in and out of the clouds as they marched northward, alternately dimming and illuminating it. It was an unforgettable day, one that would be talked about and written about for years to come. It was as if the devil himself, overtaken with jealousy for one so beloved, tried to intrude.

The corners of the altar cloth floated in the breeze, and the ancient delicate linen threatened to escape entirely with every gust. Holding it down were Father Timothy O'Rourke and another priest, wearing the scarlet vestments usually reserved for martyred saints. Behind them, altar boys carried mesquite branches on which grew sprigs of mistletoe, their clusters of white berries signifying the hardened tears of those who grieve.

Throngs of people started to arrive early that morning, and it soon became evident that the small rancho chapel would not accommodate so many. Father O'Rourke moved the funeral mass to a patchy field of buffalo grass and milkweed between the corral and the villa. As the numbers mounted, he asked three of the *vaqueros* to help keep back the crush of mourners. In spite of that, people pushed forward until they were less than a foot from the altar table, as new arrivals strained to hear and see. By midafternoon, the crowd stretched down the road past the rancho's main gate.

On one side were groups of women carrying banners they had painted in red letters reading "*Amor Conquista Todo.*" On the other, closer to the villa, were those who had wagons or horses or mules to ride, mostly *Anglos*. Only those nearest the priests could hear their words, but the others stood waiting in silence and, when they perceived that the Mass was done, started to march *en masse* to the burial site. Once the procession was under way, thousands of feet walking on the dirt road kicked up so much dust that the residents of the town of Poteet ten miles away could see a reddish-brown plume of dirt on the horizon. It streamed in the stiff wind and coiled like Satan's tail.

The first mourners to reach the grave site stood for hours, and by early evening, when the sun had set behind the far mesa, the last of them had arrived. Father O'Rourke sprinkled holy water on the cherrywood casket and its bouquet of wilted cowpen daisies, while a group of whores from a Nuevo Laredo cantina sang a simple Mexican lullaby. Then the priest said the final prayer, followed by sorrowful *aleluyas* rippling outward like waves of grief.

The *vaqueros* lowered the casket using their lariats. Just as it was about to hit bottom, the crowd pushed forward and bumped one of the men, whose rope slipped and snapped. The casket tumbled sideways; the lid caught on the edge of the grave and popped open. People nearby gasped, but at that moment a dust devil barreled through, blowing dirt into their faces and obscuring their view.

"Is that Primo?" one woman shrieked. The priest quickly shut the casket lid and cast her a harsh look, and she shrank back.

In spite of Father O'Rourke's quick actions, a murmur went through the crowd. His hair was black instead of brown, they whispered. His face was not beautiful. His skin was too dark. The man they mourned had used many identities and guises throughout his life. Was this just another of his performances? Thus began the many conspiracy theories surrounding Primo and his death.

Mourners had come from as far south as Monterrey,

Mexico, as far north as Denver, from New York and Chicago and New Orleans just to pay their respects on that day, the day before Easter 1882. Matthew Piper, a prominent writer, was among them. Later, he wrote about the true story of the funeral and the person who received the outpouring of love, and, as a result, the story became part of Texas lore.

# Part One

Texas Six Years Earlier

Chapter 1

On the morning of the annual *corrida*, long before the sun rose, Juan Miguel lay in his bed trying to imagine the perfect way to win Senora Barone's admiration. Perhaps he could take on the role of a *vaquero*, borrow the necessary weathered chaps and greasy sombrero, neglect to shave his beard—such as it was—and adopt a disdainful, steely-eyed expression. No, not that. Perhaps she would be more impressed by his education. He could slick back his hair, perch a pair of spectacles on his nose, and discuss opera. He had attended one when he was in Monterrey last year. Of course, he had hardly paid attention, but she wouldn't know that. Then it occurred to him: A feat of unbelievable daring and athletic prowess would better win her favor. Riding a bronco, doing it well, she would notice that.

His mind drifted to the image of Senora Barone, as it had most of the night. It was a bit dangerous, thinking about Senora Barone. It could lead to flirting with her, and flirting with her could lead to being with her, and that could lead to trouble, because, after all, she was Senora Barone, a married woman.

She was older, yes, but her long red hair, the color of cherrywood, her heart-shaped face, and the tiny pink birthmark on her cheek, right underneath her left eye, consumed his thoughts. She had a comical husky voice and a high-pitched silly laugh. He couldn't help but think about what it would be like to be close to her—how she would smell or feel next to him.

The sight of her was stuck in his mind. He began to sweat. He put his forearm over his eyes and sighed. There was no going back to sleep this morning.

He had other things to think about—the horse races, the roping, the bronco riding later in the day—things he looked forward to every *corrida*. This year, for the first time, he would compete with his father's *vaqueros* against another ranch.

He lectured himself in the manner of his father, telling himself not to think of Senora Barone as a woman but, instead, to think of her as another man's wife, the wife of his father's rival. If he could go back to not thinking of her at all, he would.

Juan Miguel sprang from bed, bounded down the villa's staircase, rushed out the door, and leapt up on the corral fence with no hat, his shirttail flopping around his trousers, and his light curly hair still matted to the back of his head. He swung his boots over and balanced himself on the top board, preparing to watch the sun inch its way over the row of mesquites beyond the stables.

Everyone assumed he would marry Amara Bastille someday. Last summer, when he announced to his aunt, Marina Estella, that he was in love with Amara, she asked him point-blank, "Which one of you is in love, *Senor Farsante*? All of you or just one of you?" Then she chuckled and patted his cheek. "Such an innocent ... *hermosa mia.*"

"All, *tía*," he said. "All of me this time."

"Well, well, this is serious then," she said. "Tell me all the details of your many romantic trysts." Even at eighty, she had a teasing way with men. But there had been no trysts, and he couldn't remember now the details of the infatuation, because that's what it was—infatuation. Amara went out of his mind and his heart the day he turned seventeen.

And it was Senora Barone who lodged herself there. Juan Miguel had known her since he was a small boy, but he only noticed her last year. For some reason he didn't fully understand, Senora Barone dwelt in his mind since the day of his birthday, when he saw her standing on a San Antonio street corner, waiting for a public hack. He couldn't help noticing that she looked resolute and somewhat lost at the same time—like someone who does a bit of playacting. When the carriage pulled up and she stepped up to get inside, her foot slipped and she caught herself.

Then she stepped back and tried again, her hands visibly shaking. He had never seen anyone look so alone. He rushed forward to assist her, but the hack pulled away in the opposite direction, leaving him to run down the street after her. He ran for blocks before he realized what he was doing. Looking back on it—and he did look back on it often—he didn't know why he ran after her as he did. He was embarrassed even thinking about it. Through the hack's hazy window, for some reason he saw her clearly, the way her cheeks sloped severely to a pointy chin. She turned her head and looked into his eyes. What must she have thought?

———————

Finally, it appeared. A small tip of the sun squeezed itself between two trees. The *vaqueros* drifted into the stable to prepare for the competition. It was about time for him to see to his own horse.

Just inside the stable, Pedro waited for him, a huge silver-studded black sombrero in hand. He stuck it on Juan Miguel's head and stepped back to look at him.

"It suits you, *poco.*"

The other *vaqueros* gathered round, expectant looks on their faces. He shoved the sombrero over his eyes and strapped a holstered pistol across his chest. He clomped around the horse stall with his legs bowed, his chin stuck out, and his face scrunched up with a wad of tobacco he stuffed in his jaw. "*Ai, ai, ai, ai, Canta y no llores,*" he sang in a slurred voice. Soon they were all singing along, getting louder and louder on the *Ai, ai, ai* part.

They stopped singing suddenly and looked over his shoulder, beyond him. He turned around and saw Senora Barone standing there behind him with his aunt, her eyes wide and her hands all fluttery the way they were sometimes when she was nervous. Her red hair blazed around her face.

"You remember Juan Miguel, the don's youngest son," Tía Marina said to Senora Barone, and she winked at him.

"Of course. It was years ago," Senora Barone said to him. "You were gawky and bashful, *un niño*, and now look at you. You are ..." She shook her head in disbelief, but she stopped talking without finishing her sentence.

He felt himself flush. The two women walked on, and he was left to his humiliation. The *vaqueros* looked on him with pity in their eyes, turned their backs, and drifted away.

The half-finished sentence echoed in his skull and rolled around in his brain. She still saw him as a boy, didn't she? He vowed he would make up for the sorry scene and impress her with his riding later that day. Although the vow was sincere, it wasn't a conscious vow. It lived in the inner recesses of his soul.

———————————

The morning horse race didn't turn out the way Juan Miguel hoped. His horse was slow, and then when it came time to ride the broncos, he was nervous and ill at ease. He kept looking for Senora Barone, hoping she had not abandoned the rodeo and gone inside. When he caught sight of her red hair, it was only a flash, but he felt a burst of confidence knowing she was still there.

Easing himself slowly onto the bronco's bare back, he did as the *vaqueros* had taught him, flexing the fingers of his left hand slightly to shift it a bit farther underneath the leather handle of the braided strap, then pulled the rope over his hand and behind his wrist, securing himself to the handle. He scooted up, so the handle was nearly touching his groin, and leaned forward. He looked at Pedro, one of the best of the villa's bronco riders and his principal teacher, for reassurance. Pedro was crouched next to him on the wood fence, reaching over the railing, inspecting the rope to make sure it was tight.

"Remember to bend your knees and dig in," Pedro said, trying to make himself heard over the yelling. "Keep your weight on your legs."

Juan Miguel was not a novice rider. He had been riding bucking broncos for three years, since he was fourteen, against the wishes of his father and his aunt. He could see both of them now at the back of the circle of *vaqueros*, waiting anxiously for the whole thing to be over. His father had his hand up to his face, loosely covering his mouth, ready to stifle a shout, and his aunt crossed herself repeatedly.

The bronco, Francisco, was almost all white with only a few dark brown spots on his rump. He was well past a yearling, one of the edgy, hot-tempered ones, and was known to be nasty. He also smelled nasty, Juan Miguel noted, just before he looked at the *vaquero* holding the gate and nodded for him to open it.

When the gate swung out, Francisco did his duty and bucked, twisted, leapt, and reared wildly. Juan Miguel lurched up and down, trying to follow the motions of the horse. But his chest went one way and his legs another. His hand slipped through the strap. He rode for what seemed like minutes, but was only seconds, before sliding off one side and flipping over backwards, rolling on his shoulder onto the hard ground.

Pedro rushed over and pulled him up by the back of his shirt toward the fence, away from the horse. His shirt was torn and his shoulder bruised and cut, but he hardly noticed, because his exhilaration momentarily erased all pain. He searched the crowd for Senora Barone and his eyes met hers, but they were not the eyes of someone who was impressed. The words "gawky and bashful" repeated in his head. Again, he felt humiliated.

To make things worse, his aunt rushed up to him and put her hands on his face to make sure it was still intact. She looked into his eyes with relief.

"*Hermosa mia*," she cooed, "my precious." Juan Miguel was so fair, she had nicknamed him *hermosa mia*—my beautiful one—as a child, and the name stuck.

And then his father shouted, "*Basta*. You have shown you can ride the horse. Now that is enough."

Don Emiliano motioned to Pedro, chopping downward with his hand, meaning Juan Miguel was to ride no more that day.

Pedro nodded.

"*Bien hecho*," Pedro called to him over his shoulder.

But he hadn't done well. Compared to the vaqueros, he was slow and graceless. He admired how they nearly floated atop the broncos. They knew how to ride and they knew how to fall, both important skills.

He felt his chances to please Senora Barone slipping through his fingers like the leather strap.

———

This year, when it had come time for Don Emiliano del Valle to invite *vaqueros* from another rancho to his *corrida*, he made an exception. For the first time, he invited an *Anglo* rancher to compete. In what he hoped would be an act of reconciliation, he asked the hands of Ben Barone, because a rivalry was brewing between the two men. Don Emiliano was the third-generation owner of the largest ranch in South Texas, nearly a quarter of a million acres of rolling hills, mesquite brushes, and flat pastures in Atascosa County. In 1775, his grandfather, Cameron del Valle, received the original land grant from the Spanish Crown, and because the del Valle family had few heirs, the huge tract of land had remained intact.

The old don put all his hopes for the rancho's future on his youngest son, Juan Miguel. His other sons, Jorge and Carlos, were considerably older, born to Emiliano's first wife, who died young. Juan Miguel was the son of his second wife, the daughter of a wealthy Monterrey landholder. It was from her that Juan Miguel inherited his good looks, the light brown hair and eyes. Much to his father's dismay, he also inherited her talent for performing, her passion for writing skits and roping her friends and family into acting in them. She had enlisted Juan Miguel at an early age.

When he was only eight, his family dubbed him *Senor Farsante*, Mr. Phony, a nickname that grew out of his impressive performance one winter evening when he impersonated Senora Menendez, his nanny and tutor, with a little help from a housemaid who lent him some of her clothing. He had the prissy mannerisms down pat, and the squeaky voice, but it was his imitation of the involuntary twitching of her left cheek that proved so convincing. No one could figure out how he did it.

Not amused, his father said it was "disrespectful" and promised to lash him at some point in the future—a promise he promptly forgot.

Egged on by the obvious admiration of the *vaqueros* and housemaids, he went on to imitate his older brothers, both of whom had the misfortune of being extremely bowlegged, in scathing but inventive retribution for years of teasing about his beautiful face and curly locks. His ridicule would have been funny had it not been so accurate. Other impersonations and made-up characters followed. His family looked on with admiration, then growing concern, as his playacting ability grew, until gradually, as he approached manhood, they became resigned to it.

The day after the *corrida*, Don Emiliano instructed Juan Miguel instead of his brothers to accompany him to San Antonio and help him recover some horses stolen from the del Valle and Barone ranches. Up to this point, the old don and Ben Barone had been friendly rivals who had an unspoken agreement to watch each other's backs, especially when it came to the recent epidemic of stolen livestock. The two ranchers knew exactly where they would find their stolen horses—San Antonio, a crossroads for many things, but especially for horse trading. The city had become the largest horse-trading market in the world.

Juan Miguel saw the trip as an opportunity to redeem himself in Senora Barone's eyes. He would readily admit that the day of the rodeo was no *buen dia* for him. His propensity for playacting that day in the stable had backfired when he had pretended to be a cowboy. But he remained determined, and the memory of Senora Barone's words that morning in the stable stayed with him, spurring him on.

He also considered it auspicious that they would be visiting the city on *Dia de los Muertos*, which was marked by a

Procession of the Dead in downtown San Antonio. The perfect disguise for catching a horse thief came to Juan Miguel that morning when he put on his *calacas* mask for the procession. He had asked his friend, Father Moreno, to lend him one of the voluminous brown cassocks of the Marianists so that he blended in with the other marchers, who were mostly dressed in ghostly regalia.

Leading the procession was a rotund woman with a mask painted on half her face and a garland of red roses in her hair. She waved the bamboo skeleton of an open parasol as she sang "*La Cancion del Mole*" and skipped, stepping forward three times, then back once. He followed along in his priest costume, clapping and whistling with everyone else. Next to him marched Father Moreno, whose life as a traveling priest in the Medina River Valley and south into the scrubby prairies inland from the gulf coast was a lonely existence. Father Moreno craved company, so he used just about any excuse to come to the city. The priest looked as he always looked, ruddy-faced and well fed but beatific. He was a man given to excess in drink and food as well as caring. And one of those he cared most about was Juan Miguel.

Dia de los Muertos always made Juan Miguel think of his mother. The wooden *calacas,* the traditional skull mask, was a gift from her. She had given it to him for Christmas when he was eleven, the year before she died. She had had a foreboding, he realized later. She sensed what was coming, and she wanted him to know she understood him. She understood the desire to play, to pretend, to take on another's identity. Only a few months later—in the early spring—she bled to death after a miscarriage. Although he was almost a grown man, he still longed for her, especially on this day, the day many believed the dead returned for a visit.

They marched all the way down Market Street and beyond. For Juan Miguel, it was a relief to get lost in the procession and let himself be lulled by the steady drumming. He could put away the upcoming tasks for a while and indulge his greatest pleasure—being someone else.

On the way to San Antonio, Don Emiliano and Juan Miguel had argued, not about Juan Miguel's plan to confront the horse thief and take back the stolen horses, but about the task Don Emiliano had given Juan Miguel that evening. It was nothing new for the don to ask his son to take on social responsibilities. He had done so many times before. The bone of contention was Senora Barone. Juan Miguel was to return to the hotel early, bathe, and dress in his finest, then escort his aunt and Senora Barone to dinner, entertaining them while the don talked business. Juan Miguel wanted to see Senora Barone again—he longed for redemption—but to be stuck with her for an entire evening? What would he think of to say? How would he entertain her?

Chapter 2

For the horse trader Raul Benavides, the Day of the Dead started out well: a pleasant morning in early November, with the sun shining down through air as clear as crystal, a faint breeze blowing from the north, and more people than usual in the city to celebrate the holiday. He sold three horses and bought two and pocketed enough cash to buy more. Then something began to nag at him. A priest who accompanied Father Moreno to the horse trading on Flores Street strode around looking at horses, inspecting them, patting them on the rump. He walked with his weight on his heels and gestured with slow, careful hand movements, as priests do, but the hood of his cassock was pulled down over his face. Raul Benavides knew there had to be a reason he was hiding his identity, so he slipped behind this horse and that horse to avoid the stranger's gaze.

Then someone behind him whispered close to his ear, "Do you wish to confess something, *senor*?" and the old horse trader felt the unmistakable sensation of the barrel of a pistol flush against his rib cage.

"*¿Que ... que?*" he said, sputtering a wad of spittle all over his own chin.

"You are a horse thief, the lowest of the low ... *el cabron.*" The voice was loud now and full of bravado but breaking slightly as it wavered between a deep croak and a smooth tenor. It was the voice of someone who's not quite used to the one and hasn't let go of the other.

Somehow, Raul Benavides caught a glimpse of the man behind him, just enough to confirm his suspicion that it was the priest he had watched all morning out of the corner of his eye.

"*Me doy por vencido,*" Benavides said. "You have got me." He tried to jerk forward and break free, but a strong arm caught hold of him and pulled him back.

Then the priest began to laugh—a full-throated offensive laugh. He stepped back, wheeled Raul Benavides around to face him, and pointed the pistol just above his nose, between his eyes. The hood fell back to reveal a wooden *calacas* mask painted with a white and black skeleton face. Benavides thought he remembered seeing it that morning at the Procession of the Dead.

"Let us sit down in the shade, Senor Benavides, and become the best of friends," the priest said, his words muffled but clear behind the mask. "And you can tell me how you came to be a *tonto*. That is a fine tale, eh?"

The priest pushed Benavides and pushed him again toward a sagging willow tree across the road. He pushed him down hard onto the dirt and stood over him. Reaching behind his head, he pulled at the clump of curls at the base of his neck and let his long hair fall free. Slowly, he raised the front of his cassock, exposing a pair of worn leather leggings and a holster strapped across his chest.

"You see, *senor*, I am not what I appear to be," the priest said. "Unfortunately for you, I am worse. I am *El Malo*, *senor*—a demon." He began to laugh again, so hard that Raul Benavides felt the red hot sting of humiliation come over him. To make matters worse, the crowd of *vaqueros* gathered around them stomped their boots on the hard-packed dirt and hooted and hissed. He attempted to stand up, but the priest pushed him down.

"Who are you, then?" Benavides managed to mumble.

"They call me *Senor Farsante*, my friend."

The priest bent down, lifted off the mask, and looked him in the face. His smile was insolent. He had fuzz for a beard and smooth skin the color of milk chocolate. But he looked menacing nonetheless.

"That is all you need to know. Now, down to business, *senor*. Where did you get the horses you are selling here today?"

"I bought them from another trader. That is all, *senor*."

"Perhaps this trader was one of the *bandidos* from across the border, eh? Perhaps you are in cahoots with them."

"I am just a horse trader, *senor*, not a *bandido*."

"Well, you see, my friend," the priest said, the smile gone now, "three of them are my father's horses, stolen only two weeks ago from our rancho. Three of them belong to the Barone rancho, and I recognize two others as well. So, this presents a problem."

"What do you want?"

"I want you to swing from this tree, but it is too small to hold a *gordo* like you."

"Take the horses," Raul Benavides said. "But someone else stole them, not me. I am not a horse thief."

"Oh, I will take the horses, *senor*, and you will ride away and never come back. No more horse stealing and no more horse trading for you, *senor*. You may as well ride north to the Comanches, because you are not welcome here."

Benavides stood, took off his wide-brimmed hat, tamped it against his thigh and put it back on his head.

"I will need a horse," he said.

"Father Moreno has a mount for you." The priest pointed with his revolver at the older priest holding the reins of a run-down, ragged-looking burro. "Safe journeys, *senor*," he said in a singsong manner. "Luck be with you when you meet the Comanches." He drew out the word Comanches and made it sound like a death sentence.

Raul Benavides mounted the burro, and, stripped of his manhood, his feet almost dragging in the dust, he rode north. Behind him, the *vaqueros* laughed and brayed like a donkey.

When the young priest was sure the horse trader was well out of town, he covered his face again with the skull mask and walked over to Father Moreno.

"Meet *El Malo*, father," he said.

"*Si*, you are a demon, Juan Miguel," Father Moreno said, shaking his head. "Come back from the dead." It was a joke, but Father Moreno didn't laugh. Juan Miguel was more convincing as a demon than the old priest cared to admit.

"Your father waits for you," Father Moreno said, nodding to the spot across the road where the old don stood with Senor and Senora Barone. "Go to them, and I will stable the horses."

"No, father, I cannot let them see me like this ... not dressed as a priest."

"Is that so bad?"

"No ... no, not bad ... just not alluring."

Father Moreno shook his head slowly and looked heavenward. "The follies of the young," he thought, "will they never end?" But he said, "You must go to them. Your father has instructed me."

"No, father, no, I cannot," Juan Miguel said with his head ducked down as if he were suddenly shy, although Father Moreno knew he had never been shy. He started to protest, but Juan Miguel had slipped out of sight.

———————

A stiff north wind suddenly kicked up, and the noise in

the plaza made the horses restless. They would stop and duck and start to dance sideways, their manes flowing across their eyes. The aroma of onions and garlic wafted up from the chili stands in the market where the old *abuelas* cooked their tamales and enchiladas for tourists. Juan Miguel's stomach churned, but he needed to save his appetite for the evening, for dinner with the Barones. He would need it, along with a cool head.

He stopped his horse and dismounted, then checked the tethers on the line of horses. The wind whipped the American flag over the Alamo, snapping it smartly. Juan Miguel remembered the mission only as a military headquarters. His father remembered the battle and the aftermath, the old Spanish families losing ground as *Anglos* began to predominate. His father had seen five flags fly over the mission, but he insisted that the city still had an "*Espanola del Corazon— un alma buena.*"

Juan Miguel had never seen as many people marching in the Procession of the Dead as he did that morning—the usual *mestizos*, the common people of mixed Indian and European descent, and *Tejanos*, the old Spanish families. But this time there was also a sprinkling of *Anglos* lining the streets as spectators. San Antonio was just waking up from its sleepy Spanish colonial roots. For 150 years, the town had revolved around the missions, but now newcomers brought new life to the old city. A revival of sorts was under way—an *Anglo* revival. The city's Spanish roots were becoming overshadowed by the influx of Americans, but the city retained its charm nonetheless. The most powerful people in the state—businessmen, politicians, writers, lawyers, and ranchers—still congregated at the Menger Hotel or met for drinks at one of the many saloons or haggled over prices at the market.

Juan Miguel could see that things were changing, and he blamed Ben Barone and others like him for that. Senora Barone, though, she was another story. However much he disliked Barone, his wife was blameless. Juan Miguel knew he had been rude to the Barones at the horse trading, and he regretted it. His father, standing there with his floppy old hat in his hand, had looked small standing next to Barone. The old don was one of the ranchers who often congregated at the Menger Hotel, but he was *Tejano*, not *Anglo*, and this made him different in their eyes.

"Loosen, loosen, loosen. ...," Pedro said. "Give them some rope."

Juan Miguel chuckled at the *vaqueros* behind him arguing over who got which whore at Madam Caldwell's—as if they actually got to choose.

"We will be so grateful, we won't even remember their faces," Juan Miguel yelled back at them.

"What do you mean 'we'?" Pedro said. "You won't be there, *poco*."

Juan Miguel looked downcast. Pedro slapped him gently on the back. "Someday ... we will take you someday."

Pedro had been saying someday for months. Juan Miguel continued to hope but suspected it would never happen.

Sometimes they allowed him to accompany them to the whorehouses in Bandera, but they only allowed him to watch the dancing. Pedro told the whores not to touch him.

If only for a while, he would celebrate with them at the Silver Elephant. No doubt they would buy him a drink or two and tell stories about his bravery at facing Raul Benavides. His father's *vaqueros* indulged him like companions but kept their distance like teachers. They had taught him the right position to sit atop a bronco, how to knot and lasso with a lariat, how to ride a horse at full speed, becoming one with the rhythm of the rocking gait. He watched them and mimicked their actions—holding their tongues and saying nothing they didn't mean, standing ground, bearing pain without complaint. In truth, they acted as surrogates for his father, who had grown old and weak. But about one thing, his father was right. He was not one of them.

Pedro's voice became stern. "Anyway, your father expects you. Only one drink, then on your way."

The sun had just set behind the buildings along the riverbank when Juan Miguel returned to the hotel, hours after he sent the horse thief on his way. In his room, he found his father, standing in the fading light by the window. The old don had waited for his son, trying to remain patient. He knew well when Juan Miguel was avoiding his responsibilities.

But his old heart melted when Juan Miguel put his arm

around his shoulders. Don Emiliano was almost a foot shorter than his son and seemed to have shrunk so much the past few years that his fine clothes hung on him. Juan Miguel kissed him on his white hair.

"*Padre, te quiero*," Juan Miguel said. "Don't be anxious, papa, I am with you. I will do as you ask. Go on and talk your ranch business."

The father, who found it difficult to be angry with his son, patted him on his face. Juan Miguel's pure heart shone through his eyes like a beacon.

"With the *vaqueros*, my son?"

"*Si*, padre … just a little celebration … un *poco*."

"The *vaqueros*, they are the best, but you are not one of them … *comprende*? You are different, a son of the del Valle family, which came here a hundred years ago and is venerated. …"

"*Si, padre*, I know this well. You tell me often."

"There will come a time … maybe not so far away … when I will entrust you with the del Valle rancho and the del Valle name."

"*Si*, I know this."

"Captain Barone is powerful. You must learn to deal with him … become his friend … there is no other way."

Don Emiliano slumped in the chair by the window. Juan Miguel sat down on the bed opposite him and prepared to hear the speech he had heard at least a hundred times. Out of respect, he acted attentive even though he knew it already and could recite it almost word for word.

When Don Emiliano was through, he stood up on two wobbly legs and fluffed his son's hair.

"Playing … playing … always playing," Don Emiliano said. "There comes a time for every man to forget about the playing and take responsibility on himself. That time is coming for you, my son, earlier than for others. I'm sorry for you it is this way."

He put his ancient hand under Juan Miguel's chin, lifted it and looked into the pale brown eyes, the eyes of his second wife, Christina.

"I have only you standing between the rancho and those who wish to accuse us and take away the rancho."

"I understand, *padre*," Juan Miguel said. "I will win over the wife … and the husband, if that is what is required, but …"

"But what? You have certain feelings when it comes to the wife? Tía Marina has told me."

"*Ai, ai, ai*, I told her in confidence."

"It doesn't matter as long as you rule the emotion rather than letting it rule you. Never succumb to feelings of tenderness. They will lead you down dark alleys …"

Juan Miguel turned his face away and kept his voice low although his heart was coming out of his chest. "Not feelings of tenderness, *padre*," he said.

"I see you are obsessed with her. It is plain to everyone."

"No, *padre*, not obsessed … just determined she should see me differently."

Don Emiliano constantly warned him against feelings of

tenderness even though he himself had the tenderest of souls, not very well hidden under a formal manner and forced resolve. The old don started to walk out of the room, then turned and faced Juan Miguel.

"You are the one, my son, the one who must charm his wife and convince her of our friendship. I am counting on you to do this while I talk to the husband about his suspicions."

"Why does he suspect us? We have shown our faithfulness. We don't harbor *bandidos*. That would be against our own self-interest. Tell him that."

"Because we are *Tejano*, that is why. Now, go prepare yourself. You must make a good impression on her." His father crept toward the door looking as if the day's events had already exhausted him. Then he turned and said one last thing. "You must be yourself this evening. No one else. It is time to put aside the playacting and become a man."

For Margaret Barone, a small act of defiance was enough. It had to be. She couldn't afford anything more. A small act like slumping in public instead of standing at attention or like refusing to laugh when the stories were no longer funny or like taking her dog to dinner or deliberately keeping the son of the old don waiting. She stood on the hotel stairs, the dog yapping at impatient guests as they eased past. She ran her eyes over the ornate carvings on the railings that swirled overhead to the domed ceiling and the floor-to-ceiling windows that were thwarting the headwind of a powerful storm. But inside the lobby, the hotel's splendor stayed serenely in place. She enjoyed the heady sensation of her freedom to observe, if only for an instant.

From across the lobby, she didn't recognize the young man she had watched at the rodeo riding broncos in a torn shirt and dirty boots. Then she realized who he was. On the lobby's black and white tile floor, he stood perfectly spaced between the Corinthian columns, looking as if the building had been built around him, just to frame him. It was a grand building, one of the grandest in Texas. It diminished many a man, but not him. He was dressed in a black suit—a tailored suit—and his long curls spilled over the jacket and down his back. He winced as he tried flexing his shoulder, then reached up carefully and pulled his hair back from his forehead.

That morning, in his genteel way, Don Emiliano had warned her about his son. He had a special gift his family called *desconcertar*, a word that literally meant throwing but actually meant confusing or bewildering. Just as some people can throw their voices, he could throw his whole being, the don said. "I try to discourage him, but he is incorrigible. He can be quite disarming. You must not let him get away with these games at dinner, *senora*."

However much it irritated his father, the gift gave Juan Miguel the ability to appear at home. He seemed to fit in everywhere with everyone. He called on that gift this evening, and she saw that as she approached and took his hand. The old don's warning went out of her head.

"May I escort you to dinner, *senora*?" he said.

"So you are not a bronco rider ... nor a priest. What, then?"

"I am Juan Miguel del Valle, *senora*. I am yours for the evening."

Her left eyebrow lifted slightly and she smiled a tiny, mysterious smile.

———————

The cherrywood hair was not ordinary hair. It spiraled out in all directions with no plan or purpose. He saw nothing else. Not the concierge standing next to him trying to get his attention. Not the strange-looking tiny white dog she pulled along. Not the heat lightning flashing outside the windows, warning of a storm to come.

A cool breeze rushed through the lobby every time the hotel doors were opened, flapping her black cape, exposing a lacy blouse underneath. Without thinking, he patted the cape back into place as he escorted her across the room. She was not dressed immodestly, but the combination of hair, eyes, and just enough skin was seductive. Behind the protection of her bushy hair was a canny expression. Under that, behind the blue-green eyes, she held a great mystery, the mystery only a woman knows.

Was it just that afternoon he'd felt deprived? Was it only

hours ago he'd complained?

Then suddenly the dog started jumping and tugging on the leash in Senora Barone's hands, pulling her forward.

"Something is spooking him," she said.

He reached across and took hold of the leash. "*Calma … calma … esta bien*," he soothed and pulled the leash up tight. "*Senora*, it is only the spirits. They are restless today—the Day of the Dead. They intend no harm."

"I have heard that the ghosts come out on this day."

"*Si*, they say it is so, but they are only dead, *senora*, not evil. Evil is done by the living."

He handed her the leash, and when he did, she let go and the dog took off across the lobby, pulling her black cape to the floor. He picked it up quickly and ran to catch her dog. When he returned to her, she was shivering, her arms crossed over her breasts and her wild hair almost covering her face. He spoke to the dog again, and this time the tone was stern.

"*¡Sientate! … ¡sientate! … amigo,*" which made the dog sit.

He put the leash firmly in her two hands and then wrapped the cape around her shoulders.

"*Gracias,*" she said, looking bewildered. "I didn't know he spoke Spanish."

"It's not the words, *senora*. It's the confidence in the voice he understands."

"But what of the spirits?"

"They will be still, I promise. They have had their fun with you."

At dinner, Juan Miguel tried not to stare at Senora Barone's long red corkscrews, pulled up with a mauve ribbon and flowing down her back, or obsess over the movements of her hands. Her two diamond rings sparked in the candlelight. The one on the little finger of her right hand looked like a two-headed snake. It slithered around her finger every time her hand moved.

She was so fidgety that he was tempted to find a lasso and tie her down. He watched in amazement as she drummed her fingers on the table, pulled at the strands of hair falling over her face, and smoothed her skirt over and over again until she nearly wore grooves in the material. Just when he thought she was going to settle down, she rearranged the dishes on the table and even rearranged the food on her plate. He found himself worrying about what she would do next.

Then without warning, she excused herself, stood up, and cast an angry look in his direction. He didn't know what to say. She didn't return to the table for almost a half hour. Juan Miguel looked at the doorway every fifteen seconds, waiting for her return, trying mightily to uphold his end of the conversation.

The other diners, Ben Barone and Don Emiliano, were intent on talking ranching, comparing notes on their herds and their plans. Barone's conversation droned on—talk of the price of cattle, the markets in Kansas, and the best places to hire men.

When the meal was eaten and he was left with the two women at table, Juan Miguel felt flushed, but he was adept at keeping his composure in polite company. His aunt, Marina Estella, had a habit of falling asleep at dinner. She would eat almost nothing, have two glasses of wine then nap while others finished their dessert. Juan Miguel hoped she would not do that to him this evening, that she would not leave him alone with the *senora*. But shortly after dessert was served, Tía Marina's eyes closed and her head bowed. She looked up one last time and uttered, "*hermosa mia, seguir*," before going solidly to sleep.

"She calls you *hermosa mia?*" Senora Barone asked. "Does that mean beautiful one?"

He felt his face turn red. He felt the sweat soaking his blouse. "*Si*, my family torments me with numerous pet names. It is the curse of the youngest, I am afraid, *senor*a."

"An apt name," she said. Again, the raised eyebrow.

"Tell me about the Day of the Dead, please," she said, holding her fork—with a piece of pastry balanced on it—in midair as if she forgot it. The pastry teetered precariously and then plopped without ceremony onto the tablecloth. She seemed not to notice.

"*Senor*a, it is a holiday they say we borrowed from the Aztecs. Have you not seen the *Catrina* skulls in their red wedding gowns at market?"

"And you believe the dead souls come out on this day?" she asked, placing her fork very carefully on top of the spilled pastry.

"*Si, senora*, they come out, and they are sometimes sneaky."

"Sneaky?"

"They play tricks with those of us who are still living, perhaps to get a little revenge," he said. "They can sometimes play with the emotions and lead one astray."

Juan Miguel glanced at her hands pulling at a stray piece of bread. He was about to say more when she reached her hand across the table, picked up her wineglass and took a sip, then held the glass at her chin. The red wine stained and moistened her lips. Her expression seemed as wild as the fidgeting had been. Her hand touched his when she set the glass by his plate, and her skin felt electric, as if some force of nature were coursing through her body.

"*Senora*, are you angry or upset?" he asked. "I cannot tell which."

"You have made me feel embarrassed, and it is deliberate," she said.

"*Senora*, I do not know what I have done."

"Did you not mean to touch my hand?" she gasped, looking at him like someone caught in a lie.

"No ... *senora*."

"*Perdoneme, senor*," she said standing suddenly and looking shy.

"*Senora*," he said as he stood. His eyes watched her intently as she left the room. She looked flustered and red-faced. Her right hand pulled at her hair ribbon and her left pushed the strands away from her face. She gives herself away with her hands, he thought.

"Go after her, my son," his aunt said, suddenly waking. "Your father would not approve."

He found her outside, standing under an overhang, watching the rain obscure the dark courtyard. She stared at nothing.

"*Senora*, I am profoundly sorry to have offended you," he said, walking up behind her. "Will you forgive me, *por favor*?"

At that moment, the loud voice of her husband coming from the hotel bar next to the patio intruded, and they both turned in that direction. He said something about ranching prices being deflated, about his problems with Mexican raiders. His tone was accusatory. The two ranch owners were engaged in a verbal duel. Don Emiliano had been caught off guard by Ben Barone's attitude and was at a disadvantage because of the limitations of his English and his naturally sanguine demeanor. He knew right away he should have invited his youngest son, the one with the quick mind and quick tongue, to be in the room. But he had dispatched him on another errand for just those qualities.

"Do we not have an agreement to return branded cattle?" Don Emiliano asked. "Have I not always lived up to this agreement?"

"Maybe," Barone retorted, "but how do I know you're not spiriting away some of my cattle to the no man's land north of the border to be picked up by Mexicans and taken south?"

"*Senor*, you do not have proof of this because it never

happens," Don Emiliano said, not sounding particularly convincing.

"I need your assurance, sir, that you will return every last head of my cattle," Barone said in an overly loud tone.

"You have my word, *senor*." The voice of Don Emiliano, who had been ill for months, was weak and unsure, although he was known to be a trustworthy man.

Juan Miguel could see that Senora Barone felt embarrassed by the confrontation. "*Senora*, we should go inside and not overhear something we don't understand," he said.

She looked at him with defiance and ignored his suggestion. "I am reminded of the courtyard at your family's villa, especially the banana trees. How does your aunt manage to grow them? I've never been able to."

"She is determined to have a patio like the one she had as a child in Mexico. She is my mother's aunt, really. She grew up on an estate in Monterrey, which I suppose was quite grand. As she gets older, she remembers it more and more fondly."

An uncomfortable silence fell between them. Grasping at anything to fill it, he said, "She sometimes sends me on long trips to get the plants she wants. I went to Monterrey just last fall to find the kalanchoes. She wanted the yellow ones, in particular."

"You surprise me," Senora Barone said. Perhaps she was expecting the spoiled son of the wealthy *Tejano* to be indifferent to the needs of his elderly aunt.

"You went all the way to Monterrey just to fetch a plant?"

"*Si, por supuesto*, senora, for my *tía*. She loves to teach about the plants, and I seem to be her only willing pupil. I think she also hoped I would meet a nice young lady while I was there."

"And did you?" she asked cautiously. "Did you meet a nice young lady?"

"No, I did not. I mean, of course, I met many nice ladies, but no one to marry. There was no one like you, I can promise you that."

She smiled at him with an indulgent look. "You don't owe me a promise, *senor*. And you are too young to marry. Much too young."

He took her elbow and said, "I must bring you back to my *tía,* or there will be no end to her scolding."

"Before we go in, I wish to ask you something." She spoke in a whispery voice he could barely hear.

"Please, *senora*, ask me."

"When you were confronting the horse thief at the market …"

"Yes, *senora*, what about it?"

"Were you not afraid?"

"Sometimes it is easier to be someone else. It makes me bold. For instance … times like this, when I have promised to be myself and win your favor … it is a little bit scary."

A look of tenderness appeared on her face. Her heart softened right before his eyes. Unbelievably, she reached out her hand and put it on his forearm, then snatched it back quickly.

In the days after the trip to San Antonio, Juan Miguel thought about Senora Barone even more. His feelings for her were unbidden and unwanted. But he longed to see her again nonetheless. Hope was fading until one morning after breakfast, Don Emiliano introduced the subject of a second trip to San Antonio before his son had a chance to slip out the door and ride off with the *vaqueros*. He asked Juan Miguel to travel to the city, meet again with Ben Barone at the Menger Hotel, and help him find hands for the spring roundup.

"Why are we aiding our adversary?" Juan Miguel asked in a respectful tone.

"He is convinced we mean him harm, that we are in cahoots with the raiders. We must show him our good faith and keep his suspicion at bay."

"Can Carlos not do this? He is older and more experienced."

"No, my son, it must be you. You are the one."

"Please, *padre*, do not burden me with this ..."

"You are the only one I trust to do it," Don Emiliano said. Then he walked out of the room. The conversation was closed.

Later that day, Juan Miguel stood in the villa's back room, which doubled as an anteroom to the outdoor kitchen and a storage room, helping his aunt with the potted plants she asked him to carry in from the patio for the winter. She had him line up the red clay pots underneath a row of windows, and now she instructed him on each of the plants' attributes.

He stood behind her, towering over her, listening intently as she described how to grow and care for the maroon bromeliads and yellow kalanchoes and the salvia, which his *tía* called the seer's sage. He put his hand lightly on her shoulder to steady her when she bent down to fuss with the soil.

"No, *tía*, let me do it," he protested.

"Bah," she said, waving him away. "*No me importa.*"

He was patient with his Tía Marina no matter what. He put his hands on her elderly shoulders and bent over her, putting his cheek next to hers.

"*Hermosa mia, mi amor,*" she said, then chuckled.

When they were through with the plants and the lesson, they sat at the table by the windows, drinking cups of *cafe con leche* and drinking in the sunshine.

"So, what has you in pain, my son?" she asked him.

"I cannot talk about it, *tía*."

She nodded, poured a few mouthfuls of the milky liquid into her saucer, picked up the saucer and drank from it, in the old style. He smiled as she slurped it. It meant it was just the right temperature and sweetness, he supposed.

She chuckled again as she looked at him slyly.

"A woman?" she asked.

"*Tía*, please, I cannot say."

"*Si*, a woman, then, *mi querida, lo siento*, my poor child." She nodded her head knowingly—one of her habits.

"A woman, *si*, whom I do not care to meet again."

"*Ai, ai, ai, palomito*, this makes no sense. You think of her. You have told me you dislike her … you wish to see her but you do not wish to see her?"

"I undoubtedly will see her again if I go to San Antonio to meet with Senor Barone next week."

"You must keep your head, my son, where the *senora* is concerned," she said with as much sternness as she could manage. "She is a wily one, that one. Beautiful and wily. That is a bad combination. She is a danger to you."

He nodded then winked to lighten his *tía's* mood. She lifted the saucer and took another slurp of *café* to hide the smile that his smile always elicited.

CHAPTER 3

Once she was back home at the Barone Ranch, Meg was restless and sleepless. She sat up at night and drew sketches in her journal or went on long walks to the river. She looked across the table at a husband who looked like a stranger. She hated the way he ate, suddenly. The way he chewed with his lips slightly parted disgusted her. She'd never noticed his swollen cheeks and puffy hands before, but now she did. More than that, he seemed arrogant.

"The don sends a boy to do the job of a man," he said to her from across the breakfast table.

"A boy?"

"His youngest son … the one with the hair of a woman. Don Emiliano sends him to help with the hiring of new hands."

"Do you not trust him?"

"He showed weakness letting the horse thief go, didn't he?"

"But he recaptured the horses …"

"The thief is still at large ... and no doubt still stealing horses," he said, peering at her over the top of his eyeglasses.

"Still ... it was an inventive way to get them back. That is what you wanted, was it not?"

"The trip will be useless. The boy ... is useless," he said as if making a pronouncement. Then he picked up his hat and walked out.

She felt she didn't know him any longer—but she certainly knew who he was. He made sure everyone knew who he was. Ben Barone had always had the air of a man who could make a success of things—someone to court. When she met him, he was considered a good catch for any woman seeking a husband. He was introduced to Austin's established families, one of those her family, the Palmers. They invited him to dinner often, she remembered, hoping he would court her older sister, Beverly, who was considered one of the town beauties. But it was Margaret Palmer who caught his eye and later won his heart.

He looked at her differently back then. He often said she reminded him of a wild red fox. When they went walking together, he was astonished how people stared—sometimes to the point of rudeness—at her unusual hair. In those days, she had a healthy glow from spending time outside. She often went out on long walks searching for plants and cataloguing her findings in her journal.

Her father, Sven Palmer, was a successful Austin merchant who, before coming to Texas, had been a scholar in Sweden. He had studied literature, history, and science and was a respected naturalist. Even though there was no outlet for those skills in the Texas of the 1840s, he continued his interest in the subjects by teaching his daughters about them. Maggie had been particularly fond of botany and had learned to identify many plants in the area by both their common names and Latin names.

She was both unconventional and clever, not qualities a man usually seeks out, but whatever it was that made her different, Ben Barone was just one of the many men who wanted her. Ben was the most determined of her many suitors. He wanted to win her—he made that clear. He wanted to take her to his ranch and build her a roomy home and have a family with her. After several years of offering her everything from riches to travel to even expensive jewelry, she consented to marry him.

Captain Barone turned out to be a natural-born wheeler-dealer and became more successful as a cattle baron and a businessman than anyone had ever expected. Since moving to Texas after the Civil War, he had built a ranching empire in the Medina River valley. He was one of the first to fence off his land and keep an official counting of his cattle. He recognized the coming demand for beef even before the war ended. The newly prosperous nation was clamoring for beef and leather since the Civil War years. Cheap land was for sale in Texas, oftentimes by the old Spanish families who were weary of the drudgery. He purchased several of these ranchos from their Spanish owners for deflated prices. Some said he did it through intimidation. Others said he took advantage of the Spanish landowners' desire to move their families to Mexico, where they had cultural ties.

After the government forced out the Indian population and the northern railheads were built, it was only a matter of time until the beeves could be shipped by rail. He gambled on all this and hoped to make a fortune. And he did.

Life in their sprawling ranch house in the heart of the Medina Valley seemed idyllic. In reality, it was less than idyllic. When he established his Double B brand—not much more than 100 miles from the border—Barone probably had no idea he was exchanging one conflict for another. The war between Texas and Mexico officially ended in 1848, but another war was just beginning, a border war in which the ownership of land and livestock was in dispute. He complained often about the Mexican *bandidos* raiding the ranches close to the border. But they were not the only dissonance at the Barone ranch. The Barones had reached the point of merely tolerating each other.

Meg was not fully conscious of it at the time, but the evening she dined with Juan Miguel had a great impact on her. A part of her was lying in wait for him, not as a predator, but as a woman full of anticipation. It didn't occur to Meg until days later what was happening that evening. The thought entered her mind like a guest to a party who comes in the back door and lingers on the fringes of the crowd, waiting for a greeting. She went over the evening second by second and suddenly realized—a realization that, once it came to mind, could not be easily dismissed. "I am not in love with him," she told herself. "That would be ridiculous."

———————————

The fog had settled in the meadows below the tree line, and an occasional live oak poked up here and there on the day Meg and Ben Barone traveled from their ranch to San Antonio for the second time in a month. Meg felt claustrophobic in the closed-in buggy and overwhelmed by the odors of worn boots and body odor on damp wool. She looked out at the passing scene and let the rocking buggy lull her back into the complacency she once found comforting. She pulled at the neck of her blouse as if it were choking her. The collar was so tight that she couldn't breathe.

"What is it now, Meg?" her husband asked, glancing sideways at her.

"I'm just dizzy from the motion," she said, looking out the window to get her bearings again.

Suddenly, the buggy seemed as if it would careen off the trail into one of the deep arroyos along the route. She could picture the wheels coming off and spinning into the tall weeds and underbrush. She pictured herself flying free, out of control.

Meg was near to breathless from anxiety by the time they reached the Menger Hotel. Even before they entered the lobby and she looked across the room, she knew Juan Miguel would be there, and he was. He stood behind a potted plant by the window, talking to two *Tejano* men who were well dressed, as he was, but much older. She could see the distinctive star-shaped spurs on the expensive boots, yes, but she felt his presence more than saw him. If he was trying to be inconspicuous, he was not succeeding. That would be like the sun trying to hide from the planets.

She only glanced, then nodded in his direction. When he saw her, he smiled, put his hand over his heart and bowed as she walked by.

"*Senora*," he said, "*Es bueno verte de nuevo.*"

"*Si, senor,*" she said, her voice so quiet that it made her husband look at her with questions on his face.

"He is brash," Ben Barone said when he was out of earshot. "Much too brash. The father indulges him too much."

"Yes, he is brash. That is the word for it," Meg said. "But there is more to him, obviously."

"You mean the pretty face?" Ben Barone sounded jealous suddenly. "Well, we will see tomorrow whether the young man is worth his salt. So far, he's only a pretty face."

———————

In little more than a year, Juan Miguel del Valle had grown from a blond, gangly boy to a man who no longer looked like a boy. He was tall and well built, with eyes that flirted. He was a thoroughbred, the old women of the villa often said, the result of good breeding. He has the soul of his mother and the intelligence of his father. But as he grew into a man, it became evident he was more complicated than they had discerned. He has the makings of a scoundrel, they said, clucking their tongues. On the other hand, he was his father's most trusted *ayudante* and had been for some time.

By the next morning, Juan Miguel's head was swimming as he trudged down a street still wet and muddy from the night's thunderstorms. It had been forced on him, Juan Miguel kept telling himself—the second trip to San Antonio. He had begged his father not to send him. Did he really want to go? Well, possibly, but he himself was confused by his feelings. He was young—only seventeen—and it was new to him, the desire he felt. He had spent an almost-sleepless night listening to sharp claps of thunder and watching rain pour down his window. At one point, he got up and looked out the window. He wondered whether it was the rainstorm making him feel unsettled or having seen Senora Barone again.

Above him, Meg pulled back the hotel window's heavy drapery, peering around it, trying to catch sight of Juan Miguel out in the plaza without being seen. He looked so purposeful for such a young man, but he was not difficult to look at. She let go of the curtain, sat on the bed, lifted her legs and held them to her, trying to hold in what she feared would come out sooner or later. If she met him again, what might she do?

This whole course of action is unwise, she warned herself. Unwise? No, it is dangerous. He is naïve and brash—totally without restraint. This flirtation needs to stop, for everyone's sake. But was it really a flirtation? She didn't know. She had to see his face, gauge his reaction. Look into his eyes. Yes, only a face-to-face conversation with him could avert a catastrophe.

"I'm being overly dramatic," she whispered to herself. "He's only a boy."

One minute she was convinced he had no idea the effect he was having on her. The next minute she knew he did. Still, the only way to know was see him again. She owed it to everyone to see him again. In all good conscience, it was the only thing to do. She smiled and slid down on the bed with her hands behind her head. Yes, she would meet with him in private and tell him. She couldn't wait to tell him.

———————

At Hartman's Dry Goods, across a downtown alley from the Alamo, Juan Miguel introduced Barone to the men standing outside, most of them looking for work. The *vaqueros* were experienced horsemen and beef riders. They had no fancy chaps and spurs like Juan Miguel's, but working weathered ones. They wore sombreros, dirty and greased from days on the trail and in the fields. They had hard looks, but their looks softened when they saw Juan Miguel. They knew him as a son of one of the old Spanish families, whom they still respected. They had nothing to say to Ben Barone and showed their lack of respect by not looking at him.

Juan Miguel approached the men, talking to them at

length in Spanish. After a few minutes, they squatted, so he squatted also, removed his hat and continued the conversation, gesturing with his hands. They all seemed to share a secret—although he had not met most of them before that day—from which Barone was excluded. Finally, Juan Miguel stood and nodded his head at Barone.

"Three of them will work for you, *senor*," he said. "But they require the same wages you pay to *Anglos, comprende*?"

"Three? That's not enough … not nearly enough. I need thirty at least … maybe more for the herd I'm planning to buy."

"Many of them are already committed to someone else, *senor*. Perhaps we should look elsewhere for them."

Barone sniffed, looked away, then nodded. He looked angry.

Juan Miguel scuffed the toe of his boot in the dirt and took off his hat to wipe his brow. "I do have another idea … but it is somewhat unusual."

"Let's hear it, boy."

"One of our *vaqueros* … Pedro … he is from Nuevo Laredo. He says the dry weather has been very hard and the people are looking for work elsewhere. Many are good riders. You could go there and …"

Barone hit Juan Miguel on the back with such force that it knocked him forward, but it was a gesture of gratitude. A huge grin crossed his face.

"That may be the solution," he said. "It just may be."

Don Emiliano had begun relying on his youngest son in business matters in the spring of the previous year, after he suffered a stroke that sapped him of his energy and muddled his thinking. He turned to Juan Miguel because he had paid for his eight years of private schooling in Monterrey and he was ready to get a return on his investment, but also because Juan Miguel was insightful, as his mother had been. His older brothers could read and write but weren't well educated. It was a burden for someone so young; his father understood that, but there was no one else. Juan Miguel showed an aptitude for finances when his father asked him to take over the accounting. He also dealt with others fairly and firmly, all traits that would serve him well. But for now, he would have preferred to do almost anything else.

Since his father's illness, Juan Miguel had taken on more and more responsibility and he was growing used to it in spite of his reluctance. But on this trip he felt more unsettled than usual sitting alone in his hotel room. He let his thoughts float away from his responsibilities, feeling grateful that somehow those responsibilities had led him in the right direction—toward Senora Barone. His father had thrown him a lifeline when he asked him to travel to San Antonio. When it came to Senora Barone, he found himself clinging to any shred of hope he could find.

A soft knock on the door broke his thoughts, and when he opened it, she stood before him in a prim gray suit and a funny, feathered hat sitting on top of her pinned-up hair. The strands were already escaping and floating in dark red swirls around her face.

"I wish to take a walk," she said, looking him directly in the eyes.

"*Senora*, you do not need my permission."

"I wish you to escort me."

Juan Miguel didn't jump at the chance, and she surely noticed that. If anyone should see them together, it could create a scandal. He stood looking at her face, then looked over her shoulder as if searching for answers out in the hotel hallway.

"Please, *senor*," she said in her quiet voice.

He didn't answer. He just turned and picked up his hat off the bed and closed the door behind him.

Juan Miguel and Meg walked in silence down Commerce Street to a park by the river, where swarms of black birds swooped from one spindly tree to another in the cool autumn breezes. There was no rhythm to their flights—they seemed out of control. Under one of the taller trees, she stopped him—turned slowly to face him and began with what seemed like a prepared speech.

"You should go home and forget about me and my husband. You're young. You don't know what you're getting into. Your family would not approve ..."

"*Senora*, how old are you?" he interrupted.

"Why do you ask me that?"

"Because I don't think you're that much older than me."

"I am thirty-five," she said, subtracting a couple of years

from her age.

"See?" he laughed. "We are the same age."

A grin crossed her lips, then a smile. She started to laugh, that grating high-pitched laugh he remembered.

"You're only what? Twenty maybe, at the most?"

"I will be twenty in December," he said, adding a couple of years.

She laughed softly and shook her head at hearing his age.

"I have been given a lot of responsibility by my family for years now. I know what I am doing," he snapped, like a petulant child.

She laughed even harder. The sound of her laugh made him start to laugh, too, which annoyed him even more.

"You're a child," she said. "A good-looking one, but a child nonetheless."

"Those words. You have said them before, and it is most annoying. A gawky boy, you said that day in the stable, did you not?"

She nodded. "Yes, I did, but ..."

"Perhaps you will change your mind someday."

They sat on a bench underneath the bare trees. The birds hopped chaotically around their feet, then swooped up to the branches, their yellow eyes keeping tabs on the two intruders. She put her hand on his forearm.

"Juan Miguel, please. You must forget whatever it is you think is happening."

"I know what is happening, *senora*," he said, looking down where her hand was clinging to his arm. "You are the one who does not know, who is trying to avoid."

"I'm not avoiding," she said, doing her best to keep the tone light. "That's why I asked you to take this walk, so that we can set things straight."

"That is not why you wanted to take this walk, *senora*. That is what you told yourself, but it is not true."

He stole a glance at her as he spoke. She acted as if he had caught her off guard when, in fact, she was the one who initiated the meeting. She truly was wily. He lifted her hand from where it was searing through his flesh and held it. She allowed herself to look into his eyes for only a moment.

"I should go back," she said, looking down.

Juan Miguel felt his destiny rushing toward him like a shooting star in the night sky. He reached out for something to stop it before it passed him by. He reached out for a reason to keep her with him.

"No, please, stay. Stay, *senora*. I want to show you something—something beautiful, I think. I want you to see the city, the way it really is. You cannot see from here."

She pulled back her hand firmly.

"I can't stay long," she said.

"No, *senora*, not long."

The small boat followed the clear, deep river winding behind city shops and homes, between high steep banks and places where it widened to accommodate lush tropical underbrush and open meadows covered with tall grasses. The river twisted in on itself over rapids and shoals, changing depth and width and character rapidly and offering up shapes and colors, then snatching them back before they could be taken in. Senora Barone looked at the scenery. Juan Miguel looked at her. Her face had lost the tension and her hands were at rest on the sides of the boat, not fluttering or fidgeting as he had observed before.

"It's beautiful back here, and so hidden," she said. "It's magical."

"Stop here," Juan Miguel directed the boatman.

The river was so crooked that they arrived almost back where they started, near the Main Plaza. He put his hands on her arms from behind to help her out of the boat and up the shore, along a path overgrown on both sides with wildflowers. He held onto her, perhaps, a little too long.

"There is something you must see, the San Fernando church, the oldest in San Antonio. Please," he said taking her hand with his, "I want you to see it up close."

Many times, she had seen the old San Fernando Cathedral standing watch over the town's Main Plaza. But she had never been inside the church. It seemed foreign to her.

Just inside the entrance, she stopped.

"I shouldn't go in," she said. "I'm not a Catholic, and I'm not even religious."

"No, really, it is fine, *senora*. Anybody can come in."

Meg's eyes swept up as they walked in—upward to the arched columns leading to the altar. The odors of incense and mildew hung in the air. Although it was enormous, the nave had a damp close feel.

He pulled her by the hand toward the altar.

"I want you to look up behind the altar at the ledge," he said pointing. "See? They say you can see the angels of San Fernando sitting up there. Many people have seen them. Some have even heard them, they say, singing a lullaby."

She looked up at the ledge, then looked at him with skepticism.

"You brought me here to allay my fear of ghosts, didn't you?"

"*Si, en parte*, but this is a true story. Sometimes, I think I can see them. They are the spirits of children, the children killed by Indians long ago. On *Dia de los Inocentes*, they hold a special mass for them. They sit up there, all in a line, their tiny legs swinging back and forth."

"You don't really believe in such magical things, do you?"

"Yes ... I believe."

"But it's only a legend, right?"

"For some, a legend. But for some, it is real. There really isn't any difference between legend and real. If it is real to them, then it is real. And you, *senora*, you prefer a life without magic, yes?"

"What I prefer is my business," she said, not liking his familiar tone. "Your stories are very seductive—you're very seductive. But I think you're aware of that, aren't you?"

"Yes, *senora*, I am aware. I am not embarrassed by it as you are."

"I'm not embarrassed."

"But you are. You are the most embarrassed person I have ever met."

She blushed as if to confirm his observation.

"Tell me another story, something true," she said to change the subject.

"Well, there is the story of how I sat on the horse backwards when I was eight years old. The horse reared and I fell over his ass. Now that is embarrassing."

She laughed and searched his eyes for a hint of irony.

"Tell me," she said.

"That is it. That is the story."

"So that is true, then?"

"*Senora*, many of the things worth seeing are invisible, did you know that? Not everything is as it seems. In fact, almost nothing is as it seems."

"A philosopher," she teased. She smiled, the first genuine smile ever between them. He felt he had achieved a certain victory.

"Miracles happen, *senora*," he said close to her ear.

CHAPTER 4

Margaret Barone took comfort in the concrete things of life, the things she could see. Not angels of children sitting atop the cathedral altar. Not the spirits of the Alamo heroes whose ashes were interred in the cathedral walls. But the flying buttresses or the fine German stonework of the building itself. She liked the deep blue of the autumn sky and the soft gold of the maples along the square. Or the contrast of a little girl's dark purple bonnet against her soft pale hair. Or the way the light shifted from a harsh yellow to a soft orange at sunset.

She could take refuge in the lines on the old nun's face as she passed her on her way to the cathedral for vespers. She watched her walk by, determined to remember the serene expression, the kindly eyes. She nodded slightly, and the nun bowed her head in acknowledgement. These were the tangible things she could hold onto.

It wasn't that Margaret didn't believe in serendipity. It happened to other people, but not to her. Maybe, as Juan

Miguel said, it was because she wasn't open to it. Maybe she was so blind that she wasn't seeing the signals. Or maybe she was embarrassed and cautious because her conscious mind was in conflict with the cues her soul was giving her.

Margaret knelt in the cathedral nave's back row and looked up at the figure of *La Virgen*. The original Spanish settlers had brought the tall painted plaster image from the Canary Islands, Juan Miguel had told her. Perhaps it didn't say to her what it said to others—but it said something. She connected the statue with the young man who shared it with her.

He opened her heart barely a crack. Only a sliver of light came through, but it was enough. She got a glimpse of another world, like a half line of poetry plopped down in a dry brittle tome of prose. It was difficult for her to see anything else except that light. At dinner, she sat distracted—her eyes unfocused—as her husband talked about his problems with the ranch.

"If you need someone to travel with you to Nuevo Laredo, why not hire Juan Miguel? He is well educated, and besides he knows the language," she found herself saying.

Her husband said nothing. He looked unconvinced.

"He has done well for us so far, hasn't he? Retrieving the stolen horses, helping you hire new hands ... "

"That's true ... it could be useful having someone along who speaks their language. If only I knew he was loyal."

"What better way to ensure his loyalty?" she said softly.

He nodded. "Perhaps it's worth a try."

Meg said nothing more. Anything more would be too much.

————————

On Juan Miguel's last day in the city, Senora Barone appeared out of nowhere like a phantom. He was in the hotel restaurant, trying to make himself eat his breakfast. He hadn't been hungry in days, but his appetite had returned a bit that morning.

He saw her outside the windows, pacing up and down. Then she took on an air of resolve and walked in the door. Out of the corner of his eye, he saw her squeeze herself between the tables and seated diners, looking like a person possessed, her face almost panicky, and stop suddenly at his table. She looked at him for a full minute before she spoke.

"Today is the day you are to return home, is it not?" Without waiting for his answer, she sat down next to him and blurted out, "I'm hungry as well. May I eat with you?"

He looked at her face, wanting some sort of recognition of the havoc she was unleashing in his life. Since the day they took a walk together, everywhere he looked, he saw the riotous red waves of her hair. Her face was before him when he closed his eyes and her laugh, her weird cackling, in his ears. But it was her embarrassment that broke his heart. He couldn't bear it.

He put down his fork and wondered what her sudden appearance meant.

"I can order you something, *senora*."

She didn't answer.

"Please, *senora*, can we not look at each other when we speak?"

It took a while, but finally her gaze turned on him, with more intensity than he would have liked. There is a blinding light trying to escape through her eyes, he thought, but she keeps it locked within. She reached across the table, picked up the rolled-up tortilla from his plate, and took a bite.

"Please don't do this," he said. "Please don't tease, *senora*."

She took another bite, apparently just to taunt him.

"My husband wants to discuss the possibility ... that is, my husband wants me to ask you ... I mean, would you consider accompanying him to Nuevo Laredo to hire more hands?"

Juan Miguel reached out to take back the tortilla, but she pulled it away. She had a wild, defiant look in her eyes.

"I've decided you should say yes, because it would be good experience for you and because he needs your help with the language," she said.

He tried again to take back the tortilla. This time, she snatched it away almost violently and glared at him. He sat back exasperated and looked at her sideways.

He tried to keep his voice down even though her voice was rising. "*Senora*, I don't understand."

"Also, in spite of everything, I think we can be friends," she said loud enough to receive some glares from other diners.

"In spite of everything?" he said, almost whispering. "You have been avoiding me for days, *senora*, which tells me we are anything but friends. I will consider his offer, and please stop taking my food."

He found a chance to snatch the tortilla out of her hand. She had the look of a spoiled child on her face. Then she smiled at him—or maybe it was more of a smirk—then she laughed. It was her cackling laugh that annoyed him. He started to slam his palm down on the table, then thought better of it and stood up to leave. She reached up and caught hold of his arm, then let go.

"Well, what is your answer?" she asked in a tone that seemed off-kilter—shy but plaintive.

This was too much for him.

"I know you like to tease and laugh at others, but it is not always funny," he said between clenched teeth.

He looked at her and detected something he hadn't noticed before. She had a mask of her own covering something raw and hurt and hungry for warmth.

He sat back down.

The mask fell away and he saw that her eyes were open, really open, like doors flung open to let in the spring air, receiving anything and everything. This apparently embarrassed her, and she looked down and away.

"I will do as you wish. Is this what you wish?" he asked.

She nodded.

"And if I do this, will you do something that I ask?"

She nodded again.

"Stop trying to hide. It is of no use anyway. *¿Comprende?*"

"Yes" was all she said.

When spring came to the rancho, Juan Miguel's Tía Marina laid out his best trousers and jackets as if she were preparing the burial clothing of a dead man. He was too young to go away on his own, she said. Something terrible was bound to happen to him.

He had endured the long winter distracting himself as best he could. To alleviate the boredom, he organized a *posada* at Christmastime. He played the part of Joseph and led the march of *los peregrinos*, carrying a candle inside folded paper and asking for lodging at the simple adobe homes of his father's workers. He entered each home bearing gifts and accepting their small offerings and their blessings. They called him "*el papa poco,*" and the old women kissed his cheeks.

The months that followed were strangely cold for south Texas, and as spring finally approached, Juan Miguel's patience was stretched thin. Confined to the villa with his family, he listened to every argument they could make against his going to Nuevo Laredo.

His aunt crossed her arms over her breasts and implored him. "*Mi amado ... mi amado ...*" she repeated over and over again.

"*Tía ... ya basta!*" he said.

On the day of his departure, Juan Miguel was up in his room watching his aunt help him pack his clothes and other belongings. She slipped an old wooden rosary into his bag when she thought he was not looking, then put another one in a jacket pocket.

"*Tía … ya basta!*" he said again.

His brother Carlos came in, proposing a wild plan to accompany him on his trip.

"Now, how would it look for me to go to my first job with my brother by my side holding my hand?" Juan Miguel said.

"Have it your way, *poco*. You always do. But I will tell you this," Carlos said, throwing up his hands in exasperation. "If you get into trouble, I will not be there to save you. *¿Comprende?*"

"*Si … si*. I am cast adrift," Juan Miguel said with a sheepish look.

Only his father seemed to understand the importance of his new job. He approved of it because it would help solidify the alliance between the del Valles and the Barones, but he was mourning the loss of his son already. Silent and stoic, he looked like a man who was losing his most precious possession, because in truth, he was. To ensure his safety, he sent Pedro with him with this admonition, "Guard him with your life."

When the time of parting finally came and Juan Miguel went outside to mount his horse, the *vaqueros* and their families surrounded him and wished him a safe trip. There seemed to be hundreds of them. They must have come for miles to see him off. His heart was touched by this and by his aunt's sorrowful goodbye. But nothing tugged at his heart like the sight of his father standing alone in the villa's doorway, his head slumped over almost to his chest. He left quickly with tears stinging his eyes and the children following behind him chanting "*el principe, el principe*," a nickname they sometimes called him in gentle derision.

———————

At many points along the forty miles from the del Valle villa to the Frio River where he was to rendezvous with Captain Barone, Juan Miguel thought about turning back. In fact, he almost did many times. He was leaving the family who needed him, and he had no idea what awaited him. The only thing he was sure of was Senora Barone had asked him to do this.

Before departing for Nuevo Laredo to hire *mestizo* ranch hands, Ben Barone was preoccupied with a meeting of local ranchers to discuss how to respond to the recent raids along the border, which had become worse since the end of winter. A group of raiders, called Cortinistas after the most famous of the Mexican raiders, Juan Nepumoceno Cortina, had ridden north across the Wild Horse Desert, leaving a trail of murder and robbery in their wake. About thirty of them raided Nuecestown, near Corpus Christi, brutally killing, looting, and beating the inhabitants. Anger toward all *mestizos*, even those who lived in Texas, swelled, and those seeking justice and retribution, such as Barone, began forming "minute companies" of vigilantes.

The Medina Valley group called themselves The Regulators. The night before he left, they met in secret in a grove of live oaks about a mile west of the Barone ranch house. For hours, the most important players stood at the front of the group, leading the discussion. Toward the end of the meeting, a strategy finally emerged when Barone took it upon himself to address the group. They stopped their arguing to listen.

"It's clear to me, gentlemen, we will have to take matters into our own hands, since the Rangers can't be everywhere they need to be," he said. "We will teach them a Texas lesson or two."

The others clapped and stomped their boots on the hard ground.

"The next time someone is raided, we will chase these *bandidos* down, even if we have to cross the border," he shouted.

Their clapping and whooping filled the silent, empty night.

"We will find them and kill them, and the border patrols be damned!"

It was Sunday, and the people of Nuevo Laredo were observing the Feast of the Annunciation of Mary when Juan

Miguel, Pedro, and Barone rode into town. The plaza was all but empty. Only a few old men sat on benches here and there. Soft brown sand, blown into town from the desert, was piled in doorways, next to tree trunks, and atop stonewalls. That morning, some of the women had taken a special offering of bread to the church altar to invoke the help of Our Lady of Guadalupe for rain. They knelt and prayed for a miracle, because it seemed only a miracle would save them, but when God didn't immediately answer their prayers and there was no rain on the horizon, they drifted home to nap.

Juan Miguel found the town priests in the small church across from the plaza and explained why he was there. The elder priest, Father Ybarra, put his hands together and looked heavenward. "Ring the bell, father," he said to the younger priest. "Summon them."

Naturally wary of *Anglos*, particularly since they were accused of being raiders only a few months earlier, the men sat sideways in the church benches and looked at Ben Barone with skepticism. He tried a few words of halting Spanish, then gave up and stepped aside to let Juan Miguel speak. Juan Miguel smiled, nodded at them and made a simple offer to work for Barone—food, shelter, and a small salary.

"What about our families?" one of the men said, looking somewhat taken aback by his own boldness.

"They will have to remain, but you may return for visits once a month," Juan Miguel said.

After conferring at the back of the church, most of the men agreed to go, but they had one request. It was a demand, but they called it a request. They would only work on the Barone Ranch with Juan Miguel as their boss.

He looked into their desperate faces, as drawn and parched from the drought as the cracked ground outside. He looked at the two priests standing by the altar where the bread offering to Our Lady still sat, flaky and uneaten. He looked out the door at the women and children waiting with patience in the square to hear of their redemption. He knew in his heart he couldn't say no to them. He felt a heavy weight come over him, and he had the strangest feeling that he had been sent as their ransom.

"Return to the villa," he said to Pedro, "and tell my father what has happened."

Pedro rolled his eyes and passed his hat back and forth from one hand to the other. He balked at Juan Miguel's foolhardiness, but he said nothing. He turned and walked out of the church. The old don and the aunt would not be pleased.

———

From the porch of the ranch house, she could see both the river and the road, so that's where Margaret waited, admiring the shiny, waxy buttercups peeking out from the grasses and the live oak leaves floating on the breeze, both sure signs of spring. She didn't know the time of their arrival, but something told her it would be soon. Earlier that day, she thought she saw the dust and heard the horses, but it was a false alarm. When finally they appeared and Juan Miguel, looking tired and bedraggled, rode at the head of a small band of *vaqueros*, she was relieved yet apprehensive. She covered her swollen belly with her arms. This was the day she had been waiting for—and dreading. This was the day they would both have to face the truth. But her hands would not stop shaking, so she held them tightly before her.

She had suspected she was pregnant when she met Juan Miguel in November. By December, she was sure. The winter had not been easy for her. Apparently, pregnancy was not something that came naturally to her, as it did to others. Some days she was not well enough to leave her room.

Juan Miguel stopped his horse and raised his arm, signaling to the others to halt. He took off his hat and wiped his face with his sleeve, the sun's last rays bouncing off his light hair. Even from such a distance, she could see the sweet look in his eyes. His presence was as magical as she remembered. He was the same. Nothing about him betrayed any difference, even though she looked carefully for clues. He had not changed toward her—she could see that.

"*Senora*," he shouted, waving. In only minutes, he was before her on the porch. "*Dulce amiga*, you are as beautiful as ever."

She bit her lip and looked down, embarrassed. He put his hand on her shoulder for encouragement.

"No more embarrassment, remember? No more hiding. You promised, *senora*."

"*Si* … and I will keep that promise, but things have changed … as you can see."

"So, *senora*, there will be two of you soon … two people to keep the promise," he said gently and attempted to look her in the eyes. "*Una bendicion* … a blessing … nothing else."

She was overcome at hearing his words and took hold of his hand. "Where is my husband?"

"He sent me ahead with the new hands. He will be here soon."

Juan Miguel was thrilled to see Senora Barone, but he couldn't help wondering whether it was the husband's intention to surprise him in this way. If it was, it was cruel—plotting to shock him like this. Juan Miguel felt himself growing angry and feeling protective.

"You are more beautiful than ever," he said. "Truly … *realmente.*"

Strangely, her pregnancy made no difference in his desire for her. He looked at the woman with the swollen breasts and belly before him and longed for her even more.

Though it was stretched out along the south side of the Medina River, the Barone Ranch was not one contiguous piece of bottom land but a patchwork of unconnected tracts Barone stitched together from what was for sale in the 1860s. Only one of those tracts bordered the river, and that's where Barone chose to build his house. It sat atop a hill facing the lush river valley. The house and the hill seemed to separate the deep valley from the flat prairie, where a series of horse stables, barns, and cattle stalls could be seen beyond the washhouse in the backyard.

It started out as a small, flat-roofed adobe structure with a *zaguan*, a Spanish breezeway, in the center and grew into a sprawling, sixteen-room home and ranching center. In 1870, Barone enclosed the *zaguan* and built a two-story addition with a parlor, offices and rooms for staff. The main house was constructed of timber cut from the cypresses along the Medina, then painted white. It reminded Juan Miguel of plantation homes he'd seen in drawings, but there was no mistaking who owned it. The double B brand, painted in large black letters adorning the cistern next to the windmill, could be seen for miles.

Juan Miguel soon came to realize that his duties as ranch foreman would be split. Half of the time he spent with the ranch hands, a mix of Civil War veterans, black freedmen, and *mestizos*, most of whom had learned their trade from the veteran *vaqueros* on the ranch. The other half he spent learning from Barone, who, right away, seemed to trust him with the accounting and the purchasing.

The ranch ran like a business, and the employees were only employees, nothing more. It was not at all like the congenial community Juan Miguel was used to; however, he was given privileges that the other hands were not. He was the only one allowed inside the ranch house parlor for visits, and that was only because the owners had a personal relationship with him. Since his arrival at the ranch, he was unsure about his own role there. Barone had hired him to help with the hands, but he wondered now about the rancher's real reasons.

He was also invited to dinner and other social events when the other hands were not, which made him think he was meant as a distraction for husband and wife as well as an employee. It was true that his pointless stories could make her laugh. In fact, he was intent on hearing that annoying laugh of hers. On long spring evenings, the three of them would sit on the porch and look out over the river until Meg, tired of carrying around the extra weight, would excuse herself and retire. But he was never alone with Senora Barone. Her husband made sure of that.

Even though by day it was used for business, by night the house itself was quiet, different from the noisy, sometimes raucous rancho villa where Juan Miguel grew up. While the del Valle villa was a house full of brothers and cousins and family of family and friends of friends, the Barone household was austere. The downstairs parlor had a limestone fireplace, pine wood furniture covered in dark brown leather, wood floors, and painted walls.

There were few concessions to comfort—only a quilt made by the housemaid Manuela and her sisters and a yellow curtain on the bay window. It looked as if the Barones had just moved in although they had lived there for years. Of the people who were in the Barone house on a regular basis, only Juan Miguel raised his voice above a low hum.

He was expected to be entertaining when he was invited for dinner, and he was. Meg loved to hear about his brothers' teasing and his father's hovering. He was often the butt of these stories, even when they were fiction. He talked about his Tía Marina and her obsessive mothering. He told Meg about his secret life with the *vaqueros* and how much they taught him. He told stories about disguising himself so he could ride along on deer hunts, about the old women teaching him to cook and grow vegetables in the garden next to the chapel, about his dreams of owning and racing a real thoroughbred horse.

He encouraged her to talk about her family and childhood, but she was shy about it. Her parents favored her older sister, she said, and thought their younger daughter "odd" because she liked to read and paint. Barone was usually nothing more than a fixture at these conversations. He listened but contributed little.

Then one evening in late April, the atmosphere on the porch, usually calm to the point of businesslike, took a weird turn. It was one of those small incidents that becomes larger simply because it exposes certain feelings, which were there all along but were hidden. It broke through the moat of silence around the Barones and their home. It was blown all out of proportion, to be sure, but it revealed the souls of the people who were there that evening.

It was a hot and muggy spring evening, and Juan Miguel's shirt was already soaked through with sweat. He sat on a stool by the porch railing with his sleeves rolled up above his elbows, holding a glass of cool water Manuela had brought him after dinner. He talked about his last bronco-riding adventure in the fall *corrida*. Meg, now almost full term, sat on a rocking chair by the door, happy to listen to the story about the spill off the bronco and the sore shoulder.

"I was trying to impress you, but I failed miserably," he said, holding the water glass with one hand and gesturing with the other. "The bronco, Francisco, he was the impressive one. Did you fall in love with him, *senora*?"

"Why, yes, I believe I did. He had beautiful brown eyes."

"If I must assume the guise of a bronco to win your favor, then I will."

He stood and hunched over with his head down, ready to rear, like a bronco. She laughed and grabbed her sides.

"Such beautiful eyes ..." she said.

"That's enough," Barone barked, leaping up and standing in the line of sight between Meg and Juan Miguel. "Meg is tired, aren't you, Meg? She's going to bed."

Meg blanched and, without thinking, looked around her husband to catch Juan Miguel's eye. When she did, she let down her guard for just an instant. The pretense she hid behind was gone when she looked straight into Juan Miguel's eyes. He could do nothing but look at her with all the reassurance he could muster.

Barone grew red-faced and tense. He walked over to

where she was sitting, grabbed her up from the chair by her arm, and led her toward the doorway. Juan Miguel leapt from his seat. He started toward them, then retreated.

"Please, *senor*, don't hurt her," he said before he could think about it. "It was my fault. I took liberties ... it was not her fault."

"You should go now, too," Barone said in an even but tense voice.

Juan Miguel walked off the porch with the weight of regret falling on him. He stole a glance at her on his way. She was hurt and flushed and large with child. The look on her face went through him like a knife in the gut.

Later that night, Barone sought out Juan Miguel and took him aside.

"I will forget the incident out of respect for your father," he said. "Have I not been a gracious host to you? And yet you insult me like this?" Juan Miguel felt shamed but also incensed. Out of caution, he said nothing, but he would never forget how Ben Barone portrayed himself as the victim. That would stay with him forever. That was something he would never forgive.

———

When he stayed away, she knew he stayed away for her sake. He did his job well, but Margaret contemplated telling him to go home. With each passing day, that became more difficult for her.

He spent most of his time in the bunkhouse, and it wasn't long until Juan Miguel was entertaining the ranch hands. They called him *"poco loco"* and gathered round in the evenings to hear his stories. Nothing was too much for Juan Miguel. He even succeeded in winning over Diego, a silent, gun-toting old *vaquero* who hardly ever smiled. He grabbed Diego's hat and put it on backwards one day. He put on a scowl and began to shoot off his pistol, aiming at everything and nothing. A gang of the men followed him outside, clapping and whooping. They created such a commotion that everyone in the house, including Meg, wondered what it was all about. She suspected he was luring her outside. When he was finished with his impersonation, he dawdled by the kitchen door, talking to the *vaqueros* with his head bare and his shirt unbuttoned, telling stories and sharing a bottle with them.

The humiliation Margaret felt about her husband's jealousy, compounded with her discomfort, made her want to hide in her room. The Barone household fell back into the routine it had been in for years—the years before Juan Miguel came. Breakfast at six, dinner at noon, supper at seven, then to bed shortly after sundown. It should've been comforting, and it was at one time, but Margaret was restless. She missed the stories and the laughter—the promise of something new. She got out of bed and paced.

When the pacing didn't satisfy her any longer, she left her room and sat on the porch until well after dark so she could look at the stars and wonder whether he was looking at them, too. She would linger in the kitchen, gazing out the windows, hoping to catch sight of him.

Finally one afternoon, she saw that he was up to his old tricks, impersonating one of the hands. Afterwards, he dallied, casting looks at the doorway, obviously looking for her. She stepped outside and smiled at him. The sun setting behind him lit up his hair like a halo, and she couldn't take her eyes off the soft brown skin, not much darker than his eyes. His whole body was aglow.

Even if she were free, she had nothing to give him at the moment. She was large and tired and not much to look at. She put her fingers to her cheek, then caught hold of them with her other hand and pulled them down. He smiled when he saw the by-now familiar gesture. His eyes were always following her hands, trying to read their meaning.

Juan Miguel had been uneasy, like a fish out of water, since he arrived at the Barone Ranch. The incident on the porch made him even more uneasy, but he was determined to see her. He was only beginning to learn how determined he was. It was true that Juan Miguel had never been in love before, and he didn't really know what it was. He was not aware of all the theories and stories and ballads surrounding the idea of love, but he knew there was an invisible thread between her eyes and his eyes. He knew her. He waited for a chance to be alone with her. He felt he would resort to almost anything, but he wasn't reckless. He couldn't afford to be reckless or impatient. He learned well the lessons his fa-

ther's *vaqueros* had taught him—on the outside, bravado;
on the inside, *razon*.

CHAPTER 5

One evening, right before sunset, Juan Miguel struggled with a wooden gate on the outside fence of a far corral when he heard shouting and what sounded like gunfire. At first, he thought it was just the *vaqueros* celebrating the end of the day a little early. When the noise got louder, he jumped up on the gate and strained to see the ranch house and its surroundings. He could see enough to know it was no celebration. He leapt down, drew his pistol, and ran toward the noise.

A swarm of *bandidos* darted quickly through the west pastures, running from bush to bush and tree to tree, flanking the house and outbuildings. He could see what they were after, the broncos in the horse corral. They were headed for the gate, and the ranch hands were all but helpless to stop them. The two or three who had guns managed a few shots now and then, enough to keep them back for the time being. The *bandidos* were cagey. They saved their ammunition, keeping themselves hidden and drawing fire but moving steadily toward their destination.

Later, when Ben Barone returned from a business trip and Juan Miguel told him about the raid that night, he said it was more chaos than fight and it caught everyone off guard. The ranch hands ran around in a disorganized fashion, trying to find weapons, he said, shooting wildly without purpose. In spite of that, Juan Miguel and Diego succeeded in backing the *bandidos* up behind a row of bushes beyond the pasture to buy some time.

He remembered thinking that someone had to do something. It was act or be killed. He stepped up to the fence below the pasture, steadied the barrel of his pistol with his left hand on the top board, and aimed for their heads, just as his brothers had showed him. His first shots were wide, but he kept aiming. Finally, one struck one of the *bandidos*. He fired again and again, and finally he hit another one.

Juan Miguel shouted at them in Spanish, hoping that would make an impression on them. "Get on your horses and ride or you will all surely die here."

He waited for a reply. None came, only silence. So he addressed them again in Spanish. "Throw out your guns and get on your horses and we will allow you to leave."

To Juan Miguel's relief, he saw a few of them throw down their guns, and then a few more. Soon, they rode off toward the south. Juan Miguel and Diego crept up closer to inspect the dead ones. Two of the *bandidos* had bullet holes in their heads and oozed blood onto the pasture clay. Juan Miguel bent down and put his hand on one man's chest to find a heartbeat. He removed the man's blood-soaked hat and covered his face. His own heart was racing and his head felt light.

Then the ranch hands ran around yelling, celebrating and patting Juan Miguel on the back. He didn't like the celebration, and yet he felt some pride in what he'd accomplished. He felt sick and exhilarated at the same time. He had never shot at a man before, much less killed one.

"Cover their faces," he said. He turned away and tried to fight the sick feeling in his gut. "Take them away, then bury them away from the house."

He stood up and steadied himself, then stumbled unsteadily to the ranch house. Manuela was waiting for him in the kitchen.

"The *senora*?" he asked.

"She is upset," Manuela said. "She wants you to go up to her room right away. She is afraid you are hurt."

Yes, he told Barone about the raid, but he didn't tell him what happened later, although the gunfight and the kiss would always be linked in his mind. They were linked and they were related. Quite possibly, he would never have kissed the *senora* if the gunfight hadn't happened. Quite possibly, their story would have ended quietly without passion or purpose. But the story went on because he climbed the stairs, sweaty and exhausted, his shirt bloody and his pistol still in his hand. He climbed the stairs slowly, trying to catch his breath and clear his head. His heart beat was so loud that it reverberated in his skull. He needed to see her like he had never needed anything.

It was twilight, and the light was dim in Meg's bedroom when he walked in.

"Are you hit?" she asked. She sat on the bed, looking heavy and immovable.

"All is well now, *senora*, they are gone," he said with all the bravado he could marshal.

She looked at him with wide eyes, terrified eyes. She wanted comforting, but he had nothing left to give her. His hand shook as he took off his hat slowly and placed it on a table. He dropped the pistol, then took off the jacket and let it drop on the floor. He unbuttoned his bloody shirt and wadded it, then threw it down. He stood there looking, for all the world, like the man-child he was.

Meg lifted her swollen body carefully, pushing down on the bed with both fists. He rushed over to help her, but he was reluctant to touch her because he knew he felt cold and clammy—like one of the dead men lying on the dirt.

From the beginning, his reaction to Meg was like the ocean tide responding to the moon. Every time her emotions changed, his insides shifted, and he was connected to her in a way that left him no choices. He should have left her at that moment, but the thought never entered his mind. He was always taken into her realm against his will, ravished by her presence.

Finally, he reached out and put his arms around her. She gasped. He held onto her, his arms encircling her, engulfing her in his world, the odor of sweetness and need emanating from his touches.

He bent down and kissed her. It was a small, hesitant kiss. Then he kissed her again, and he knew it was as it should be. It was a real kiss. She pulled him by the hand to her bed.

"Come with me," she said.

He lay down on his back, looking up at the ceiling, struggling to calm himself. She lay down next to him, put her arms around him and held him tight. She stroked his face and kissed his cheek.

"I must tell you something, Marguerite," he said. "I must tell you why I came here ... why I really came here."

"No ... don't," she whispered. "I know the reason ..."

"I have to say it. Please let me ... let me say it. I came because you are everything to me."

She put her hand lightly over his mouth to stop the confession.

"You're just a boy. You're so young."

"Give me a chance to show you that I am a man. I drove away the *bandidos*, did I not?"

Yes ... yes, you did. But there is still so much you don't understand ... about me ... about life."

"You are wrong, Marguerite. I do understand, and I will show you if it takes forever. I haven't been alone with you in a long time. I have so much to say ..."

She tried to keep her face composed. "Please don't … not now."

"But, *senora*, this is our chance to speak …"

"If anyone should see you here, you would be fired and we would never see each other again."

He cocked his head away from her and looked into her eyes.

"*Senora*, is all this a test of some kind? Because if it is, give me a hint what sort of test it is so that I can pass."

Then he put his hand on her belly, and the feel of his hand made her insides contract. She grabbed his hand, but he held onto her and wouldn't release her even though she struggled.

"I will wait," he said.

"You should leave," she said softly.

"I will wait for you. I will wait as long as you ask me to. But you have to ask, *senora*."

"Wait for me," she said. Her eyes were manic, but he could see it was not anger. "Just wait a little longer," she whispered, not daring to look at him.

"Forever, *senora*."

She smiled at his impetuosity. She put her head on his shoulder.

"Just sleep," she said. "Just sleep."

In the middle of the night, he raised himself on one elbow and saw, on the bureau, the moonlight coming through the window lighting her gold and diamond wedding band sitting in a pink seashell dish.

She pulled him back down.

"Stay ... please stay," she whispered.

"Marguerite, you ask so much ... " he said.

He sat up against the headboard most of that night, patting her damp forehead when she twitched in her sleep. When the baby moved inside her, he caressed her belly. It suddenly became clear to him—everything he loved was in that room.

CHAPTER 6

Ranchers up and down the Nueces River valley suffered many losses that summer as Mexican raiders struck at will. Bands of vigilantes, including The Regulators, organized to protect the livestock, but thousands of cattle were spirited across the border in only a few months. And the raiders didn't stop at stealing. They sometimes terrorized the ranchers, particularly the small isolated families. Seven members of one family lost their lives in a raid, an especially bloody one, further inflaming the sore feelings between *Anglos* and *mestizos*.

The reconstituted Texas Rangers, charged with law and order over all of Texas' frontiers, were busy fighting Indians on the northern frontier. The *bandidos* started raiding north of the Nueces River valley, even sometimes the ranches near Bandera along the Medina River. Although the raids were less frequent than along the border, the ranchers and their families lived in fear. They petitioned the government in Austin to send a company of Rangers their way, but the wheels of government process were slow.

Ben Barone, who had in the past been even-handed dealing with men of all races, began to show resentment in his dealings with *mestizos*. With Juan Miguel, he became distant, but he kept him and the *mestizo vaqueros* on hand as insurance against more raids. Mexicans from south of the border were a little less likely to raid ranches where they knew *mestizos* worked. He was also grateful and impressed that Juan Miguel had thwarted the *bandidos* while conflicted because he felt threatened by the young man's charms. Juan Miguel had told the story of killing *bandidos* one too many times. His countenance was easy and seductive to everyone, especially his wife.

Manuela had grown fond of Juan Miguel, and she missed his presence in the ranch house. She decided to tackle the subject head on, as was her custom. She inherited a tendency to be quite blunt from her mother, who was from the Karankawa tribe.

"Do you not miss Juan Miguel, *senora*?" she asked Meg one afternoon in the parlor. "Do you not want him to come back and tell stories?"

"Yes, I do, but there is nothing I can do about it," Meg said.

"Invite everyone to something, *senora*."

"What do you mean?"

"If we invite everyone to a dinner, perhaps a dinner on the ground, how could Senor Barone object to that?"

So the two women conspired to get Juan Miguel back

into the house, using food. They invited the ranch hands, some neighbors and Manuela's sisters. Manuela contributed a casserole of chicken and dumplings, some spring squash, and dewberry pie. Others brought tortillas, *pan*, beans, and beef cooked over an open flame.

But when the day came, the dinner on the ground was not as festive as they hoped. Meg and Ben sat stiffly in wooden chairs under a spreading live oak, swatting away an occasional fly, Juan Miguel across from them, an invited guest for the first time in weeks. Because of the heat that day, only a few of the invited guests actually came, and the atmosphere between Ben and Juan Miguel was cold. The three were quiet; there had been little conversation or storytelling recently. The feelings between Meg and Juan Miguel hung in the air like a phantom, a phantom they hoped no one else could see.

They ate in virtual silence. Juan Miguel glanced at Meg every few minutes to make sure she was not going into labor. He seemed the most worried about the birth. He fretted. Would they be able to fetch the doctor in time? Would the baby be healthy? Would Meg be in terrible pain? Of the three of them, he was by far the most anxious. Then, as if to fulfill his worst fears, she doubled over and clutched her belly, her face turning dark red. Juan Miguel jumped up and held out his arm to support her.

"Is it ...?"

She nodded as she doubled over.

"I'll ride for the doctor," he said, and, in seconds, he was running to saddle his horse.

"Juan Miguel!" Ben shouted, "Let one of the hands go."

But it was too late; he hadn't heard. He galloped full speed down the road, his hair flying in the wind.

Juan Miguel had a detailed description of where to find the doctor and how to get there, but it took so long, much longer than he anticipated. So it was many hours later that he rode up the road with the doctor beside him, Juan Miguel urging him to ride faster every step of the way. But he knew as they climbed the porch steps and entered the house the event was done. There was no hustle and bustle, no hurrying about in preparation. The house was quiet, and the mood was grim.

Manuela came downstairs and told them in Spanish the baby had arrived, that it was a girl, and she was never able to catch her breath.

"*Ella murio, senores*," she said in a shaky voice, "*ella murio*."

The doctor looked at Juan Miguel to translate.

"She said the baby is dead."

The doctor climbed the stairs to see what he could do for the mother. For the dead infant, he was too late. Juan Miguel sat in a nearby chair, hung his head and fought back tears.

They buried the infant on the ranch grounds near the house. Four people attended the short ceremony: Ben and Meg, Juan Miguel, and Manuela. Nothing was said over the small coffin. Juan Miguel and Manuela crossed themselves and looked at each other with stealth. It was as still as doomsday.

The petulant young Juan Miguel blamed everyone for Meg's sorrow. He blamed the doctor for being so slow. He blamed the husband for getting her pregnant. He blamed Manuela and the hands for their untidy presence. He blamed himself—it was his fault, after all. He was the one who desired her when she was large with child. He was inconsolable for weeks, staying in bunkhouse most of the time, only emerging to work.

The consequences of the infant's death were hard to calculate when it happened. Only later would they look back and know how many things were broken as a result. Juan Miguel buried his grief in his work. Late spring was a busy time on the Barone Ranch. The cattle had to be rounded up by May to get an accurate count. Barone had hired extra hands, but all the ranch hands had to work long days, and sometimes into the night, to get the job done. The hard work was a godsend for Juan Miguel. As for Meg, she took the baby's death badly. She fell into deep mourning, and she chose to do it alone, in her room. She seldom emerged, leaving Juan Miguel on his own, adrift in a strange environment without purpose.

One afternoon after roundup, sitting on the porch catching up on paperwork, he looked up at a spot far in the distance, across a field of coral paintbrush, where a summer thunderstorm loomed on the horizon. He could feel the first wind gusts and hear a soft rumbling of thunder. He looked at the storm clouds, but his attention was on what he could hear inside the house, the muffled tones of what sounded like an argument. He strained to make out the words, and he thought he heard his name mentioned. He feared he was the subject of the discussion, and that bothered him, but he couldn't leave Meg; he couldn't leave her now while she was grieving.

He picked up his papers and moved inside when the first pellets of rain struck. He brushed off the blown leaves and branches from his hair, then stopped abruptly. He could hear more plainly the contentious conversation, that Ben was planning to be away, probably chasing *bandidos* across the badlands and into Mexico, as he had many times recently. The Regulators had become more active, requiring Barone to spend weeks at a time away from the ranch. Meg sounded plaintive, her voice high and strained from tension.

To Juan Miguel's relief, Barone left the next day and didn't ask Juan Miguel to go with him. He dreaded the day Barone would try to involve him in The Regulators' forays. It would go against his nature to chase down *bandidos.*

With Ben and most of the hands gone and Meg confined to the ranch house, he was at loose ends all day, inventing tasks for himself and casting glances toward the house, hoping to see Meg. Finally, he got up his courage and stepped inside the kitchen door, hat in hand, looking around for a glimpse of her. Manuela asked him to carry a barrel of fresh well water, then she found some other items for him to carry, then she asked him to reach something on a high shelf. When she was completely out of excuses to keep him inside, she put her hands on her hips and faced him.

"*Senor*, you are invited to dinner this evening," she said matter-of-factly.

"By the *senora*?"

"Well, yes, she will invite you, I'm sure. Just be here at dinner time ... and wash up."

He smiled sheepishly at her and put the hat back on his head.

"You are like a sister to me ..."

"*Si ... si ... si*. Now go on and come back looking handsome."

After days of saying almost nothing directly to each other, Meg and Juan Miguel ate dinner alone. They ate without talking for most of the meal, saying only what was necessary. After the dishes were cleared, they sat opposite one another, hardly moving. She smiled faintly, then asked him, out of the blue, whether he could sing.

His aunt used to sing a lullaby to him, he said, but he couldn't really remember the lyrics.

"Sure you can, *senor*," she said emphasizing the *senor*. "Sing some of it."

He looked at her, his eyes pleading to be excused from the singing.

"Sing something," she said, waving Manuela out of the

dining room.

"Please, *senora*, don't tease," he said.

She only glared, waiting for some response.

Then, in a voice she could barely hear, he began. "*Mira la luna; comiendo su tuna*. That's all I can do ... "

She rose from her chair, walked slowly around the long dining table, and stood beside him. She put her hand lightly on his shoulder. He looked up at her as a man looking up at a judge.

"It wasn't your fault," she said.

The feeling came over him that she looked to him for answers—about life and death, about important things for which he had no answers. He took her by the hand and pulled her up the stairway to her room, softly closing the door behind them. She stood before him, her hands clenched in fists and her face looking drawn and tight.

"I don't feel anything anymore," she said, searching his eyes.

"You are still you. I am still me. I will not abandon you."

He put his arms around her and held her like a brother holds a sister, then sat on the bed and pulled her down on his lap. Rocking her back and forth in time to the tune, he sang softly.

"*Mira la luna; comiendo su tuna. Echando las cáscaras; en la laguna.*"

One solitary tear flowed down her cheek. He reached up to wipe it away.

"Is this the Spanish lullaby? The one the angels sing?"

she asked.

"Yes, it is true. There are angels and they do sing. You can believe that."

"Do you promise?" She looked and sounded like he imagined her as a little girl.

He laid his hand on her knee and stroked it. He put his other hand on her hair and caressed it. She began to feel connected to the universe again. When he left to go to his room, she held onto his hand as long as she could before he left.

The next morning, he came back and ate breakfast with her in the kitchen. She looked younger than he had ever seen her, her hair in braids and an innocent expression on her face. She was in a playful mood and teased him without mercy as he ate his eggs. To get back at her, he snatched a towel and began to taunt an imaginary bull. He mimicked the stance, the movements, the facial expression.

"El matador?" she said smiling. "The great one. Where is your *acero* ... your sharp sword?"

Juan Miguel performed a balancing act trying to stay close to the woman he loved and work for her husband at the same time, a situation he knew was not sustainable, but he was helpless to change. When he left the Barone Ranch and traveled to Bandera for confession with Father Moreno or to buy supplies or visit the bank, his mind cleared enough to wonder at himself and his situation. He missed his father and Tía Marina and worried about them. He missed his fun with Pedro and the other *vaqueros*. But he gladly sacrificed everything to be near Meg even for fleeting moments and could think of nothing that would pull him away from her. He felt oddly invincible. Nothing could take him away.

On one of these trips, Juan Miguel dawdled in town after his errands, stopping for a cup of coffee. As he put his coins on the store counter, a deep-voiced man next to him asked, "Aren't you Ben Barone's foreman?"

"My name is Juan Miguel del Valle," he said nodding.

"Of the del Valles who own the ranch down south?"

"*Si, senor*, that is my family."

"So what brings you to these parts?"

"You could say, *senor*, I am learning the ranch business."

"I guess they won't be raiding your place anymore now that Ben's joined Der Kreis," the man said.

"What is Der Kreis?"

"It's part of The Regulators, sort of. It's a group of us businessmen," he said as they strode out the door together. "We're banding together to make some strikes of our own—you know, get them before they get us."

Juan Miguel nodded again, mounted his horse, and rode on. He had questions about Der Kreis. He didn't understand why Ben would be involved in striking others rather than just defending his ranch. But when he got home and brought it up in conversation, Ben was evasive.

Ben looked and sounded stern. "It's nothing to concern yourself with, and don't mention it to Meg,"

It always surprised him when people were cross with him. In truth, people were rarely cross with him. Later that evening, he approached Diego in the stables to get more answers.

"What do you know about Der Kreis?" he asked.

Diego spat to the side, wiped his chin, and snorted. "This is the *Anglos*," he said. "They are after the *mestizos*. They want revenge. They want to rid the state of *mestizos*. I swear to God, they do."

"All *mestizos* or just the ones from Mexico?"

"All," Diego said. "That is what I heard."

"But Barone has *mestizos* working for him."

"That's different, I guess. Hey, *Anglos*," he shrugged as if to say, who can understand them?

Left alone with time to contemplate Juan Miguel's curiosity, Ben Barone grew angrier and angrier that he knew about Der Kreis, which was intended to be a secret organization. Juan Miguel was friendly with the *mestizos*; he might even tell them about it. Hell, he might even be considered one himself. Ben smiled at the thought. All those centuries of the Spanish families breeding their genteel sons. It didn't mean much now, he guessed, but he still felt a modicum of loyalty to Juan Miguel, who had been a good friend and a good worker. As he stewed, he began to wonder, was it a coincidence that Juan Miguel questioned him about Der Kreis, or had he been snooping into his business, asking around in town about where Ben was going on his trips away from home? Maybe he asked too many questions in Bandera.

Barone waited for Juan Miguel when he got back to the bunkhouse later that night. He pointed to one of the chairs, and Juan Miguel sat his tall body on the small chair.

"What is it?" he asked, as calmly as he could.

Suddenly, Ben leaned down, his face only a few inches from Juan Miguel's. He grabbed hold of Juan Miguel's shirt and pulled him up.

"Do you even remember what happened here a few months ago? Do you want to see us in that kind of danger again?"

"No, of course not. I mean *si*, I remember, and no, I do not wish for it to happen again."

"Well, this is one way to stop it. Stop it before it starts," Ben nearly shouted. He pushed Juan Miguel back down roughly. Only for the *senora's* sake, to preserve her honor, would Juan Miguel have let anyone touch him like that.

"*Senor*, I am your employee," Juan Miguel pleaded. "I am loyal to you."

"You could be suspected ... they're arresting citizen spies, you know. Stay out of this. It's none of your business."

"What do you mean ... citizen spies?"

"Anyone who is *mestizo* is suspect ... could well be helping the raiders ... harboring them."

"*Senor*, I would never do that."

"You aren't as innocent as you look, I would wager. Just do your job and stay away from the house ... and Meg ... or I'll send you packing ... back to south Texas."

Ben stood up straight and looked down at Juan Miguel,

then stomped out, slamming the door. That was the day he let his suspicions that Meg and Juan Miguel might have had secrets of their own cloud his judgment and tip his hand. It was plain to all who saw them together, including Ben Barone, but he told himself it was far-fetched—feelings of love between an older married woman and a boy.

Chapter 7

The cypress trees lining the banks of the narrow Medina River rose from their serpentine roots on the edge of the clear water to the sky overhead. Their limbs met in the center and created a canopy, a refuge from the rest of the world. Early autumn rains had filled the creek, and fishing was good, Juan Miguel said, when he insisted on taking her with him. The sun would sometimes peek through, and Meg would take advantage of that. She pulled up her skirts, stretched out her bare legs, and let a tiny scrap of sunshine warm her skin. Propped against a limestone rock jutting out from the northern bank, she watched Juan Miguel cast his fishing line into the rushing water three feet below.

The fishing was a ruse. She knew that. It was Juan Miguel's way of getting her out of the house and into the fresh air. She had scared him—and herself—with her recent illness. From the outside, it appeared to be a physical illness, but it was an illness of the heart, the illness of grief and doubt.

The secluded spot, upstream from the ranch house where the river made a deep turn, was a place Juan Miguel found in his wanderings and claimed as his own. He started going there on Sunday afternoons to fish. But mostly he would hold the fishing pole and let his mind wander to Marguerite. He set an artificial deadline for himself of late August. If he had made no progress in winning her by then, he would leave and return to his family's rancho. Late August came and went, and he remained.

Only a twig broke in the breeze now and then, or a broad-winged hawk occasionally glided silently overhead, looking to prey on the darting cave swallows. She turned her head to watch Juan Miguel as he struggled to remember his brothers' fishing lessons. His long sleeves bothered him, so he had peeled off his shirt and laid it on a rock. He was doing fine. He had already caught some small perch.

He walked up the steep embankment and showed her the five fish in his makeshift catch basket. It was a small accomplishment, but she had never seen him look so proud.

"They will make a good *caldo*," he said.

The thought of fish soup made her insides roil. A wave of nausea came over her. He put down the basket and stretched out his body next to hers on the bed of brown cypress needles, turned toward her and put his arm across her waist. Her face was pale, and her lips were parched and dry. Her hair hung lifeless next to her face.

"I don't like for you to see me like this," she said, looking embarrassed.

"*Senora*," he soothed. "Everybody gets sick. Did I tell you about the time I had the measles and my brother put sheep dung on my sores?"

She looked up in his not-very-serious face.

"No, tell me."

"That is it. That is the story."

He put his hand on her abdomen to feel the muscles contract just a little in a small laugh.

"*Senora*, what do you want me to do?" he asked, attempting to catch her eyes with his.

"I don't know," she said, not looking at him.

"If I don't love you, then I don't love anything—I don't breathe. Do you not understand that?" He looked at her for an answer but did not find one.

"*Senora*, let go," he said in a pleading tone. "Let yourself feel again. Let yourself float free."

Tears were beneath the surface, but she wouldn't allow them to come out. Choking back her tears was making a lump in her throat the size of a boulder. He took her chin in his hand and turned her face toward his, but she still refused to look at him, keeping her eyes downcast.

"If you continue to hold in your feelings, you will never get well. You make yourself sick."

She pulled his hand down with her hand. "Do you think because I am older than you I know what to do? Well, it's not true," she said, her voice cracking slightly.

She had the look of a caged animal, locked within herself. He brushed back the stringy stray strands of red hair from her eyes and sighed a long, heavy sigh. Everything had gone awry since he'd been there. Nothing had gone as he planned, but he didn't blame Senora Barone. He didn't blame her because he loved her. He was helpless.

———————

That afternoon, Manuela crossed her arms over her ample bosom, tapping her foot against the kitchen floor. The young *principe* instructed her on how to cook. He stood at the kitchen basin scraping and paring the small gutted fish.

"Just cook the fish bones and fish heads," he said. "Then remove the meat and add the fillets later."

"I know how to make the *caldo*," she said with impatience.

"And don't put any *chiles*. Make sure the potatoes and carrots are well-cooked."

The Mexican *caldo de pescado* was one of his Tía Marina's specialties, and he wanted his *caldo* to be just like hers. She had told him many times it was soothing to the stomach.

"*Senor*," Manuela said, motioning her head toward the open back door. There stood one of the hands, trying to get his attention.

"A rider is on the road, *senor*," he said.

Juan Miguel dropped his paring knife and reached for his pistol. He peered down the road at the lone rider approaching when suddenly the rider looked familiar to him. He recognized the black long hair and full mustache of his older brother. He stepped off the porch and waved.

"Carlos," he shouted running to meet him.

The two brothers embraced as they hadn't done for years.

"I came to take you home," Carlos said. "Father is ill, and he probably will not last ..."

His words trailed off, but Juan Miguel knew what they meant.

"You must come with me now," Carlos said.

"*Si*, I can see that ... just let me take my leave."

Juan Miguel made Manuela promise she would finish the soup and see to it that Meg ate some of it. He made Meg promise she would eat the soup and drink some of Manuela's special tea.

"I will be back as soon as I can," he said, taking his leave at her bedside.

When he bent over to kiss her cheek, she whispered something, but he couldn't make out the words.

"What is it, Marguerite?" he asked, sitting down next to her.

"I said, come back to me soon. I am dead without you."

Margaret Barone's soul was as dead as a tree stump, her insides empty, so empty she felt like the cold autumn wind was whistling through her. Nothing brought her comfort except writing in her journal, where she unburdened herself, hoping the contents would remain secret. As soon as he left the room, she began to want Juan Miguel and yearn for him, not only in her heart, but in her body. Just the thought of him created a physical craving unlike anything she had ever experienced—an actual pain in her gut. She rolled over and covered her mouth to stifle a scream.

She ate his fish soup that evening but ate little after that. She rarely joined her husband for meals, so he took to eating with the hands.

Juan Miguel carried Meg's last words with him, weighing heavily on his heart.

Chapter 8

In the weeks that followed his fathers death, Juan Miguel and Carlos returned to the rancho villa every evening dirty, tired, and hungry, then ate huge portions of beef and beans and flopped into their beds, only to rise again before sunrise. Since he had arrived at his family's rancho, Juan Miguel's days were all the same, doing daily what he had done only occasionally growing up: rounding up cattle, riding the outer boundaries to pick up strays, helping with the branding, mending corral fences.

He had no time for dreaming, yearning, or even praying in the chapel. He missed Meg, but he had little time to think about her—Carlos made sure of that. The days blended together with no special purpose and no break from the work or monotony. One might have thought it was some kind of self-imposed suffering had it not been for the older brother constantly pushing him to work harder. More than anything, he felt he had to live up to his father's desires for him, to be a rancher in the old tradition. He would've liked just one day to think about his life, just one hour to himself, but it was never granted. Even on Sundays, the two brothers skipped Mass and worked all day, trying to fill the vacuum left by their dead father and the brother and the many *vaqueros* who had deserted them soon after their father's death.

At the end of a day in late fall, Juan Miguel felt weary as he rode up to the rancho house. He stepped off the horse and stumbled slightly from exhaustion. Inside, he plopped down, his body heavy, on one of the couches and laid back his head.

When Celita came into the room, he said, "Please, *senorita*, could we have something besides beans?"

"*Senor*, I have some bad things to tell you."

He looked at her, steeling himself for what was to come.

"Tía Marina has taken to her bed, *senor*."

He closed his eyes and felt the hot stinging tears rolling down his cheeks. They were the tears of fatigue and frustration, and the bad news only added to his burdens.

"What else, *senorita*?"

"Senor Carlos has left," she said.

He waved her away. "He will be back, I am sure."

"No, *senor*. He took his clothes with him."

Juan Miguel sat up straight, then stood up. He rushed up the stairs to his brother's room and found it almost empty of clothing and personal belongings. He sat down on his brother's bed, hung his head, and held his head in his hands. It was his brother who had given up first; he was left to carry the whole weight. He went downstairs to his Tía Marina's room, walked in quietly, and stood next to the bed.

"*Mi amado*," she whispered. "My time is coming."

"You have said so many times before," he said teasing. "When am I to believe you ... *mi tía?*"

"This time ... this time you should believe."

He could see that this time was different. He had been so busy that he hadn't noticed her body had grown frail, her face pale.

"What can I do for you, *tía?*" he asked. He sat down next to her and took her tiny hand in his.

"The *senora* you desire ..."

"*Si, tía*, what about her?"

"Do not let it slip away. Love comes seldom ... seldom. Maybe only once. Maybe never again."

"I know ... you have told me."

"Promise me this ..."

"*Si* ... what is it?"

"You will act as a man ... This is your rancho now. Go get her and bring her home."

Those were Tía Marina's last words. She died that night. Her body lay in repose in her room for many hours, because Juan Miguel couldn't bear to part with her. When finally he consented to let the *vaqueros* bury her, he chose a small plot next to her patio.

At her burial, he wept inconsolably, to the point where the old women began to wail and beat their breasts for him. He felt emptiness like he had never felt before, and he knew he was feeling what Senora Barone felt after the baby died. It gave him some comfort. As they lowered Tía Marina's casket, he whispered, "*Tía, mi primer amor.*"

———————

Once his aunt was buried and his grief began to abate, Juan Miguel looked in the mirror for the first time in a long while, and what he saw surprised him. His brown hair was long and turned blond from the sun, his skin was dark and streaked from the sand and sweat, his body was thicker, more muscled from the work. He was going on a trip, and yet he had no fine clothing to wear. The fine clothing was all worn and faded; even his hat was tattered.

His hands shook as he fastened his jacket and pulled on his boots. He didn't know what he would say or how he would act. He hadn't been around people in polite society in a long time. He'd forgotten what to do. And what about the illness? Would his visit make things worse or better for her?

"I have to go," he said under his breath. "I promised Tía."

There was also the advice from Father Moreno. On his recent visit to the rancho villa, he had come with an ulterior motive. Father Moreno didn't just hear confessions when he made his rounds through the Texas hill country, he also heard gossip—lots of it. He was like a traveling news source of personal problems and politics. Not much escaped him. Even though the Barones were not Catholics and he rarely visited them, he did visit with Manuela and other Barone workers on a regular basis. Manuela told him Senora Barone was still ill, and he saw for himself that this was true.

"*Padre*, please tell the young *principe* about her illness. I can't tell you why," Manuela said, raising an eyebrow.

But Father Moreno suspected why. He had heard the whole story in Juan Miguel's confessions. So whether they were fantasies or truths, he didn't know, but he worried because he had a special affection for Juan Miguel.

Father Moreno had succeeded in eliciting a certain promise from Juan Miguel on a recent visit, when the old priest came for Sunday lunch and afterwards they sat talking on the patio in spite of the chilly wind. Juan Miguel wrapped his sheepskin coat around him, and Father Moreno had a heavy wool cassock over his plain brown one. The wind blew through Juan Miguel's long light hair. He had neglected to shave for weeks, and the moustache and beard made him look older. Father Moreno didn't approve of his unkempt appearance, but he sympathized with him. Juan Miguel had been abandoned, left to run a ranching empire on his own.

"Son," the priest began. "I have some news from the Barone ranch. The wife is still ill. They say it is an illness of the spirit."

He waited for a reaction.

Juan Miguel's eyes clouded over as Father Moreno continued, "I want you to take a trip and visit her. I'll stay here and take care of the rancho for you while you go."

Juan Miguel looked skeptical. "Father, I cannot leave now, not with Carlos gone."

"I know what to do. I grew up on a ranch, as you did," the priest lied. "It would only be a few days. Everything will be fine here. I can send word to her."

"Did Tía Marina have something to do with this?"

Again, he lied, "No, no, my son, of course not."

So, cornered by his beloved dead aunt and his friend the priest, Juan Miguel consented to visit Senora Barone. Celita packed his food for the trip and put in some of her pralines to cheer him up. She patted his arm as he left.

"This is good," she said. "Don't be embarrassed. Go and find out whatever it is you need to know."

Celita appeared to know as much about the situation as Father Moreno and Tía Marina.

It would be the simplest thing, he thought, to take her away, just stretch out his hand, give her a boost onto his horse and ride off with her. But instead, it was the most complicated problem he had faced. She was not his. She belonged to someone else. Second to spiriting her away was convincing her to leave. But how to do that? How do you ask a full-grown woman to leave her husband of more than ten years? He had no answer, but he was determined not to let it best him. He still wanted her. His love for her grew stronger, and he longed for her.

On the day he went to see her, the sun was shining, but it was cold, and a dark purple-blue cloud on the north horizon threatened something—possibly snow, probably ice. She waited for him at the agreed-on spot, the same spot where Juan Miguel had fished for perch. She stood on the river shore on a winter landscape of browns and golds and grays, wrapped in her black cape with the dark red hair floating in the breeze. Her face and hands were red and chapped from standing for almost an hour in the cold wind. The brittle, flat leaves of a single maple tree scattered across the landscape with every strong gust.

She caught sight of him coming down the riverbank, walking fast, crunching the dead needles and leaves with his boots. Saying nothing, he put his hands out and took hold of hers. She reached up to tug at his long hair falling over the collar of his coat. She touched the two weeks of beard on his face.

"I haven't had time to shave in a while, *senora*. But maybe tomorrow. It is my birthday." He rested his forehead against hers.

"Happy birthday."

"I once got a goat for my birthday. Did I tell you that?"

She smiled slightly, and the wind seemed to grow colder.

"So, you are to be 21 at last."

"Well, I have a confession to make, *senora*. I lied about my age—I will be nineteen. I hope you will not be angry with me."

"I missed you," she said, letting go of him and turning toward the creek. "The walls of the ranch house are closing in on me."

"I know, *senora*, you are trapped there." He put his hand on her head and stroked her hair. "Come with me. I can take care of you."

"I cannot do that."

"Why, *senora*? There is no reason to stay."

"I cannot," she whispered.

He reached into his pocket and pulled out the old wooden rosary, then turned her palm up and placed it in her hand.

"My father and aunt have died," he said. He still had the stricken look of the grieving on his face. "My brothers have left, and I am the only one to run the rancho now."

She didn't respond but only put her hand on his arm and looked into his eyes.

"Don't give up hope, *senora*. Promise me you will not give up. I will find a way for us to be together."

"I promise," she said.

"A storm is coming—we had better go back. You asked me once to wait for you, and now I am asking you to wait. Can you do that, *senora*?"

"I will wait for you," she said softly.

Meg got back to the ranch house just before the ice storm hit. The temperature was dropping fast, and the ice pellets blew in the wind, sticking to the oak trees. She worried that Juan Miguel wouldn't make it home before the storm hit him, but she comforted herself, knowing he would be going south, away from it.

Juan Miguel rode home at almost a full gallop, trying to outrun the coming storm. When it hit him south of Bandera, it was cold windy rain soaking through his clothing and freezing on his back. He arrived so exhausted that he lay down to sleep for a full day.

The other truth was even more difficult for Juan Miguel to face, but he knew it. The failure of the del Valle rancho began with his departure. He left his elderly father and aunt with no one to care for them or run the ranching business. His brothers were weak and afflicted with problems—Jorge, the oldest, was prone to drinking, a curse that ran in his father's family, and Carlos, who loved gambling to the point of an obsession, spent long periods away from the rancho pursuing his own selfish pleasures. The guilt of having left them and the reason he left weighed on him. He was buried by it.

When he returned, he and Father Moreno decided to assess the situation. They went to the parlor and sat on two chairs facing each other. They rested their elbows on their knees, deep in thought.

Father Moreno straightened up and put his hands on his thighs.

"We need to find some more *vaqueros*," he said. "I will go to San Antonio on your behalf and find them and bring them here."

"I don't have the money to pay them right now, father. That is why the others left."

The two sat thinking for a while longer.

"Maybe you could do what the sheepherders do. Make them *caporales*, give them each part of the herd to tend. Let them be the responsible ones, and if they do it well, they get part of the asking price at the end. Eh? What do you think?"

Juan Miguel didn't immediately dismiss this idea. He sat up and folded his arms.

"This would be something new for cattle ranchers. Only sheepherders do this."

"So?" the priest asked. "Who cares about that? I will ask around until we find the right ones. There are many, I think, who would want to do this."

"If it is such a good idea, why has no one else done it?"

"*Ai-ai-ai*, my son, beggars can't be choosers. Do you want to solve the problem or not?"

"Yes, father, but I am beset with problems right now."

"All the more reason to start solving. So, let's see what happens then. Shall I ask around?"

Juan Miguel stood and walked to the window, gazing to the north as if he could catch sight of Meg from this distance.

"Yes," he said. "Ask around and come back by next week."

"The young *principe* gets bossy," Father Moreno said, winking. "I will return as soon as I can and I'll stop by the Barones' just to say hello to Manuela." He slapped Juan Miguel on the back.

"Now, about Senora Barone," he said, more seriously. "What transpired on your visit?"

"Father, I cannot talk about it," Juan Miguel interrupted.

"Fine, my son, but the ice has to break sometime, eh?"

———————

That night, after Father Moreno left the house, Juan

Miguel walked outside and saw the light from Father Moreno's candles in the chapel. He had been lying on his bed with no prospect of sleeping. The night air was so close that he could barely catch his breath. During the day, he was a rancher. At night, he was a mystic, listening to the wolves and coyotes exchanging howls, listening to the voices of the dead ones, listening to the weeping. Or was it his own weeping? He could no longer tell the difference. He stepped into the chapel and startled the old priest. He crept in and knelt in front of the small altar. Father Moreno walked up behind him.

Juan Miguel began, "Father, I want what I cannot have. Is there a greater sin?"

Father Moreno patted him on the shoulder.

"Rest easy, my son," he said. "Love is never a sin."

"And lust, father? What of that?"

"We should say a prayer," he said, bowing his head but keeping his eyes on the young man. "Our Father, we honor your name and all that you have made—the perfect and the imperfect. Even the imperfect is yours. Amen."

"Father, I pray constantly to be with her."

"Don't be troubled, my son. God knows what to do. Do you think we need to instruct him?"

Juan Miguel stood and faced him. "Father Moreno, it is more complicated than that," he said.

Father Moreno patted him on the shoulder again. "Sit, my son. Go on—what is so complicated?"

"Her husband is not just a barrier between us. I don't

trust him, father. What if she is in danger because of me?"

"Do you think he would harm her?"

"I have seen his anger, father, and that was only the tip of it. There is more under the surface, boiling and festering. And, yet, I have not convinced her to leave."

"Then you will have to trust her, my son. I have heard she is quite intelligent. She will come to her senses at some point if that is what is required."

"That is not the worst thing, father."

"What is worse?"

"I really don't know whether I have seen what will happen or whether I have caused it. I am afraid of what I have unleashed, father."

Juan Miguel took a deep breath, but still, it felt like there was no air to breathe.

Chapter 9

When Margaret and her sister, Beverley, were children, they made mistletoe balls for Christmas, and every year since, they had made a point of getting together for that purpose. In December Beverly and her husband and son, Tommy, visited the Barone ranch, and the two women set about gathering what they needed for their creations.

They would start with an apple or potato as the base, then add sprigs of sage, lavender, anise or oregano with generous of amounts of the white-berried mistletoe that grew everywhere in the trees of south Texas. They decorated them with ribbons, usually red or dark purple, and small silver bells and gold trinkets taken from old jewelry. Sometimes they added autumn leaves or dried flowers for bits of color.

Despite their differences in temperament, the two women worked together well. They would sit for hours at a table with all the necessary ingredients spread out before them, talking about an array of topics, offering their opinions on the artistry of each mistletoe ball, sometimes humming or singing a tune from their childhood. They loved the ritual of it; it was perhaps the only ritual they possessed. It was the first time Meg smiled and laughed since the baby's death.

Meg was sometimes wary of her sister's visits. Beverley March could be pleasant at times, but she had the quality of a busybody about her. She was always dipping into other people's business, as people do when their lives are dull. She had married a Methodist preacher, hoping it would give her status and make her feel secure, but as is often the case with those types of marriages, it was boring. On top of that, she envied Meg's good fortune at marrying a wealthy rancher.

Beverly started snooping almost immediately when she got to the Barone ranch. On the second night of the visit, she found her sister's journal in the sideboard, and even though her conscience pricked her, she opened it and read it. She was overwhelmed with Meg's carelessness, writing about her longings for a young man and leaving the book for anyone to find. She became judgmental but convinced herself she should tell Ben Barone about the journal for her sister's sake. And that's what she did the next morning. She waited for him outside the kitchen and waylaid him under a cottonwood by the side of the house. She didn't tell him everything she had read. but she warned him nonetheless, and that warning only served to confirm Barone's worst fears.

Meg knew someone had been snooping, and she suspected her husband. That evening in bed, Meg confronted him. "Did you find what you were looking for?" she asked, then regretted what she had said as soon as it escaped her mouth.

"I don't have to look for anything," he said. "I know what has been going on. I know you met with him."

He snapped the blankets over himself, obviously angry. She was stunned.

The next morning, Beverley waited alone for her when she came downstairs, expecting to engage in small talk.

"You know," her sister said in her most singsong voice. "You need to be more careful. You don't want to lose your marriage, do you?" Her voice rose even higher at the end of the question. "Anyway, you probably lost the child because you weren't happy."

"What? Who told you that?"

"Ben told me right after the birth. Now, you know, Meg, your husband's happiness is your happiness." She sounded as if she were giving a prepared lecture. "Remember, that's what Mama used to say."

Meg blanched at the audacity. "Where did you get that, from a tract on marriage?"

"You need to recognize that Ben is a good man and you're lucky to have him. Now, there must be some reason why he feels the need to snoop in your journal."

"What are you saying?"

"I'm saying there are rumors. I'm sure they're not true. I would never, ever believe such things. But you just need to be careful. Don't spoil it, Meg. That would be embarrassing to everybody, now, wouldn't it?"

"I wouldn't want to embarrass you and Tom," Meg said angrily, rising to leave the room.

"Meg, if he's willing to overlook ..."

"Just stop it," Meg said, walking out the door. "There's nothing to overlook."

Her sister and her family left that morning, earlier than planned. There was some excuse about Tommy being allergic to the pollen, blowing like clouds of smoke, from the nearby cedar trees. When Meg walked them out to their wagon, Beverley put her arm through Meg's and leaned over.

"We had a wonderful time," she said with the familiar smile that usually served as a mask.

———————

Raiding continued along the Texas-Mexican border and north to the Medina Valley. Rancor toward the raiders had reached the point that many Texans thought of all people living below the Rio Grande as *bandidos* and all *mestizos* above the Rio Grande as conspirators.

Within only months, Der Kreis became an important organization in the Medina Valley. It was a vigilante group but also a cattlemen's association, and it was prestigious to be asked to be a member. The organization also took on political overtones, planning slates of candidates for local office. Ben Barone, one of the leaders, was asked to sit on the group's governing board. To celebrate the installation of officers, he planned a gathering at the Barone Ranch on New

Year's Eve. It was important to impress others with the solidity of his marriage and with his commitment to Der Kreis and to protecting the Medina Valley. He felt a certain zealotry about it now that he was playing such a conspicuous role. He was not just a rancher, he was a crusader for justice.

The night of the event, he surprised his wife with a necklace he had bought on a trip to San Antonio, partly to please her, partly to signal to the group how important he was. The black velvet choker held an oval locket with a filigree design surrounding a black enameled pear. Inside the locket he put a piece of one of his watch fobs, a black grosgrain ribbon, as a memento.

Looking at her reflection in her bureau mirror, Meg fingered the locket around her neck. She couldn't conceal feelings of dread when her husband walked up behind her, bent down, and looked in the mirror.

"I bought it especially for the occasion," he said somberly.

She touched the locket. "It's lovely ... thank you."

"I guess I thought you would be a little more appreciative." He kissed the back of her neck and fingered the choker, then put his fingers on her neck, encircling it just as the choker did.

"I am appreciative," she said, pulling his hands away from her neck.

When the evening's discussion turned to the raiders, Barone mentioned several times how his own men had killed two of the *bandidos* earlier that year. He ended his talk with words of contempt not just for the Mexican raiders but for all *mestizos.*

"We will do whatever it takes to punish them. One good Texan is worth twenty-five Mexicans," he said. "Texas belongs to us, not to them. We showed them that at San Jacinto, didn't we, boys?"

The room erupted with applause and hoots.

"We will choke off the steady stream of cattle going to Mexico," Barone said. "The Rio Grande is not a barrier to justice or a dividing line between *bandidos* and law-abiding citizens. As far as we are concerned, they can no longer hide down there in their haven."

After the speech, Ben made a point of mentioning the choker to his guests whenever possible, as if its existence nullified any doubts about his devotion to his wife. People were suitably admiring. He considered it a compliment; she considered it an affront. Her irritation grew over the evening until finally, she could take it no longer. She gave an excuse about feeling ill, went upstairs and stayed there. She couldn't bring herself to go back down and say goodbye to his guests.

She should have known what would follow, but she had not anticipated it. Half drunk from whiskey, he came up the stairs with heavy steps, threw open the bedroom door, and took her by the arm where she sat on the bed.

"How dare you act like that," he yelled. "How dare you be rude to my friends?"

He raised his hand to strike but stopped himself.

"Don't ever embarrass me like that again, do you understand?"

"I didn't leave to embarrass you," she said, trying to free her arm.

He pulled her up roughly, holding her wrists tightly in front of him.

"I've done everything to keep this house and family together," he barked. "You've done nothing. Well, maybe it's time I put my foot down. Just see what happens now to your precious boy."

He pushed her down onto their bed. Meg sensed saying anything would be a mistake, so she kept silent, and she only exhaled when she'd heard him leave the ranch house.

———

· The del Valle rancho ran as it always had but with Juan Miguel as its center. He became a cattle baron not by choice but partly by birth and partly because of the affection others felt for him. Out of necessity, he became decisive, convincing, and sure-headed. And when he wasn't, he simply acted that way. If he was in danger of taking a wrong turn, the others prompted him. They wanted him to play his role well. On New Year's Eve, Father Moreno returned to the rancho with the good news that he had found thirty *vaqueros* who wanted to be *caporales*. Some of them were the same men who had followed Juan Miguel from Nuevo Laredo to the Barone Ranch.

"I think you could give them about three thousand head each," Father Moreno explained to Juan Miguel, who was busy stabling his horse. "But you shouldn't just trust them with the beeves. I think you should ask for a small deposit, but not too much. They can't afford too much. That way they won't just off with the beeves, you see?"

"Fine, but it had better be a substantial amount," Juan Miguel bargained. "I cannot give up my cattle to just anybody. They have to know what they are doing."

"You will ask for a small deposit, then another amount to rent the pastureland. That way the cost is spread out and they don't realize."

"Father, don't you think they will add it up? But, I agree, renting the land should be separate."

For New Year's Day, Celita cooked his favorite dish, chicken and rice *poblano*, substituting red *chiles* because she didn't have the *poblanos*. She invited Father Moreno, and for dessert she served them empanadas with cinnamon she traded for at the market. The young *principe* and the old priest stuffed themselves. After the meal, Father Moreno and Juan Miguel moved to the parlor to sit by the fire. The fragrant odor of burning mesquite wood filled the room. Father Moreno reached in his robe and pulled out a small bottle of homemade mescal—the Mexican drink made from the maguey plant—he had bartered for with a few extra prayers.

"Eh? This will warm the innards. The mescal is for everything bad, or everything good, either one," the priest said with a sly smile.

He removed the cork and handed the bottle to Juan Miguel. He waited until they both had downed several drinks before confronting him.

"Now I wish to discuss Senora Barone," Father Moreno said, attempting to look serious.

"What do you wish to know, father?"

"Perhaps you desire to confess something?"

"There is nothing to confess. Only thoughts and feelings."

"*Ai-ai-ai*, my son, are you going to wait forever?"

"The whole thing doesn't make sense," Juan Miguel said. "She is married. She is older. My life is ... a mess."

"Nothing makes sense, my son. Have you not noticed that yet? Love least of all. Love is, well ... " He waved his hand as if to encompass the whole universe. "Love is outside of all; it's an intervention, not a part of the plan."

Juan Miguel nodded in agreement.

"That is true, father. It is like a lightning bolt."

"So are you content to stand aside and forget about her?" he asked after they both took a few more drinks.

"I am not content with any of it, father, but I have nothing to offer now but a failing ranch."

"*Si, si, si*," he nodded, "But of course, that is how you wooed her, with your great ranching abilities."

They both laughed and took several more drinks.

"Is she not worth fighting for?"

"What would you have me do, father?"

"God is with you, but you must make your own case here on earth. If you want something, then take it and pray about it later."

"That is your advice, then, father?"

"In love, the conqueror and the vanquished are one and the same, my son. You are either part of that or you are part of nothing."

The priest shrugged. Juan Miguel drank the rest of the mescal. In the morning, Celita found the two men sleeping by a cold fireplace, the empty bottle beside them.

One evening as Juan Miguel dozed in his chair by the fire after herding cattle all day, three *conspiradores* appeared. Juan Miguel opened his groggy eyes. Celita said, "This is my sister, Beatriz, *senor.*"

It was quite apparent that within the newly constituted cattle baron, Juan Miguel del Valle remained a man with a kind heart. The *vaqueros* treated him with deference, and the women, both old and young, with love, but they also didn't hesitate to ask him for what they wanted.

Juan Miguel looked from the women to the priest, then sat up and endeavored to clear his head. Although the *caporales* system had stabilized the rancho business over the past two months and made it possible for Juan Miguel to pay his debts and think about a possible profit the next year, it still required him to work with Pedro and the others every day to protect the investment.

"Beatriz needs a job, *senor*, and we need her help with the cooking now that there are more *vaqueros* to feed," Celita said. "She has a son to support, *senor.*"

Juan Miguel nodded. "She can stay."

"Well, *senor*, she has a husband, Jose, who has left and gone …" She waved in a southerly direction, indicating he had gone to Mexico. "He misses his son, Roberto, who is now twelve years old and will soon be a man. He wants to come back and live with them again."

Juan Miguel started to get the picture.

"He has some money now, *senor*," Celita said.

I'll bet he does, Juan Miguel thought to himself; raiding and stealing broncos is probably very lucrative.

"Anyway, *senor*, he wants to be a *caporale* … for you … to help you out. Father Moreno will vouch for him."

The priest nodded.

Juan Miguel was feeling a little cornered. "I will think about it," he said. "Let me consider it."

"One more thing, *senor*," Celita said. "Roberto wants to help you with the broncos. He's getting bigger and he could be helpful if he learns what to do. I can send him to you to-morrow, and you can see for yourself how big he is now."

Juan Miguel smiled in spite of his skepticism. "Fine, send him."

Father Moreno remained as the two women left the room. He sat down opposite Juan Miguel, as had become their custom.

"You know I was in the Bandera region before I came here this time," Father Moreno said. "I heard something that will upset you, so you have to remain calm while I tell you."

Juan Miguel's heart pounded and his throat felt dry.

"Senora Barone has left, they say. No one knows where she is."

Juan Miguel started to jump up, but the priest restrained him.

"Calmly, my son, calmly. Even Manuela doesn't know where she is, but she has listened to Senor Barone's conversations and thinks she went to San Antonio."

Juan Miguel shook his head slowly. "Why? Why would she just disappear?"

"There was a fight, I think. The husband treated her badly, I hear."

Juan Miguel put his head back with a defeated look on his face. This was the worst possible news and the thing he had feared the most. He rubbed his eyes to disguise the emotions.

Father Moreno patted him on the knee.

"We will find her," he said. "Don't worry, I have a way. Pedro will be going to the city. He can ask around for her whereabouts."

Chapter 10

Juan Miguel felt no pain, looking up at a clear black night. Unable to sleep, he sat outside shivering in his sheepskin coat, clutching a bottle of mescal Father Moreno had left for him. The bottle was empty, but he liked the feel of it in his hand. A half-moon was almost set on the western horizon—a tiny red ray of sun appeared on the eastern one. The sun became so enormous, lolling just over the low hills, he feared it might drop back under the horizon.

Nothing made sense to him now. He felt alone. He tried to imagine how Meg must feel; he tried to tell himself she was not hiding from him. He tried to draw on something from his short life to give him hope, but there was nothing he could think of now—not this night.

The sun coming up meant another day of work. He tried to remember what it was like only a year ago when he worked at the Barone ranch, enjoying his time with Meg.

He picked up the bottle and looked at it, then threw it out against a post. When the bottle shattered, he thought he heard a noise in the distant field—maybe a reaction to breaking glass. He stood up and walked farther from the house to see more clearly. He heard footsteps and could barely make out the outline of a man running away. Or maybe it wasn't a man, maybe it was just a coyote or one of the phantom camels that roamed the area at night.

"Who is there?" he yelled. He stepped inside and grabbed his pistol, but when he got back outside, no one was there.

The shadowy figure in the field bothered Juan Miguel for days afterwards. He feared he was being watched, and it made him uneasy, day and night. He kept his pistol strapped on all day; at night he insisted that one of the *vaqueros* stand watch close to the house.

One of the things he worried about most was the stash of money in the rancho safe. Contracting with *caporales* had brought in much-needed money, as Father Moreno thought it would. In fact, Juan Miguel had so much business to do, he moved his father's old desk to the parlor next to the fireplace. He had taken to sitting at the desk a good part of the day, doing paperwork and keeping track of the now more lucrative cattle business at the rancho.

But after the day's work, Juan Miguel often sat looking morose in the parlor, staring into space. In the evenings, Beatriz, Roberto, and Jose did what they could to lighten the heart of the young *principe*. Jose might strum his guitar, and Beatriz and Roberto would show him how to do the *jarabe tapatio*, a dance Jose had learned in Mexico. But Juan Miguel could only be distracted for a short time, because his distress over the *senora* sat on his heart and weighted him to the earth.

Ben Barone was—above all else—a practical man, but that didn't mean he didn't have his own fantasies, his own aspirations, and he inhabited his fantasies as a man of integrity. He was brave—he'd demonstrated that. He was resourceful—he'd demonstrated that. He was even willing to be forgiving up to a certain point—he'd demonstrated that. But in his own mind, he was never a fool—never that.

He had come a long way since moving to Texas, marrying a new wife, building a successful ranch, finding his place in the community. But this new turn of events was definitely a setback. It wouldn't be easy to explain his wife's absence; it could even create suspicion among his friends. Better to attack the problem head on.

Barone looked exhausted but exhilarated sitting on his horse in a clearing, waiting for the other men to arrive for a meeting of The Regulators. He had been awake almost all the night before, anticipating this meeting. Captain Neel was making a special appearance to talk about the Ranger activities in the area, and he wanted to make sure he said just the right thing and made just the right impression.

He repeatedly took out his watch, his impatience showing. Finally, some of the others started to arrive. They nodded to him as they rode up, not overtly friendly, but not unfriendly, either, he gauged.

One thing he noticed about Captain Neel as he spoke to the group—he was cocky even in the presence of law-abiding citizens. The Rangers had new plans, he said, not only to subdue the *bandidos* and their Indian cohorts in Texas, but also to cross over the Bravo into Mexico and pursue them there, if need be. The *bandidos'* forays into Texas had become deadly serious, one of them recently costing as many as eight lives in ranchos and sheep ranches along the Nueces River.

"Boys, understand there is no surrendering to these criminals," Neel said, his voice quiet but stern. "We will learn them a lesson if they cross over again from the Mexican side."

Barone stepped forward from the circle of men surrounding Neel.

"What about the ones who live right here in this country?" he asked.

"American ranch owners are exempt. You know that."

"How do we know they're not helping them?"

"If they are citizen spies, we have ways to deal with them. Some have been hanged for that. If you know something, spit it out."

Barone put his hands on his belt and pulled up on his trousers.

"One of my men has seen one of the *bandidos* living and working on a rancho south of San Antonio, on this side of the border," he said. "He happened to be on the del Valle rancho to pick up some ponies, and he recognized one of the raiders who struck my ranch last year."

"If the del Valles are harboring *bandidos,* we will deal with them," Captain Neel said.

It was enough, Ben thought, just to plant the idea. He wanted to be smart about the whole thing. He didn't want to go too far and mention the *bandido's* name, even though he had gone to considerable trouble to find it out. Yes, it was just enough, he told himself.

Father Moreno's network of gossipers took their time, but they finally came up with the information that Meg was staying in a women's boardinghouse in San Antonio. The thought of her alone and friendless was something Juan Miguel couldn't abide. He knew he had to find her if he had to go to every boardinghouse in the city.

So Juan Miguel went to San Antonio and finally found the right place, when he returned to Mrs. Cummings' late in the day after visiting four other boardinghouses south of down-town and asking a slew questions. With Mrs. Cummings by his side, he knocked on Meg's door. He had knocked on the same door earlier in the day but gotten no answer so he re-turned and asked Mrs. Cummings to accompany him to the room with her keys.

"Mrs. Barone, there's a young man, a Mr. del Valle, who says he's a friend. Shall I let him in?" Mrs. Cummings said after knocking softly. There was still no response, but he had convinced Mrs. Cummings that Meg was in the room, so she unlocked the door for him.

It had been rainy and windy all day; what his *tía* called an "ill wind" was blowing up from the gulf. It reminded him of the night he spent in a San Antonio hotel longing for Senora Barone. That seemed so long ago, in a different lifetime somehow.

The room was so dark that he couldn't see her, and there was an unpleasant stench. Juan Miguel closed the door, walked in slowly, and stood next to the bed. He said nothing. He waited until his eyes adjusted and he could see she was curled up in a ball on the far side of the bed. Her hair and clothing were a mess. She looked at him as if she didn't recognize him.

"*Senora*, what has happened to you?" he asked, approaching her with caution.

Her eyes were piercing him like bullets. He sat down on the bed and reached out his hand to pull back her hair. She jumped back. He reached over and pulled her toward him, and that's when he saw that her face was red and puffy and her arms were bruised.

"*Ay dios mio*," he said. "Who did this?"

Still, she said nothing.

"Say something," he said. "Did someone attack you? Marguerite—who attacked you?"

She hesitated. "The one with blonde hair."

"The one who works at the ranch?"

She nodded.

His anger was so intense that he could've killed at that moment, but he stayed calm for her sake. The desire for revenge entered the heart of Juan Miguel in one swift moment, and it would take time and much pain for it to leave.

He carefully removed her dress, pulling it from the shoulders down. When he put his hands on the bruises on her shoulder and side, she jumped with pain.

"I am sorry," he said. "I am sorry, *senora*."

He filled a basin with water to wash the wounds. In truth, she needed a good bath, but he did the best he could under the circumstances. He packed her valises and laid out her traveling clothes on the bed.

"I am taking you home with me," he said.

She started to protest, but he just shook his head.

"No objections, please, *senora*. Just get ready to go."

They rode in her buggy in the darkness and drizzle to the del Valle rancho, with his horse tied behind. She remained silent. He could see that she was in pieces, and not just physical ones. He was angry with the one responsible, to be sure, but also angry with himself for letting it go so far. He smiled at her to reassure her, but behind the smile was a hateful rage.

That evening, Meg was surprised when a crowd of people —the *mestizo* women who served as house staff, a young boy, and two yelping dogs—ran out of the house to meet them. Another dozen *vaqueros* walked up from the nearby fields and outbuildings, and Father Moreno stepped out of the chapel. Obviously, Juan Miguel was the center of their world, and they were relieved to have him back.

"Take care of her," he said to Celita and Beatriz, then walked away, his body rigid, barely able to contain his anger any longer.

The two women were gentle with her. They put her to bed in the downstairs room, the one that had been Tía Marina's room for years, in a large oaken bed with an overstuffed mattress and freshly pressed linen. The unfamiliar room had walls covered with adobe, washed a rusty red, and log facings on the doorways. On one wall was a painting of the Virgin and a tiny painting of a blond boy she knew was Juan Miguel.

Beatriz laid a cool wet cloth on her face and brushed back her scraggly hair. Later, Celita brought in a bowl of warm creamy corn chowder, with biscuits and a slice of cured pork.

"Eat the pork, *senora*," Celita said. "It's good for the blood."

———————

Meg recovered over the next few weeks, with the help of Celita and Beatriz, but she seldom saw Juan Miguel, and when she did, his demeanor was formal. As her wounds healed, she went on walks around the villa grounds, trying to become familiar with it. Early one morning, a chill still in the air, Meg found her way to the rancho chapel. She nodded to Father Moreno, who fussed with some plants by the door, and walked inside. The wood plank floors were freshly swept and the walls white-washed up to the high round window over the altar. Two lighted votives sat on a table next to it.

"Can I do something for you, *senora*?" Father Moreno asked.

"No, father, but *gracias*."

"Do you have a question?"

"Yes, father," she said. "Where is Juan Miguel?"

"He was here this morning—he lit the votives. He wanted to give you time to heal, I think, before he left."

"Tell me, father, where is he?"

"Well, I don't know for certain, but I think he has a score to settle. But maybe you know more about that than I do."

"He has not gone to the Barone Ranch, father. Tell me that is not true."

"Are you religious, *senora*?"

"No, I suppose I'm not."

He motioned for her to sit down on a wooden bench. "I have something to tell you, if I may."

He sat next to her.

"Juan Miguel is not like others, you see. He is above us in some ways, and in some ways, he serves us. Blessings can sometimes be curses, you know, and he has too many of both."

She looked at him blankly. "What are you saying?"

"His power is also his burden," the priest tried to explain. "He cannot lay it down and forget it. He has to carry it—and he will all his life."

"He's just a boy, father."

"That is true, but a boy unlike others. Naïve, yes, but unwise—never. You don't know this yet, but he has great strength, the kind of strength that carries others. Anyway, something to think about, to meditate on while you're here—since, as you say, you are not religious."

"I can't undo anything, father."

"No, no, *senora*, you cannot undo. You have to go on from here. Just remember, the last year has been difficult for him, without his father or brothers, and he has worked very hard. He is responsible for all these people." He swept his arm as if to encompass the whole village. "Without the young *principe*, they have nothing."

Meg had never heard Juan Miguel called *principe* before, but perhaps the name fit him. Perhaps she was only beginning to see him clearly.

———

Juan Miguel had his pistol strapped across his chest and a knife in his hand as he hid behind an oak tree and waited for just the right moment to approach the Barone ranch house. He was disguised as a *bandido* although he had no doubt that the object of his hatred would recognize him well enough. He had tied an old blue bandana around his face and borrowed Pedro's boots and hat. He put the knife—a cold steel shaft and ivory handle—between his teeth and picked up the rope he had brought with him.

He waited patiently for Manuela to leave the house. When he was sure she was well away, he nodded to Pedro and his other *vaqueros* hidden by a row of bushes behind him. They had made short work of teaching the blonde one a lesson.

He walked up the back steps of the house, used the knife to pry open the back kitchen window quietly, and slipped inside. He remembered the layout of the house well, so even though it was dark, he could easily find his way. At the end of the hall, he saw a light in the parlor. He waited again, listening for sounds.

When he heard a slight rustling, he started down the hallway. At the door, he could see the back of Ben Barone's head. He appeared to be drinking straight gulps of whiskey from a bottle he had balanced between his knees.

Quickly, wasting no motion, Juan Miguel looped the rope around Barone's neck and pulled it so tight that he could make only a low gagging sound. When he was sure the rope was secure, he pulled him toward the door.

"*Senor*, you will regret having her beaten," Juan Miguel said through clenched teeth, as he pulled him out the door into the darkness. He held the rope tightly with one hand, drew his pistol, put it to Barone's head and cocked it.

"Do not make a sound or I will blast your head in a thousand pieces, *senor*," he said. "Now tie the end of the rope to my saddle."

When that was done, Juan Miguel mounted his horse and

rode away at a full gallop. The *vaqueros* looked at each other, amazed. Pedro was afraid, for the first time, what Juan Miguel might do. But he dared not intervene.

Juan Miguel dragged him only far enough to make his point, not far enough to kill him. Then he stopped, dismounted, and cut the rope. Barone said nothing as he struggled to get back on his feet. Juan Miguel pushed him back down to the ground.

"Don't touch her again, *senor*, if you hope to live."

By the time Barone was able to stand and call out for his hands, Juan Miguel and his *vaqueros* were gone, riding south without looking back.

————————

The next evening, Beatriz brought stacks of Meg's laundered and ironed clothing into her room and put them on the bureau by the bed. She put a pale blue blouse on top and pointed to it.

"He said this one would be good to wear tonight," she said. "He wants everyone to have dinner together. Come to dinner soon, *senora*."

"Why does he want everyone there?"

"He does not give reasons, *senora*. It is his house."

At dinner, Meg sat between Father Moreno and Roberto. Beatriz, Jose, and even Celita joined them for the meal of beef and beans, with peaches canned the previous spring. Juan Miguel had washed and put on his best clothes.

Meg was like a visitor among family. She tried to catch Juan Miguel's eye, but he spent his time joking with Roberto about his roping skills. Toward the end of the dinner, Juan Miguel rose from his seat at the head of the table.

"*Bienvenido*, Senora Barone," he said, bowing his head formally and toasting with a glass of honey wine.

Juan Miguel was not forthcoming about his visit to the Barone ranch for many reasons, but especially because he didn't want to burden the *senora* with the knowledge. After dinner he waited until the others were gone, then followed Meg to her downstairs room. She turned to him before going in; he put his hand on the door frame and leaned forward.

"Thank you for the dinner," she said. "It was enjoyable, but not necessary."

"*Solo para ti, senora*," he said and bowed his head.

She reached out for him, but in an instant, he was gone.

This was a new experience for her—this distance from him. Since she met him, she had always been able to see his feelings. She shivered thinking about that distance, and more than anything, she had to know the reason. She sat alone in her room until curiosity got the better of her. When everyone had settled down for the night and the house grew quiet, Meg gathered her courage and went up to his room. She had pulled down her hair, and it hung around her face like a billowing cloud, the red waves rippling outward.

"May I come in?" she said, standing by his door.

He sat on his bed, his bare feet propped up. He looked so young. She was reminded of how young he really was.

Glancing up, he said, "Of course, *senora*, you can do any-thing you want."

She closed the door with one hand and rested her other hand on her bodice.

"Are you going to tell me what happened at the ranch?" she asked quietly.

"I have been waiting for you, *senora*."

"So, you knew I would come?"

"Yes, I knew, but I am not embarrassed by it as you are."

"I'm not embarrassed ..."

"But you are. You are the most embarrassed person I have ever known."

She walked over to where he sat back with his head against the headboard. She sat down, reached out, and lightly touched his hair, pushing it away from his eyes so that she could see them—so she could better read his mood.

"Please, *senora*," he said, smiling. "Don't tease."

She put her hand on her cheek because she felt herself blushing.

"When are you going to be rid of this embarrassment?" he asked, pulling back her hand.

"My feelings for you are not about sex," she said.

"Of course they are, *senora*. You know they are."

She smiled slightly and looked at him with her head down. The red waves seemed to grow wilder. He reached up to smooth them down.

"It is not sex I'm asking for," she said.

"But it is. That is why you came to my room."

She was suddenly very angry—angry that he had made her come to him. She started to stand up and leave, but he caught hold of her arm. He pulled her to him and kissed her. He held her arm with one hand and with the other hand took the wooden rosary from around her neck and put it on the table next to the bed. She tried to pull away, but he had a tight grip on her arm.

"*Senora*, I will listen to no more of this," he said. "It is nothing but the lie you have been telling yourself. No more lying. Do you understand?"

"But there is something more between us," she said.

For the first time, he laughed at her.

"*Si*, much more, but first we will deal with this, then we will move on to the rest."

At the same time he said the words, he reached out and put his hand on her bodice, feeling with his thumb the breast underneath. His fingertips burned like fire.

He lifted her blouse slowly over her head. He put his hand on her face, then ran it down her neck and chest. She could feel the warmth pass through his hand into her body, diffusing her anger.

Then suddenly, without warning, as if unable to contain himself any longer, he pulled down her camisole, exposing her breasts. He leaned forward, put his arms around her tightly and placed his mouth on her breast.

Peeling off the rest of her clothing, he asked her, "Is it still not about sex, *senora*?"

He lay next to her and caressed her lightly, but she was

stiff and tense, suddenly embarrassed to reveal herself to someone so physically perfect—his naked body was beautiful, fresh and sweet and untouched like succulent fruit. He propped himself on one elbow, looking into her eyes, put his fingers on her face, and said, "Can I tell you something, Marguerite? Can I tell you about the time I saw you at the hotel in San Antonio?"

She nodded and looked away.

"I saw you standing on the stairs, wearing a lacy blouse and black cape. Your hair was the most beautiful color I had ever seen, and your face was shaped like a valentine. When you bent over to pat your dog, your movements were graceful like a ballerina's. I loved you immediately, that very moment, and I have never changed, only loved you more."

She looked into his eyes and saw he was not mocking her.

"It is only the two of us, Marguerite," he said, putting his cheek next to hers. "No one else is here. No matter what happens, I will still love you."

He kissed her, lightly touching her breast, and lay back down. Then several minutes later, he touched her breast again. All the nerves in her body felt it. By the time he touched her yet again, her body was screaming with desire.

She let go and felt the explosion coming from far away, entering her body freely, effortlessly. It was an unfamiliar but welcome visitor.

Father Moreno was up early, fidgeting in the kitchen, feeling impatient waiting for Juan Miguel to come down. He picked up yet another of Celita's biscuits and put it in his mouth. He had ridden into the del Valle rancho during the night to perform mass and discuss business. But Juan Miguel had not come down for breakfast—and neither had Senora Barone. Father Moreno and Celita looked at each other. One of her eyebrows raised. He shook his head knowingly.

"*Ai-ai-ai*," Father Moreno said. "What now?"

Celita shrugged.

The day wore on, and when the two lovers didn't emerge, Celita put a tray of food outside Juan Miguel's closed door. When she checked later, the food had not been touched, so she took it back to the kitchen.

Finally toward evening, Celita took another tray of warm food upstairs. She knocked on Juan Miguel's door, determined not to be deterred.

"*Senor*, I brought your dinner."

After a long pause, Juan Miguel opened the door a crack, then just wide enough to take the tray.

"*Senorita, gracias*," he said.

"Is the *senora* well?" she asked, trying to peer around him into the room.

Juan Miguel looked slightly embarrassed.

"Tell everyone I will be down soon."

The next morning, Juan Miguel arose at his usual time, went down to the kitchen, and sat eating his breakfast as always.

"Are you ready yet to discuss business, my son?" Father Moreno said to open the conversation.

"No lectures, please, father. I know it is wrong. You don't have to tell me."

"I was merely trying to discuss business."

"I know what you're thinking. I know what you want to say. If you have something to say, please say it to me, not to the *senora*. Promise me you won't speak harshly to her."

"Of course not. But you are being reckless, my son. She is still the wife of a powerful man. Do you think he will let her go without a fight?"

"*Si* … you told me once to take what I want and pray later. So I did, and now you question it?"

"Just be careful. Senor Barone has many friends, and when he finds she is here, he will take revenge."

"Good … I am ready for a fight. She is worth fighting for." He rose and strode out the door.

Father Moreno was stunned at Juan Miguel's harsh tone. The priest finished his breakfast and walked out to the chapel. He gazed after the young *principe*, who rode away from the villa without saying anything to anyone. Father Moreno spent the day thinking about Juan Miguel—stewing about Juan Miguel and avoiding the *senora*.

Meg sank onto a quilt on top of Juan Miguel's bed and pulled part of it over her.

Where have I been? she asked herself. She had been submerged in his world of emotion for hours, swimming in a sea, a stormy sea. Floating atop the waves, then beneath them, buffeted to and fro, rudderless. She had been looking for the shoreline and reaching for it; then he would pull her back again.

He was unfair. He was ruthless. He was totally without scruples. He was totally without conscience. He knew what he was doing. He used her up—consumed her.

It surprised her. She had no idea. It was shocking.

She smiled—the first genuine smile of her life. It lit up her soul. She could feel it through her skull and down to her toes. She could not stop smiling.

———

Never one to miss an opportunity to benefit from another's misfortune, Raul Benavides, the former horse trader, became a mercenary, a hired gun. So when the opportunity arose to hire on with The Regulators, chasing down *bandidos*, he jumped at it. And when he was asked to help punish Juan Miguel del Valle for harboring *bandidos*, satisfaction welled within him at the prospect. Not only would he get paid for the work, he would be able to exact revenge on the man who ran him out of town on a burro. He hadn't known until later that the young "priest" was the son of a wealthy rancher, but when he learned that, it had inflamed his hatred even more. Being born poor had made him resent the wealthy, especially landowners.

What they were asked to do was unusual, not a simple project. But Ben Barone and his cohorts laid out the details convincingly. Benavides and the others mounted their horses and rode south to search for Juan Miguel del Valle, who unfortunately had gone out alone the day they arrived in Atascosa County.

Juan Miguel stopped and sat still on his horse. His eyes were open, but he didn't see what was before him. He had been blinded. His mind roamed over the day before, the *senora's* beautiful body and face, all they had done together.

That morning, he had ridden miles away from the villa to talk to the *vaqueros*, to get their opinions on when the cattle drive should begin and how many beeves there would be. He deliberately rode far so he could clear his head, figure out what to do. But the distance did not really help.

He had moved Meg into his house, and now she was in his bed. He was defenseless against his desire for her. He was enveloped in it. He had broken his promise to wait for her to be free because he could wait no longer. Would God forgive him for this?

A low rumble in the distance interrupted his thoughts. He turned his horse slightly and listened carefully. It sounded like horses' hooves—maybe men riding. He looked off in the distance past a low line of mesquites, and he could see dust. Yes, that's what it was, a gang of men riding.

Finally sensing the danger, he dug his spurs into the horse's side and took off galloping as fast as the horse would go. Horse and rider tore through the field toward the villa, jumping bushes and gullies. Just past a wide gulley, his horse stumbled slightly, not enough to come up lame, but enough to slow them down. Before he could recover, the men were upon him. Juan Miguel was surrounded. One of the men, a paunchy white man with a flowing gray mustache, took his horse by the reins. He recognized several of the men from the meeting at the Barone Ranch, but most of all, he recognized the leader of the gang, Raul Benavides.

"Whoa, son," Benavides sneered. "Who is the horse thief now, eh, *amigo*? You have a certain infamous *bandido* working for you, one known throughout the land for riding with Cortinistas."

"This is my rancho," he protested. "I am Juan Miguel del Valle."

The men looked at each other, then laughed.

"That may be," Benavides said. "But that means nothing to us. We have proof you have been helping the *bandidos*. You will pay a price for that."

152

# PART TWO

MEXICO AND TEXAS 1879

CHAPTER 1

Squatting down in the middle of a group of men in the alley beside an old building in Nuevo Laredo is a bandit worthy of his fame. Dressed in black except for a blue kerchief, with boots worn almost gray and a nickel-plated pistol strapped across his chest, he looks the part of a desperado. His dirty dark hair hangs down his back in a long ponytail sticking out from a black hat, and his five weeks' growth of beard is flecked reddish gold.

In one hand, he holds a stack of Mexican currency and, in the other, a bottle. Standing over him, another man holds a rifle at the ready.

The man in black sets down the bottle and divvies up the

money among the men. When he is finished, he levels out a place on the alley's dirt surface, takes a cigarette butt out of his mouth, flicks it to the ground, and begins to explain his plan.

"Hey, Primo, can we not rest for awhile?" one of the men says in Spanish.

The one with the rifle raises it. "You can give back your share and leave anytime," he says, a menacing look in his eyes.

The one in black, who calls himself Primo, keeps his head down and his voice low.

"We will go up through the Nueces Valley, then the Frio, as usual, but this time, we will double back along the Medina," he explains drawing a map. The men crouch down to listen to the plan.

The others don't question Primo. They don't question his plans, and they don't question his past. Some say he is from down south, maybe Oaxaca; some say he is from up north. But no one really knows.

The one thing everyone knows about Primo is that he lives on the run—free and clear—no ties to anyone except his partner, Pedro.

When the men have dispersed, Primo stands up and leans against the crumbling wall, rolls himself another cigarette and pulls his hat off sideways. Pedro turns to him and claps him on the shoulder.

"Let's go see Lucia, eh?" he says.

They head down the street toward the cantina, Pedro

hovering as if to protect his partner. Primo keeps his head down. Lucia will have a plate of hot food for them. They will listen to Maria strum her guitar or watch her play a little cards. Pedro likes the whore, Teresa, so he may have a go with her. Primo, as usual, will sit by the window and gaze off in the distance until early morning, then find a place to sleep upstairs.

Primo and Pedro have been on the run now for well over a year. It has been easy enough to stay away from the *federales*, who tend to look the other way. North of the border, it's a different story. Captain Neel has beefed up the Rangers, adding several hundred men to his force. And he spends most of his time chasing down *mestizo* and Indian raiders, sometimes boldly chasing them across the border, well into the interior of Mexico.

The outlaw Primo never intended for his exploits to become widely known. He never intended to become a famous *bandido*. It was a surprise to him when the people in the border towns started telling yarns about his raids, the stories spreading like a wildfire on both sides of the border.

"Primo is smart," the people say. "He is educated. He outsmarts them every time."

Beneath all the stories, his fast pistol, and his weathered appearance, Primo is a single-minded man. It's not the notoriety he is after; it is the money.

Upstairs in the cantina later that day, the infamous outlaw Primo sat naked in a tub of soapy water surrounded by the three whores, who quite frankly, were enjoying the sight—the well-formed chest and shoulder muscles, the long legs. They had wanted to get their hands on him for quite some time. Lucia pushed down on his shoulders, shoving him farther into the water. Grease and dirt floated to the surface when she laid his head back and let his long hair flow into the water. Maria gently scrubbed his arms and legs with a cloth and then poured clear water from a pitcher over them. Primo closed his eyes and gave in to the women. At this point, he had no choice. They had approached him as he ate a plate of eggs and beans for breakfast. Lucia held a bar of soap; Maria held a cloth. He was caught; he had no escape route.

The rest of the day, in back of the cantina, he sat wrapped in a blanket in the autumn sun, his laundered clothing laid out on boxes next to him. He leaned back in the chair to let the sun warm his face and chest. Every now and then he would doze, then his muscles would contract in a spasm of tension and wake him up, and he would finger the pistol in his hand under the blanket.

At the end of the day, Primo walked into the cantina newly scrubbed, shaved, and dried, in his clean clothes. The sight of him made the three women stand and walk up to him, inspecting him as if they had never seen him before. His light brown hair hung around his face in ringlets. His face was young, younger than they remembered. His eyes were a soft doe-color and were ringed with heavy black lashes.

Pedro smiled. "Hey, *pistola*, good to see you again."

Looking embarrassed, Primo pulled his long hair back, tied it, and clamped his hat down over his eyes.

"We have a long way to go," he said, strapping on his holster.

When it came to raiding, Primo had three simple rules. Always raid by the dark of the moon. Never announce your presence. And never shoot unless shot at. Once, when one of the men—a bloodthirsty, unruly ex-buffalo hunter—broke the last rule on a raid north of El Paso, Primo shot him off his horse and left him lying in the dust.

Most of Primo's men were wanted on both sides of the border for crimes ranging from petty theft to murder. Primo didn't want to know about their crimes—or their families—or what they did when they were not riding with him. As odd as it might seem for someone already celebrated in *mestizo* ballads, he was trying to keep a low profile.

Once assembled just outside a small town south of the border, the raiding party amounted to about thirty men. Primo allowed only *mestizos* to take part in his raids because he felt he couldn't control Indians or Americanos. This way, they all spoke the same language, so there was no doubting his orders.

Because this raid was to be different than any they had performed so far, Primo went over the plan once again. He had heard from a good source that Captain Neel and most of his men were riding out west, chasing down the remnants of the Quahadis. He judged it a good time to raid some of the ranches and farms close to San Antonio that they had never had the opportunity to hit.

Primo sat on his horse with his knees bent and his feet out of the stirrups. He had on shiny silver spurs shaped like stars. "Once we're done and the horses are delivered," Primo told the group as he lit his cigarette, "we go our separate ways. *¿Comprende?*"

They all nodded. He stuck his boots in the stirrups, nudged his horse, and rode through the group to lead the way. Pedro followed close behind.

———————

Primo decided early on to steal horses rather than cattle because they were swifter and easier to transport across the border. He and Pedro could ride north, pick up a small herd of horses, and sell them south of the border in a matter of days, whereas stealing cattle could take weeks of hard work. Cattle were selling for about a fourth of their American value in Mexico. Horses could bring a much higher price if they were good ones. Primo's main target was *Anglo* ranchers, but he was not opposed to raiding stores, military posts, or wagon trains transporting goods, gold or silver, all of it done at night. Staying out of sight was the chief priority.

That's why it was so odd that a week or so after the last raid, Pedro found himself standing outside the San Fernando Cathedral in San Antonio, trying to blend into the scenery.

He stood up against the door by the main entrance, his rifle tucked behind his right leg out of sight. Pedro scanned the street for any sign of trouble, his hands shaking slightly. There was no overstating the danger they were in. Two of the most wanted outlaws in two countries were paying a visit to the middle of the city on a busy Saturday in broad daylight.

Pedro had not wanted to ride into San Antonio at all. That was against all their rules about laying low. But Primo took him aside after they delivered the horses south and told him he planned to ride in now while the Rangers were out of town.

"You won't go without me," Pedro said. "Going alone would be suicidal."

"I'm going alone."

"Either I go or you don't go," Pedro said.

Primo was inside the cathedral, sitting in a back pew in the shadows. His hat was pulled down over his eyes, but he kept glancing up to the statues, the fine arched columns, and the ledges behind the altar. A youngish-looking priest walked toward him from the front of the church. Primo stood up suddenly and said to him in a low voice, "Pardon me, where can I find Father Moreno?"

The priest looked him up and down and took several steps backward.

"What do you want with him?" he asked warily.

"Would you tell him an old friend wants to see him, please, father?"

A few minutes later, Father Moreno walked down the aisle toward him, his arms folded across his simple brown cassock, totally unaware of what he was about to encounter.

Primo held up his hand when Father Moreno got close to him. "Don't say my name, father," he said.

"My son, my son," Father Moreno said, starting to approach him.

"No, father, stand back and act like you don't know me. And don't tell me any stories, please. I know what happened to the rancho. I just want to know where Senora Barone is."

"I don't know where she is. She disappeared, just as you did."

"Father, find out where she is—you have ways to find out. I will be back in two weeks."

Father Moreno shook his head slowly. "What has happened to you?"

"Don't say anything else, father, just do as I say."

Father Moreno watched as the two men rode away down the crowded street. This could not be, he told himself. I am mistaken. It is not him.

Then the difficulty of the task he had been given dawned on him—find a woman who had seemingly disappeared off the face of the earth. He had already made many inquiries about her whereabouts, just as he had tried to find Juan Miguel.

This would take a concerted effort, and he had to be careful whom he asked.

"Who was that, father?" asked the other priest walking

up behind him.

"I don't know. I've never met him before."

Matthew Piper was an ambitious man of twenty-nine, with a gift of gab and a quick pen. He had the kind of ambition that propels a man forward without regard for money or consequences, that makes him want to be the best, the first, the most noteworthy. In short, he was a born newspaperman.

Matthew had a narrow range of needs for a young man. He didn't need a sweetheart, or children, or family dinners on Sundays, or celebrations at Christmas—all he needed or wanted was one good story. He thought about it when he woke up, as he went about his day, day in and day out. Nothing else mattered—nothing superseded the story.

He had spent his teen years as an apprentice printer in Iowa, then worked for a Kansas City newspaper, first running proofs, then setting type, and finally he got a chance to show his stuff writing a news article now and then. Matthew had what it takes—he was willing to ask questions, to trudge through all manner of unusual environments to get the news, and he could write down the basics really fast. It wasn't long until he was writing and reporting full time, but he longed to be writing about something more interesting than local service clubs and mayoral races.

When he was offered an opportunity to move west and

cover something a little more rough-and-tumble, he welcomed the chance. He arrived in San Antonio at a time when the city was peppered with all manner of interesting people. Cattlemen and outlaws, merchants and schoolteachers, immigrants and natives, *mestizos,* Germans, Irish, *Anglos,* Indians—enough colorful characters to fill a newspaper and then some.

Matthew sat at his desk in the newsroom of the *San Antonio News* on a sunny Saturday morning thumbing through a copy of *Legendary Cow Men of Texas*, a dime novel written by a New Mexico newspaperman and published and printed in New York. It was the latest craze, these cheap paperbacked books of fantastic and often fanciful adventures of westerners. They presented a new way of life, a new culture about "cowboys."

It was a busy day in downtown San Antonio. The cooler weather brought people out to shop at the market and in from their ranches and farms to do business. But it was a slow news day for Matthew, and he was beginning to feel boredom setting in. Reading through the novel, it suddenly hit him. He could write as well—no, better—than the person who wrote this story. There was plenty of material right here in San Antonio; all he needed was a contact with the right people back east.

Matthew walked into the office of the managing editor, Lou Silas, and leaned nonchalantly against the doorjamb.

"Hey, Lou, who do you know in New York?"

"Nobody," answered the crusty old editor.

"No, really, know any publishers?"

"Don't you have somewhere to go? A news story's not going to walk in that door, you know."

"I know. I'm on my way out, but don't you know any publishers back east?"

"Try William Jackson at the *Daily News*. Now, go on and find a story."

Matthew wasted no time. He sat down that afternoon and wrote a letter to Mr. Jackson, asking for a contact at any of the publishing houses that produced dime novels. It would take a while, he judged, maybe even several weeks, but it would be worth the wait. He felt his heart start to pump again. Yes, this is what it's all about, he said to himself—the chase.

———————

Matthew strolled down Main Street looking in all directions for anything to catch his eye. The courthouse was locked up, the cathedral was virtually empty, the banks were closed—only the stores were open, and they didn't make good news copy. He stopped in one of the shops and considered a new shirt, but he couldn't really afford it, so he passed on by.

Walking past the *establo*, the city stable, he decided to take a break in the closest bar, the Silver Elephant. He ordered a beer and sat down at a table by the window, propped up his feet and got ready for a long, dull afternoon.

Matthew was known about town for his quick wit and friendly manner. A chubby, short fellow with a bit of an Irish brogue he inherited from his mother, he would and could talk to anyone. In fact, Matthew was not really happy unless he was chewing over yesterday's news, fishing for today's news, and speculating on tomorrow's news with someone—and just about anyone would do.

It wasn't surprising that it took him only a few minutes to attract an audience. Cowhands, *vaqueros*, shopkeepers, and a few local whores were gathered at his table listening to his tales and telling a few of their own.

One of the cowhands, Johnny Bristol, stayed on when the others drifted away.

"Say, did you ever hear of the outlaw Primo?" Johnny asked.

"Yeah, I've heard some stories. Why?"

"Well, that's him right there," Johnny said, pointing out the window as two hard-looking types rode by. "That other one's his partner, Pedro, I expect."

Matthew craned his neck to get a better look. So that is the famous outlaw Primo, huh? He certainly looks the part. But what is he doing riding down the middle of Main Street in broad daylight? Before he had much time to think about it, the two men disappeared down a side street.

"Are you sure that was him?"

"I know it was. I've seen him before, and not only that, I know where they hang out."

"You know where to find him?"

"Yeah, but it ain't easy to get there. It's way down south in Mexico."

This was the lucky break Matthew had been waiting for. If he could write about someone as genuinely notorious as Primo, he could really make a name for himself. He might even have a good chance of doing a dime novel.

<hr>

On the same day, Primo and Pedro stopped to water their horses in a stream. They had ridden west, rather than south, to confuse anyone who might follow them. The north shore of the Medina, with its limestone rocks and tall cypresses, brought back a flood of images that Primo was struggling to contain. He could not afford to let his mind drift back for a long, self-indulgent trip to the past, because just such drifting had been his undoing.

Pedro bent down and scooped up a handful of the cool clear water to drink, then rubbed some of it over his face.

"Do you trust this priest?" Pedro asked, not looking at his friend.

"I have to."

"You know, Primo, three years is a long time. Think of all that has happened to you in that time. The same is probably true for her."

Primo allowed Pedro to talk to him in a way that he wouldn't allow from anyone else. Pedro had a way of smoothing his rough edges, knowing when to speak and when not to.

"I have to know," Primo said. "Don't bring it up again, eh?"

"Juan Miguel is dead now, *pistola*, he doesn't exist anymore. He died three years ago."

Primo was all too aware he owed Pedro his life many times over, and he felt an obligation to his friend and partner. It was Pedro who searched for a full year and finally found him rotting in a Mexican prison; who somehow raised the money to pay off the prison warden; who carried him, arms around his chest, Primo's feet dragging the ground, out of the prison; who sat with him in the hotel room and watched him retch up his food almost every day for a month because he couldn't digest it; who restrained him from returning to Texas, where he would've been hanged as a citizen spy. And it was Pedro who had been by his side every minute of the day and night since then, guarding him with a rifle.

"It is not your affair, *amigo*. Stay out of it," Primo warned.

Pedro, who knew Primo like no one else, knew his friend was only bluffing. He was a master at it.

CHAPTER 2

Upstairs in a small dressing room of Galveston's Dune Hotel, the widow Maggie Palmer surveyed her image in a gilt-framed full-length mirror. Around her long neck, she placed a gold chain and pendant centered with a large desert turquoise cabochon—the blue-green nearly matching the color of her eyes. She wore a white satin gown overlaid with the finest lace and tied with a sash of dark chocolate *moire* silk. On her left hand sat a diamond ring.

Maggie tucked up some straying strands of hair and took one last look at her reflection. She still looked young, her figure was still slim, and her pale vanilla skin was clear and unharmed by the sun. In a few minutes, she would walk down the curved staircase and enter the hotel solarium, where her fiancé would announce their engagement to the cream of Galveston society. She planned a Christmas wedding to Nathan G. Carlton, one of the most celebrated architects of Galveston, perhaps in the whole state of Texas. Considered the city's most eligible bachelor, Carlton was not only intelligent and talented, he was an exuberant man, if a bit shy. Although short in stature, he had a handsomely shaped head, an aquiline nose, and light gray eyes.

Along with his partner, master builder David Lynch, he was responsible for many of Galveston's new buildings, mostly built in a highly ornamental gothic style that reflected Carlton's sensibilities—detailed, precise, mannered.

He had come to Galveston, Texas, from Ohio after the Civil War and right away began designing everything in sight, from large stately homes in downtown Galveston to the Dune Hotel to cathedrals and libraries all across the state. He was a young marvel.

Maggie met him one hot summer day at the Dune Hotel, where she had been working as a hostess and assistant manager, putting to good use her business expertise. That and her uncanny instinct for how a good hotel should be run helped her rise quickly on the hotel staff to a fairly responsible position.

The Dune was Nathan G. Carlton's grand accomplishment. The huge structure, known for its mauve and green exterior, was three stories high and had 200 rooms. The verandas were wide—18 feet wide—and looked out over nothing but sand and ocean. Streetcars delivered visitors right up to the front door, and in the summer, fireworks and live bands entertained them. The hotel offered a kind of gaiety that had been lacking in Maggie's life, and she took to it.

Nathan and Maggie hit it off from their first meeting. Maggie found him easy to talk to, and he, in turn, had interesting stories to tell about his architectural philosophy and designs. He was good company. The relationship started out on a light-hearted note, Nathan sensing that Maggie was not in the mood for passion or intensity. They would have lunch together on the days he visited the hotel on business, then they would walk along the beach or stroll downtown and buy a flavored ice or a stick of taffy.

Over the course of the summer, they grew closer. Finally, two weeks earlier, on a sweltering late summer evening on the hotel terrace under the stars, Nathan had asked Maggie to be his wife. She hesitated for three days, saying only that she had some "serious considerations." Nathan knew that one of those serious considerations was Maggie's previous marriage. He didn't know exactly what had happened to her husband, and she didn't like to talk about it.

Maggie was genuinely happy on this day, not because she was in love—that was a feeling she would never tolerate in herself again. Nathan offered her not only security and permanence but also a place in society, the recognition and esteem that would come from being his wife. She let her mind flash back to the past for only an instant, long enough to remember her suffering when Juan Miguel disappeared and then died, those days of waiting and worrying and having nowhere to go and nothing to do but worry about him. They were days she wanted to forget, and Nathan was helping her do that.

A light knock on the door brought her back to the present. She smiled and opened the door to her future husband.

"Don't muss my dress," she said.

He kissed her lightly on the cheek, then walked up behind her, reached around her and put his hand on the turquoise necklace, a move that made her shiver with its similarity to something from her past she would rather forget. She dismissed the memory as quickly as she summoned it.

———————

It was the middle of the night after the betrothal reception—an affair with champagne, piano music, and lilies and roses in crystal vases—and Maggie could not sleep. Whether it was the excitement of the event or something else, she could not tell. She walked out onto the balcony and looked across Galveston Island toward the Gulf of Mexico, where lightning flashed on the horizon and the wind whipped up the whitecaps. There had been talk at the party of merchant ships spotting a cyclone out in the gulf.

Maggie leaned her elbows on the balcony ledge and let the wind blow through her long hair and billow out her white nightgown. She could feel the breeze cooling the nakedness underneath her gown. It was a free feeling, a feeling that took her back to a time when she was free, when Juan Miguel was alive and touching her.

No, she told herself sternly. I can't think of that.

Maggie put her hands on her breasts and moved them down the front of her body. Sometimes she could almost feel him there with her, she could almost see his face and body, she could almost reach out and touch.

Suddenly, she tasted saltwater. She reached her hand up to her burning cheek and wiped away tears. She had not allowed herself to cry for a very long time, probably not since she heard of Juan Miguel's death. So why was she crying now? She was happy—she had everything a woman could wish for, a man who wanted to care for her. She put her face in her hands and started to sob, the grief coming in silent waves, shaking her body, making her head and heart feel hollow.

"I hate you, Juan Miguel," she whispered. "I hate you for leaving and I hate you for dying."

When she was spent from the crying, she went back inside and lay on the bed, exhausted.

Maggie had been asleep only a few hours when the cyclone hit. First the wind banged the windows, then the rain and lightning and thunder hit. After one particularly loud clap, she pulled the quilt up higher to protect herself. Maggie's body shook under the quilt as the storm raged on for hours. She felt herself in a deep black void and almost cried out for help. She had never been afraid of storms, but she was afraid of what was inside of her. She comforted herself by singing a song from her past.

Mira la luna; comiendo su tuna. Echando las cáscaras; en la laguna.

"This is the lullaby the angels sing," she whispered.

Father Moreno's main problem was finding out something fast. The *bandido* had given him only two weeks; that wasn't much time. He backtracked in his mind through all the people he had already asked about Meg Barone. They were mostly people in his old parishes along the Medina, not any of her relatives. But who were her relatives? He thought back of all that he'd heard about her, and he remembered that she and Ben had met in Austin. Maybe she has relatives there, he surmised.

The old priest was a favorite of the bishop, so when he asked special permission to travel to Austin for personal reasons, the bishop approved the trip. It took several days of querying, but he finally found out the name of Meg's sister, Beverley, and was able to ask her some questions.

"We don't correspond regularly," her sister said, with her haughty expression. "But I think she is in Galveston."

Father Moreno felt relieved and also a little guilty that he had not found this out earlier. But if he had, whom would he have told?

Happy he had at least some information about Meg, Father Moreno waited with a little fear in his heart for the man to return. The man he met was someone to fear, he could tell that, and he was beginning to suspect he was the one they called Primo. He certainly fit the descriptions he'd heard of the infamous outlaw.

Exactly two weeks after the first meeting, Pedro found

Father Moreno sitting in the church's garden.

"Father, come with me quickly," Pedro said.

The priest followed the man with the large rifle out the garden gate, down the street, and behind a gentlemen's emporium on the riverbank.

Primo sat on a bench behind some trees and bushes, looking at the river. Pedro left them alone but stayed in sight.

"Sit down, father, please," Primo said. "What do you have to tell me?"

"She is in Galveston, but she is probably using her maiden name."

Primo betrayed no emotion.

"That is all you know?"

"I know one more thing. Everyone thinks you are dead."

Primo turned to the priest, looking him in the eyes for the first time since they met again. Father Moreno saw the stern countenance, but the eyes were the same.

"Thank you, father. Now you must forget that you have seen me, *comprende?*"

"*Comprendo.*"

Primo and Pedro stayed hidden beside the river until darkness came. Primo smoked and drank from a bottle they had brought with them. When the bottle was empty, he leaned over with his elbows on his knees and his head down.

"Shall we go now?" Pedro asked.

"Pedro, I am going to ask you to do something for me, and you have to do it."

"*Senor*, of course, what is it ...?"

"I want you to leave and go back to Mexico without me."

"I won't do it. Don't ask me."

Primo stood up, put his hand on Pedro's shoulder, and looked into his eyes, smiling. It was a smile much like Juan Miguel's.

"Go now, Pedro," he said, giving him a gentle pat, then a shove.

Once before, he had sent him away—the day he decided to cast his lot with Barone. Pedro was reluctant then and was reluctant now. But Primo was not easy to argue with.

"I will see you again, *amigo*," Juan Miguel said as he watched his only friend walk out of sight.

———————

As the train to Galveston sped along the track in the late evening darkness, Primo sat in the coach car pretending to read a book he had found left behind in the train station. His mind was racing, and his eyes were vigilant. Two men opened the outside door at the front of the coach and stepped inside. Primo could see right away they were marshals, or maybe Rangers. He resisted the urge to check for his pistol tucked in his inside coat pocket. One of the two men nodded at him; he nodded back. When he heard them exiting the coach's back door, he let out a long silent sigh.

Out of the corner of his eye, he stole a look out the window and studied his reflected image—gray felt Stetson, dark brown suit, tan leather vest, white shirt, silk tie. On his feet were the best tooled leather boots and his silver spurs.

Primo had spent the previous night in the *establo*, sleeping next to his horse with his saddlebags hidden under the hay in the corner. He had taken only his share of the money; he had left a sizable amount for Pedro. He slept uneasily with his hand on his pistol—alone and unprotected for the first time since prison.

In the morning, he paid the stable boy to let him shave and bathe in the old tub behind the *establo*. He also paid him to borrow his clothing and to let him stash his own clothes under some floorboards. He picked up the heavy saddlebags and headed for the shops downtown. Once outfitted with a new suit, he slung the saddlebags over his shoulder and stepped into the Frost Bank next to the cathedral.

The bank's skinny, mousy teller didn't question him about opening an account, nor did he question his identity—Martin Zamora. Primo presented a letter of reference he had written himself on stationery he had stolen from a Nuevo Laredo business office. The teller didn't bat an eye when he deposited thousands of U.S. dollars. Primo tucked his deposit book and the money he was taking with him in his inside pocket. He threw the saddlebags in an alley on his way to the train station.

Primo smiled a faint smile as he let the train's motion lull him back to a more peaceful state. It had all been so much easier than he had thought it would be, this hiding in plain sight. He leaned his head back, pushed down his new hat over his eyes, and slept a bit. But his sleep was fitful—any small noise in the coach woke him up and made his body twitch.

The train pulled into the Galveston station early in the morning before sunup. When he stepped off the train and smelled the ocean breeze, Primo was immediately aware of being in a strange environment. It would take time to get oriented and figure out how to find the *senora*. It would take even more time to figure out how to approach her once he found her. This was a part of the puzzle he had not yet put together.

Primo had sedated his sorrow with tequila and bourbon for a long time now, since well before his stomach healed. He couldn't remember exactly when it had become a necessity instead of a distraction.

For a awhile, he stayed in a cheap boardinghouse on The Strand, spending his days asking questions, searching for Meg. At night, he could not resist the bottle. One night, he clutched his bottle of bourbon in one hand and walked to the beach. He had his sleeves rolled up and his boots off on this unusually warm fall evening. The sea air blew stiffly, and a huge almost-full moon rose over the ocean, lighting up the entire horizon.

Primo sat down on a part of the beach protected by several dunes and continued to drink. He could hear music wafting across the air from one of the beachside bars. He was almost tempted to feel sorry for himself this evening. His searching had not yielded any leads; he was no closer to Meg than he had been back in Nuevo Laredo. Perhaps the information had been wrong or someone had led him astray. God knows, he thought, it wouldn't be the first time.

He left the bottle on the sand, walked back up to the boardwalk and leaned against a pier railing just to get his bearings for a moment. Watching the couples strolling on the boardwalk put him in a worse mood, so he decided to go back to his room before he passed out and risked being arrested.

His eyes were blurry, so when he caught sight of the red hair, he had to try to focus. Looking again, he could see that there was no mistaking that dark red, the loose strands escaping around the face. She was far enough away that he didn't risk being seen, so he walked up a little closer to get a better look. His heart skipped, then pounded in his chest. It was her, to be sure. The shape of the body and the heart-shaped face were hers.

He stood transfixed as she walked by, arm in arm with a short well-dressed man. Primo stared as the two walked out of sight. This was absolutely the worst thing that could've happened at this time, he thought. He had found her, but he hadn't found her. She was happy and married, perhaps. He was drunk and unpresentable.

On the way back to his room, he picked up another bottle—this was going to be a two-bottle night.

It was well into the next morning when Primo woke up with a head the size of that rising moon. He sat on the side of the bed for a good while thinking about his next step. If I found her now, would she even want to know me? he asked himself. He had to admit, the man she was walking with looked like a fine fellow. Probably not a criminal. Primo had to smile in spite of himself. He was two men, both of whom were wanted in two countries.

Yes, there were many obstacles between him and Meg, but that had always been true, and it had never stopped him before.

As his mind started to clear, he remembered he had heard one helpful bit of information the night before. He had heard the man call her Maggie.

Chapter 3

Matthew knew how important it was to broach the subject of Primo with his editor in just the right way. He couldn't start out with some half-baked sketchy bit of information and expect Lou to go along with it. He needed some solid information to make his case, so he had spent several weeks milking the cowhands and *vaqueros*, trying mightily to come up with an angle Lou would go for.

Most of the people he talked to knew stories about Primo, but so far he could find no one who really knew him. Still, he had put together a good amount of information about the outlaw, and he was ready to lay it all out.

Matthew strode into Lou's office late one afternoon, when he hoped the editor had had a few drinks to soften his attitude, and began.

"What would you think of a series about a real outlaw, Lou? You know, the real story, not these fancy stories about the 'cowboy code' and 'outlaw gangs?' "

Lou looked up from his page proofs with skepticism on

his face.

"I think I could find one of them," Matthew continued. "I think I know where one hangs out in Mexico. They say he stays around Nuevo Laredo. I could go down there and look for him and ... "

"And how long would this take?" Lou asked, still skeptical.

"It would take two weeks at the minimum, I guess."

"And what would we do for two weeks while you're gone?"

"I'll do it without pay. You can start paying me again when I get back and start writing. C'mon, Lou, I have a good lead on this. It could turn into something."

"So, tell me, what've you got?" Lou asked leaning back in his chair.

Matthew laid out the story as he knew it so far. He embellished a little, but that didn't matter.

"Fine," Lou said. "I'll bite, but don't come back without a story—a series of stories—or you don't work here anymore."

"That's great, Lou. I won't. I'll get it. I know I can get it."

Primo—the intrepid outlaw—stood outside Galveston's Dune Hotel, where he knew he could find Meg inside. It had taken several days for him to gather the courage to be there, neatly scrubbed and wearing his new clothes. He felt nervous and self-conscious for the first time in a long time.

"This is not going to be easy," he said under his breath.

He started to walk up the path to the main entrance, then turned around and walked back. He stood behind a post and adjusted his coat and tie, then stomped the sand off his boots.

Finally, he walked forward slowly, hesitantly. Once inside the hotel, he removed his hat and had a quick look around. It was a very nice place, as nice as the Menger, he thought. He walked into the solarium lobby trying to appear normal. He had stood there only a few minutes when he saw Meg across the room, walking toward him. He stepped in front of her and said, "May I speak to you, *senora*?"

Maggie looked at him with absolute shock for several minutes, then she covered her face with her hands and doubled over as if in pain.

Primo took her by the shoulders and led her out the door and onto the terrace. He tried to put his arms around her, but she jerked away and faced him.

"I hate you," she said, sobbing. "I hate you for this."

Again, she doubled over, then slumped to her knees.

Primo knelt on one knee in front of her and put his hand on her hand.

"Please, *senora*, don't cry. Please, *senora*, I can explain."

The people on the terrace had started to stare, so Primo straightened her up gently and led her down the front walkway away from them. Once they were out of sight, he picked her up and carried her to a grassy place under some palm trees by a cafe. He was helpless to stop her pent-up grief and pain, which came pouring out like a rush of water. All he could do was hold her in his arms and wait for her to grasp what was happening.

When her strands of hair came tumbling out of their pins, he reached up and pinned her hair. He took out his handkerchief and wiped the tears and moisture from her face and neck. When finally she started to get quiet, he pulled back her hair and kissed her behind her jaw.

"Do you hate me now, *senora*?" he asked, putting his cheek next to hers and rocking her gently back and forth.

She turned to him, her face flushed and swollen, and looked him in the eyes as if to confirm what she was experiencing.

She reached out her arms, put them around him, and held him close.

"*Senora*, I have so much to tell you," he whispered.

"I can't believe you would do this to me," she said, sounding angry but looking joyful. "I can't be here ... I can't do this."

"No, no, *senora*, come with me, give me just this one day ... please."

In the early morning hours long before the sun rose, sitting next to Primo in bed, propped on her knees watching him sleep, Maggie was still amazed he was there—in her bed, in her room, in Galveston.

She pulled back the blanket and exposed his naked body. It had changed in the last three years; he looked more rugged and more mature. She picked up the limp hand that rested on his chest and examined it. The hand that once looked sensitive was now more muscular and competent.

She laid her head on his shoulder softly, so she wouldn't wake him, and caressed his hand. She ran her fingers over his arm, his shoulder, and his chest, touching him gently. When she looked up into his face, his eyes were open, watching her.

"What are you doing, Marguerite?" he asked.

She looked embarrassed.

"If you are looking for Juan Miguel, you will not find him. He is dead now," he said. "This is the bargain that I made, so I have to keep my side of the bargain."

"You made a bargain? What kind of bargain? You traded Juan Miguel for what? For fame, for money?"

"For you, *senora*. It was to see you again."

Maggie couldn't comprehend this talk of bargains. Feeling herself growing angry, she sat back and leaned her head on the headboard.

The two lovers felt self-conscious sitting next to each other, even though they had been intimate only a few hours earlier. The ocean was at high tide, and they could hear the waves crashing against the beach with more force than usual. The room was illuminated by a full moon, almost as bright as the sun and high in the sky, not even trying to hide its all-out assault on the earth.

"But there are other reasons you haven't mentioned, aren't there?" Maggie said quietly after long minutes of silence.

"Yes, there are other reasons. I have other responsibilities that I cannot forget."

"And those other reasons, do they include other women?"

Primo sat up and took her by the arms.

"You are the only woman I have ever wanted, *senora*. Do you believe me?"

Maggie looked him in the eyes, looking for the truth. Incredibly, his eyes had not changed.

"Maybe, I don't know. You've been gone for three years."

"And this man I have seen you with—what of him?" he asked.

She was surprised. She didn't know he knew about Nathan.

"We are engaged. We were engaged."

"Tell me about him, *senora*."

"There's nothing to tell. I won't see him again."

"But he is a man with money and position, am I right?"

"Those things don't matter ... "

"But they do matter," he interrupted. "They obviously matter to you."

"Is that what you think I care about?"

"It is obvious, Marguerite. It is obvious."

"Can't you just stay with me? No one will find you here. This is the last place they would look for you."

"*Senora*, I wish that were true, but it is not. They will find me; they are looking for me now."

Primo got up without looking her in the eyes.

"I have to leave this morning, before it is too late."

He put on his clothes without speaking, then kissed her on the hair, made even more unruly than he remembered by the humid ocean breeze.

"I will see you again soon. I promise."

Maggie reached out her hand and said, "Hold me once more ..."

After he left, she sat looking out the window, feeling foolish and befuddled.

She walked out onto the balcony and took a long deep breath of sea air to clear her head. She was able to think logically again for the first time in days. And ... logically ... she couldn't count on him to return.

On the train back to San Antonio, Primo felt considerably less cocky than he had on the ride to Galveston. With his hat perched on his knee, he watched the empty landscape of the south Texas lowlands go by.

He tried to be inconspicuous as he surveyed the people around him in the coach car. Only a handful were traveling that day, and they looked harmless enough. He might as well relax while he could. The next few days might be dangerous.

He could have told the *senora* all that was in his heart,

but he didn't. He could have told her he would miss her terribly, that he would be with her every moment while he was gone, that he lived only for her. But that would've made it even more difficult for her, and it was difficult enough, he imagined, having him there.

A weight of guilt sat on him like the low-lying clouds hugging the plains. Quite possibly, it was a selfish act, visiting her as he did, taking her as he did.

She had been tentative and shy on his first night in her room. He sat on her bed waiting for her to undress, humoring her while she dallied and talked about inconsequential things. Finally, he held out his hand to give her a chance to accept or refuse him. She didn't take his hand but started to unbutton her blouse, then stopped.

"I am older now, you know," she said.

"Yes, *senor*a, you are, and so am I. Just take my hand. Forget about the clothing."

She put her hand in his, and he pulled her very slowly toward him, trying not to frighten her away. He kept pulling until she was in his arms, then held her close.

He smiled, looked her in the eyes, touched her lips, and said, "However … it would be easier for me to make love to you if you take off your clothes."

She began to, but she felt embarrassed. He reached up and pulled down her hair.

"*Senora*, you are still beautiful. You are more beautiful," he said reaching around to help her with the rest of her clothing.

When she was completely undressed, he laid her down on the bed next to him, and she seemed to forget about the shyness. As the familiarity of it washed over them, he could feel her body start to respond. He tried to hold back for her sake, but the years without her came pouring out, and he couldn't control it. He put his mouth over her mouth and kissed her when she cried out.

"Forgive me," he whispered.

That had been only the beginning of their lovemaking. As he had in the past, he took advantage of her feelings—of how sure he was of her feelings.

He thought about the man she was to marry, the man whose name he didn't even know. Did he hate him or did he feel sorry for him? Probably the latter. He might marry her, but he would never know her—that he was sure of.

As the train slowed, approaching the station, Primo looked out the window at a small contingent of buffalo soldiers seated on horseback. When the train came to a stop, he put on his hat and watched, ready to exit the back of the train if necessary. The doors of a car down the line opened and the men dismounted, then carried an obviously heavy safe to one of their waiting carts and loaded it up for transport.

He wondered, who was guarding that safe before the train pulled in?

CHAPTER 4

Buzzards circled what appeared to be a coyote carcass in an arroyo ahead as Matthew rode south out of Nuevo Laredo. He was looking for a certain cantina he'd been told about that was just enough out of the way to be a good hangout for *bandidos*, whores, and *federales* on the take.

He could smell the dead animal as he rode downwind of it, so he pulled his coat collar over his face to keep out the stench and the dust. It had taken him almost a week to get this far—to put his affairs in order and get his gear ready for the ride to Laredo. The trip took five days of riding, with very few stops. Matthew was tired and dirty by this time. He'd eaten only one meal a day and had been without a bath or even a shave for all five days. It would have been enough to make other men give up, but not Matthew.

Even though the trail from San Antonio to Laredo was well-traveled, Matthew had been on edge riding through the south Texas plains alone, on a strange horse that spooked easily, his clothing not suited to the task at hand. He had on his bowler and a flimsy old wool jacket he'd been wearing since Kansas.

He became more frightened once he reached Laredo and entertained the prospect of crossing the Bravo into Nuevo Laredo. The river had risen, making for a difficult passage this time of year, but he also feared he would be noticed by the wrong people. Traffic from the other side of the border into Texas was common, but *Anglos* riding alone into Mexico were rare.

Before making his way to the ferry, Matthew sought out some of the so-called sources he'd been given by the *vaqueros* he'd interviewed in various San Antonio bars. They all told him the same thing—they'd heard the elusive Primo and his partner, Pedro, were sometimes in the Nuevo Laredo area, but no one knew where they were at any given time.

"Living on the run means you don't stay in one place more than a day," said one Laredo bartender, who seemed determined not to be helpful.

Matthew had fought his nausea and fear as he traveled across the Bravo by boat. On the Mexico side, he decided to find a cantina and quiet his nerves and his stomach. That's where he heard about *La Herradura*, the place he was looking for now.

Once past the coyote stench, Matthew spotted a small adobe building ahead with no sign out front and an open doorway with no door. That's got to be it, he thought, relieved not to have to travel any farther. Walking to the cantina door, he heard a familiar combination he heard often in

Texas—the German accordion and the Mexican twelve-string guitar keeping time to a polka rhythm. Maybe thirty men were gathered round listening, some of them stomping and clapping to the driving rhythm. The scene made Matthew feel at home as he sat down in the back and ordered some food and a beer.

When he was well into his beans and tortillas, he noticed another man sitting in the back of the room, not joining in the fun. Matthew picked up his beer and walked over to him.

"Can I trouble you for a light—*¿tienes fuego?*" he said, holding up the stub of a cigar he had tucked in his pocket.

The man reached for a match and handed it to Matthew.

"Do you mind?" he asked, sitting down in front of the man.

Matthew decided to ease into the conversation with some stories about San Antonio cantinas and whores he'd known, just to break the ice.

The man sat silent for a while, then, without speaking, got up to leave. After he was gone, the bartender walked over to Matthew.

"He doesn't talk much," the bartender said. "That's Primo's partner, Pedro, I hear."

Matthew grabbed his hat and was out the door before the bartender could say anything else.

———————

Matthew felt someone stick a rifle butt in his back just

as he walked by a sign on a deserted Nuevo Laredo street. He felt him push down hard with the rifle, indicating for him to kneel. Out of the corner of his eye, he saw it was the man he'd tried to talk to in the cantina. Then a woman walked up behind him on the Nuevo Laredo street and addressed Matthew.

"He says don't follow him anymore. If you do, he will kill you," she said.

Matthew stood up when he felt the rifle butt withdraw, but both the man and the woman were gone—out of sight. He picked up his bowler hat from the dust and pounded it with his hand, then walked up and down the street looking for a sign that someone was there, but there was no one.

He walked down the mud-smeared wooden walkway, looking for a place to duck out of sight. As he passed a small grocery, a man stepped forward out of the shadows.

He pointed inside. "A man will speak to you in here."

The store was packed with what Matthew guessed was mostly stolen goods: American-made cloth, barrels of dried beans and rice, stacks of ammunition, and what appeared to be army weapons contraband. A short middle-aged man stepped from behind a counter.

"You are looking for Primo, eh?"

"I just want to talk to him."

"The one with the rifle is his partner, Pedro. If Primo were here, he would be with Pedro. If you want to know where he is ..." Then the man held out his palm.

Matthew put two U.S. silver dollars in his hand.

"They say he is in San Antonio now. Only Pedro knows when he will return."

"You are sure?"

"Everyone says."

"So, you have seen him yourself?"

"Yes, I have met him."

"Can you describe him?"

"Tall, has a *pistolero* across his chest, silver spurs shaped like stars."

"What is he like?"

"He is cordial and honest, but also without pity for those he hates."

"Who is that?"

"The *Anglos* who wronged him, *senor*, the ones who took everything, who sent him to prison."

"What do you mean 'took everything'?"

"He was the son of a rich family, they say, the richest in Texas."

Matthew was surprised to hear this. "So his name is not really Primo, then?"

"Oh, no, *senor*. No one knows his real name."

"What else do you know?" Matthew asked, placing another silver coin in the man's hand.

"He is very young, only a few years a man. Try Lucia's cantina, *senor*."

Matthew studied closely the photo of three Mexican *bandidos* hanging on the cantina's wall. One of them was Pedro, he could see that. The other two were not familiar but looked similar, with their swarthy black mustaches and broad-brimmed hats.

"Is one of these Primo?" Matthew asked one of the whores who had apparently been given the task of keeping an eye on him.

She laughed out loud. "No, *senor*. No one takes his photograph. He doesn't look like that."

"What does he look like?"

"*Bello*," she said. "*Muy bello*."

Matthew looked quizzical. He had made a nuisance of himself at the cantina for several days, hoping to get at least a glimpse of Primo before he had to head back to Texas. He leaned his elbows on the bar and took a sip of beer, feeling bored enough to nod off, if it wouldn't bring attention to him.

He heard a commotion outside and turned to look. Someone had walked in—someone tall, and, yes, it must be him. In spite of all the descriptions he had heard, Matthew was surprised at Primo's appearance. He was dressed like an outlaw, and he had the menacing look of someone who might draw his gun at any moment. But when the man removed his hat, then ran his fingers through his long light hair, Matthew smiled. My God, he thought, he is perfect— the perfect hero.

"Will you introduce me to him?" Matthew asked the woman.

Teresa motioned to Primo with her hand, then pointed to Matthew.

"This man has been waiting for you," she said.

Primo bowed slightly and put his hand reflexively on his pistol.

"My name is Matthew Piper. I'm a writer. I want to write about you."

When he looked down, the pistol was cocked and pointed at his chest. Primo's face was absolutely expressionless, but his eyes were not unkind.

Teresa walked up behind Matthew, put her hands under his arms, and felt for a gun or a badge. When she was satisfied that he had neither, she pushed him down onto a nearby chair.

Primo put his pistol on the table and sat down opposite him. Matthew looked down at the star-shaped silver spurs.

Primo leaned back in his chair and lit a cigarette. "Who do you work for, *senor*?"

"The *San Antonio News*. I'm a reporter."

"So they sent you all the way down here to write about me?"

"Yes, a story from your point of view."

"I cannot allow that, *senor*."

"But it would ... "

"*Senor*, you have ten minutes to leave Nuevo Laredo and go back to Texas. If I read about myself in your newspaper, that will be the end of your career and the end of your life. *¿Comprende?*"

Matthew looked into Primo's eyes, and he saw no room for negotiation. He got up, left the cantina, and started back. He didn't get the interview he was after, and he couldn't write about Primo in the newspaper, but he had enough information for a good dime novel; he was sure of it.

Pedro had a mother-hen quality about him, sitting in a chair with a rifle on his lap watching Primo squirming in his sleep upstairs in the cantina. He had come to feel comfortable that way, so he didn't mind. He crept silently across the room and took the almost-empty tequila bottle out of Primo's hand. Once Matthew was gone, Primo began to worry, and his worry had led to tequila.

With his defenses down, Primo looked like the rich, pampered boyhood friend he once was. It was a relief for Pedro to have him there where he could keep an eye on him. He had worried about him incessantly for the two weeks he was gone.

Lucia opened the door, walked in quietly, and picked up a partially eaten plate of food.

"Did he eat at all?" she whispered.

"No, not much."

"Do you think he's getting sick again?"

"I don't know. Maybe he's just upset."

"The woman?"

"*Si*, always the woman ..."

Primo turned over in his sleep and groaned loudly, usually a sign to Pedro he was in pain.

Pedro knew Primo better than anyone, but the one thing he knew best was how unpredictable he was. He could never guess Primo's next move. That was one thing that made him so good. So Pedro had been caught off-guard when he walked into the cantina for a late afternoon drink and there sat Primo, at his usual perch by the window. Without saying anything, Primo motioned to the back door.

The two outlaws had stood leaning against the back wall of the building. Pedro turned toward Primo and asked, looking somewhat embarrassed, "So did you see her, then?"

"*Si*, I saw her."

"And was she still beautiful and ... willing?"

Primo rolled his eyes slightly.

"So, what are you doing here, *pistola*?"

Primo resisted the urge to smile at Pedro's use of his childhood nickname.

"I know a way we can take the Texans for a lot of money," Primo said.

"So why do we need even more money?"

"I need more money. I should have put it that way."

Pedro turned away from his friend, leaned his head back on the wall and took a deep breath.

"Will we be going back to San Antonio, Primo? Because if we are, I don't know. Do you not think people there will figure out who you are?"

Primo stood in front of Pedro and looked at him evenly.

"Yes, but maybe the time for hiding is coming to an end."

"*Ai-ai-ai,* it's the eye of the storm, my friend. Why not stay here where no one bothers us?"

"This is something I will do with you or without you."

Pedro shook his head, bewildered.

"I will go. On one condition."

"What condition?"

"Get some sleep first, *pistola*. It's obvious you haven't slept in days."

———

A small crowd of city officials, hotel representatives, and other admirers gathered outside on a downtown street in San Antonio waiting to hear from the state's first, and busiest, architect. In the last year, he and Maggie had been present for many of these dedications—the Electric Pavilion in Galveston, the MacHugh residence in Dallas, a new cathedral in Austin. Maggie laid her gloved hand on Nathan's arm as they walked to the front steps of the Marshall Hotel, one of Nathan G. Carlton's many ornate High Victorian-style buildings.

As the remarks and recognitions droned on, Maggie shivered in the chilly wind and looked up at the intricate carvings around the hotel's first-floor windows and doorways. She marveled at the stonework, the sheer size of the solid but slim building. She felt pride knowing her husband-to-be was one of the creators of this wonder. It was a physical expression of his intellect.

She smiled when Nathan stepped up to make his brief speech. The weeks since Primo's visit had been difficult, but she was beginning to emerge.

Three days after Primo left, she discovered the old wooden rosary tucked under her pillow. She held it in her hand, trying to guess what he had meant by putting it there. She pressed it to her mouth—it was a poor substitute for his presence. Did he think she would be comforted by it? She slipped it around her neck and tucked it under her bodice, caressing the smooth wooden beads. She didn't need a memento—everything reminded her of him. It seemed not a minute had gone by she didn't think about him—the way he moved, the look on his face, the things he whispered.

"You are mine, *senora*; nothing else is true," he had said.

Maggie thought about what lay ahead of her. The freshness of his absence ached like a blow to the stomach right now. She could almost tolerate such a sharp clear pain, but what would it be like when the autumn days grew darker and colder, when fall turned into winter and he was still not there? How would she bear his absence then, when the sharp pain had turned into a dull heaviness, weighing her down, making her forget what she believed when he was there? This was her fear, that he would cease to exist and she would go on hoping.

"Miracles happen, *senor*a," he had said as he walked out.

The two of them had walked down to the beach, past the farthest buildings where there was no one. Maggie spread out a quilt she had taken from her bed. Primo, with his shirt open and feet bare, sat wordlessly for a long time. Looking at the low waves breaking on the sand, he began to tell her what happened on the day he disappeared. The words sounded like he was choking on them when he told her about being sentenced to prison and being ill. When he said the word "fugitive," she blanched.

"Does that mean you are wanted still?"

That was when he told her his name and explained—as best he could—his identity. She put her hand on his long hair and pulled it back to look at him. When he returned her gaze, he had an expression of pain that she didn't know how to interpret.

Now in San Antonio, in what had become an unconscious habit by this time, Maggie placed her hand on the rosary underneath her dress as she stood listening to Nathan make a short speech about the building. He had a way of being self-deprecating and prideful at the same time, drawing attention to himself without drawing attention to himself. His voice had a different tone and his face a different look when he spoke in public like this. It was as if he turned into someone she didn't know.

Maggie stood watching with both hands over the rosary, the wind growing chillier. She didn't really like these events, because they brought to mind something from her past life she preferred to forget—something to do with hypocrisy she couldn't quite wrap her mind around—something to do with husbands and wives and how they behaved.

What she did know, however, was that there were layers

and layers of silence between her and her fiancé.

Between her and Primo—in spite of the time and distance—there was no space at all.

CHAPTER 5

On the Sunset Route of the Galveston, Harrisburg and San Antonio line, the engine took little time to get up a good head of steam on its way from San Antonio through the rolling south Texas plains to the coast. On its way back, the train went more slowly, climbing the gentle but steady grade from sea level to the Texas hill country. This was where Primo judged that the train would be most vulnerable. At certain points along the line, he remembered, the train slowed to almost a crawl, whether it was a steep incline or just a courtesy slow-down through one of the small farm communities.

There was one place, he remembered, where the train went slowly through a forested area, well away from any settlement. He decided that this would be the prime spot to stop the train and take the safe.

Primo thought he had a good plan, and there was no shortage of men to go along with it. But he spent the better part of the winter in the room over the cantina, suffering from a relapse of a stomach ailment that had plagued him since prison.

Pedro and the whores took care of him, trying to get him to eat, snatching the bottle out of his hand when he tried to sneak a drink. He would start to recover; then the fever would overtake him and he would go back to bed, sweating and groaning in delirium.

Finally, after weeks of seeing him suffer, Pedro could stand it no longer. He loaded him up in a horse-drawn cart, covered him with blankets, and took him to a doctor in Monterrey. The doctor insisted on putting Primo in the hospital where the nuns watched him even more closely than Lucia and fed him cooked cereals. Pedro stayed with him in his room all four days. Once again, Primo recovered and gained strength, but his body was ravaged and thin.

Back in Nuevo Laredo, Primo began eating again. Lucia made apple-filled enchiladas for him and served them with goat's milk. Gradually, his face filled out and took on more color.

He was able to talk to his friend for the first time in weeks, sitting in the sun staring down the empty street outside the cantina.

"Tell me, *pistola*, what happened when you were away?" Pedro said in his low voice.

"I thought it would be easy to leave her there with another man," Primo said hesitantly, looking down at his still-unsteady hands. "It wasn't."

Pedro shook his head. All this for a woman.

"It will be easier to rob a train, eh, *amigo*?"

Primo smiled, maybe for the first time since he got back from Texas.

"So, let's hear the plan."

Several days later, the two men rode out of Nuevo Laredo on their way to Texas. Primo's hands were steady now, and he sat a horse convincingly, but Pedro was even more protective than usual, riding close by his side rather than behind.

———————————

The spring rain had just passed, and the pink-tipped tops of thunderclouds hung on the eastern horizon. The aromas of wet wood and wet soil were in the air. At the bottom of the cliff, water rushed along in a small stream.

Atop the cliff, Primo, Pedro, and six others sat on their horses in a clearing, surrounded by cedars and scrub oaks. Primo held up his hand, signaling for everyone to shut up and keep their horses as quiet as they could. He listened intently. He thought he could hear a faint chugging, but he wasn't sure. Then he knew he could hear it. He nudged his horse, and the others followed.

The band of robbers walked their horses through a stand of trees and waited for Primo to give another signal. He could hear the train slowing as it hit a fairly steep grade while curving around the bend of the Brazos River. When it got nearer and the chugging got slower, Primo raised his hand, swiped it downward and yelled, *"Vamonos."* The horses plunged down the cliff, jumped the stream, and emerged into the clearing along the tracks. Primo and Pedro rode forward, galloping alongside the slow-moving engine then leaping aboard, while the others rode toward the back of the train.

Once on board, Primo stuck his pistol to the back of the engineer's neck and yelled over the sound of the engine, "Stop the train." The engineer started to turn around, but Primo yelled again, "If you look, you die."

It took a while, but finally the train came to a stop. Primo stayed up front with his gun on the cowering engineer and fireman. Pedro went to the back to help unload the safe. The dozen or so passengers looked out the windows of the coach car in amazement at Pedro and his men breaching the doors of the mail car with little difficulty and dragging out a safe labeled Frost Bank.

On the same day, in New York, boxes of dime novels were being loaded for distribution to cities all over the country. The publishing firm of Baer and Jacobs had done a booming business in these cheaply produced paper-backed books, and they turned them out as fast as they could. Readers seemed to have an insatiable appetite for stories about the west, particularly stories about larger-than-life heroes and villains. Taking their money was as easy as robbing a bank.

The firm's latest, called *The Adventures of Primo and the Vaqueros*, was written by a new author, a young man from Texas with a big imagination. But the story fit the genre, so they bought the manuscript for a small price, hired an artist to create a cover drawing, printed it, and were ready to send it out. Little did they know that the book would be so wildly popular it would go through four printings after the initial one. Matthew Piper and his stories were destined to be in great demand.

Several days later, Martin Zamora deposited $30,000 in his account in San Antonio's Frost Bank. Once again, the teller didn't ask questions; he just made the notation in Martin's bankbook. Martin smiled to himself as he returned the money to the same bank from which he had stolen it.

On that same day, Matthew Piper quit his position as reporter at the *San Antonio News* because he needed more time to research his new book, a sequel to *The Adventures of Primo and the Vaqueros*, called *Primo's Hidden Treasure*.

———

In her hair, Maggie wore a sprig of fresh baby's breath Nathan had ordered from a florist several weeks earlier. For their debut in San Antonio society, she chose a dark burgundy dress trimmed in eggshell satin with a skirt drawn up at the empire waist with a brooch of pearls in gold. Her face and hands were slightly swollen from the pregnancy, but other than that, she looked rested and serene.

She sat in the front row, uncomfortable in the limelight but joining in with the others. Nathan sat next to her, genuinely engaged in the night's entertainment. He would laugh, then look at Maggie to make sure she was doing the same. She was trying to help him make the night a success—she knew it was important to his growing business.

Maggie wanted to present a welcoming scene to her guests and give them a first impression of grandiosity—something she had not cared about in the past, but it seemed important this particular evening. The Carlton home was well lighted and decorated with evergreen wreaths. The Carltons were opening the spring entertaining season with a gala at their new home on Windsor Street, and they were expecting numerous state and city officials as well as the social elite.

The couple had gone to great lengths—and considerable expense—to provide light entertainment on a stage set up in the back parlor. Having entertainment had been Nathan's idea. Maggie was not especially fond of playacting. It made her feel uneasy and unsettled.

Miss Ella Mason sang "I'll Take You Home Again, Kathleen," followed by a lively comedy skit starring two famous actors, James McIntyre and Thomas Heath, who constituted one of the country's most popular minstrel acts.

The Carltons had moved into the two-story home, with its red brick facade and ornate ironwork gates, just after its completion in mid-February. The structure, which Nathan had originally designed for another family, was already being talked about as a modern wonder. It was one of only a handful of San Antonio homes with gas lighting.

After Primo left Maggie in Galveston, she had been inconsolable—there was no other way to describe it. She was alone with no one to comfort her. She would sleepwalk through her days, saying little, showing nothing on the outside. She tried to follow Nathan in conversation, but she couldn't concentrate long enough to respond to him. He would ask her if she was ill, until one evening her patience snapped. She turned on him suddenly, looking like someone barely under control and shouted, "Quit asking me what's wrong." He quit asking.

Then a few days before her wedding, with no warning, she started to feel light and weightless, as if she could fly. As the days passed, the irony of the situation struck her. How can you feel lighter when you're getting heavier every day?

Maybe it was a case of selective memory, but if you had asked her, Maggie would have said she still didn't believe in serendipity, or luck, or "God's will" at work in the world. Nothing in her life had convinced her she should believe in such things. But she couldn't help wondering, when Nathan came home one day, only two weeks after their Christmas wedding, and said they were moving to San Antonio.

Even the possibility—however small—she might see Primo again lifted her into a perpetual state of anticipation. At least, now there was a chance he would one day know she was having his child.

The two performers in blackface were acting the buffoons, one of them playing a zany stable boy, the other his smooth friend who outwits everyone at every turn, using a succession of artful disguises. They took turns dancing and singing a series of outrageous routines, all in a bid for fame and fortune. The all-white audience howled at their high jinks.

When the entertainment was over, Nathan rose and faced his guests.

"Please join us in the front dining room and parlor for the buffet supper," he said, gesturing with his hand.

Maggie only nibbled on her food as she went from one group of guests to another. She didn't feel hungry; instead, she felt anxious for the whole affair to be over. Nathan guided her to a group of distinguished looking types. He nodded toward a slight man with a white shock of hair and a white beard, introduced him as Governor Ogden Mason, then said. "And this is Captain Neel."

Maggie searched her memory for where she had heard the captain's name. It was from her past; she was sure of it.

"We were just discussing this new novel about San Antonio, Mrs. Carlton," Captain Neel said. "Have you heard of it? It's called *The Adventures of Primo and the Vaqueros*. Supposedly, it's about a real Mexican outlaw."

Maggie flushed; her face felt like it was on fire. She remembered the nickname.

"Primo? Isn't that a common Mexican nickname, captain?" she asked. "It's just fiction, right?"

"Why, no ma'am. it isn't common at all. We think he's

real, all right, and he may be responsible for many of the robberies in the last two years. But don't you worry, Mrs. Carlton, we'll catch him."

Maggie excused herself and walked away. This had to be a coincidence. It couldn't be about him. Who knew enough about him to write about him like that?

She suddenly felt the oppressive weight, not just of the child she carried but of the secret she carried. She stepped into the kitchen, grabbed her swollen belly with both hands and reached for the side of a cabinet for support.

Maggie crept up the staircase while most of the guests were still downstairs, pulled out her black cape from the armoire and put the hood up over her head to hide her face. She grabbed her handbag, went quickly down the back stairs, and signaled to her driver, who loafed by the back door as usual.

It was almost unheard of for a lady to be out alone past dark in San Antonio, she was aware of that, but this could not wait.

The driver looked dubious when she told him to take her to the cathedral.

"It's too late, Miz Carlton; they won't be open this late."

"Just take me. I'll find a way in."

Sitting in the small front parlor of the cathedral residence, Maggie pulled off her hood, feeling there was no need to hide at this point. She had gone there only on the off chance someone would know how to find Father Moreno, and she was stunned to find out he was a priest there.

"Senora Barone," Father Moreno said as he walked in.

"No, father, it's Senora Carlton now."

"I see. What can I do for you?" The priest sat across from her.

"Do you know how I can find Juan Miguel, father?"

Father Moreno glanced down at Maggie's pregnant belly.

"I don't know where he is, but I have seen him—as you have."

"Can you somehow get a message to him?"

"I will try, but I can't promise. What is the message?"

"Captain Neel is after him. He's figured things out from some dime novel."

Father Moreno hesitated, then asked the obvious question.

"The child is his, then?"

"Don't tell him that, father."

"Have you not done enough damage to him, *senora*?"

Under the old priest's gaze, Maggie felt guilty for the first time.

"If you will pardon me, please, madam, after all that has happened, why do you not forget him?"

Maggie put the hood back over her head, stood up, and started to walk out.

"It's not possible to forget him. You, of all people, should know that."

———

Father Moreno couldn't bring himself to look Matthew in the eye. "Can you find him again?" he asked bluntly.

"I might be able to, father, but he is dangerous, you know."

"Fine, then tell me where to find him, and I will go."

Matthew sat back in a chair at the Silver Elephant and considered whether this was a good idea.

"How do you know him, father? He doesn't seem like the religious type."

"I knew him in the past. I don't know him now."

This intrigued Matthew. The priest was the first link he had discovered to Primo's mysterious past.

"I will tell you where he hides out if you tell me his real name."

Father Moreno demurred. He weighed which was more important—keeping Primo's past a secret or finding and warning him.

"I can tell you he is from a Spanish noble family, one of the original ones in this area—over a hundred years as landowners and cattle ranchers."

"The name, father, what was the name?"

Father Moreno frowned.

"The family name is del Valle."

"And his name ... ?"

"That's all I can say. To say more would betray him."

Matthew sneered. The family name was all he needed anyway.

"He stays mostly in the Nuevo Laredo area, father. Lucia's

whorehouse and cantina—that's where your boy lives."

Father Moreno left the bar wondering—could he find Primo before Matthew Piper gave him away? It was a chance he had to take. To do nothing would be even more risky. After finding and reading *The Adventures of Primo and the Vaqueros*, Father Moreno thought the *senora* had a right be even more worried.

Matthew Piper's book painted a vivid picture, not of a villain or outlaw, but of a hero, a victim of some past obscure persecution. He had been deprived of his position and his good name, so he sought revenge by performing holdups and raids. He had a fast gun, but he was brave and generous, not depraved and evil. It was just the sort of story that would attract attention—and admirers—to Primo. Many, not just the captain of the rangers, would start searching for him. Already, exploits he had nothing to do with were being attributed to him.

Once again, Father Moreno took his case to the bishop. This time, he needed a good cover story, something more than just visiting a friend, so he concocted a story about the mission in Nuevo Laredo needing assistance. He talked, he embellished, he cajoled, he finally convinced him. The bishop gave him permission to go, plus a covered wagon with supplies and the young priest, Father O' Rourke, to accompany him. Father Moreno couldn't believe his good fortune.

When a young boy delivered a handwritten note addressed to "Senora Carlton" at the house on Windsor Street,

Nathan was the only one at home. He knew he shouldn't, but he broke the seal and read the note. It read simply, "I know where he is and I've gone to talk to him. Fr. Moreno". Nathan reread it several times and checked the envelope to make sure it was for her. He wasn't usually a suspicious man, but this note made him wonder—and worry.

———————

Father Moreno walked into the cantina alone. He stood just inside the doorway with his arms folded and looked over the customers.

He was tired—as tired as he had ever been. The four days on a horse-drawn wagon listening to Father O' Rourke complain were almost more than he could bear. And when they arrived at the small Nuevo Laredo church with supplies from the San Antonio diocese, Father Ybarra was unappreciative and cantankerous. He refused to help unload the supplies, so Father Moreno and Father O' Rourke had to do all the work. It had taken all afternoon—carrying heavy boxes in the May sun.

Lucia hurried from behind the bar to talk to him. The last thing she needed was some priest snooping around.

"*¿Cómo puedo ayudarte, padre?*" she asked. "Are you lost?"

"It's fine, Lucia," a voice said from the back. "Let him come in."

Pedro stepped inside the room and nodded toward the back door. Father Moreno crossed the room and looked around for Primo.

"What do you want?" Pedro said, not looking the priest in the eye.

"I'm looking for Primo. I have something to tell him."

"He's not here. Tell me and I'll tell him."

"I can talk only to him."

"Father, I'm sure you mean well, but ..." Pedro turned to look at him just as Father Moreno slumped. Pedro laid down his rifle and tried to grab the old man, but he fell to the ground.

He felt for the priest's heartbeat. He put his ear to his chest and listened.

"Lucia ... Lucia," he yelled into the cantina. "Bring some water."

At last, Father Moreno gasped, "Senora Carlton is in San Antonio." He said those words several times, then passed out.

Pedro and Lucia did all they could for Father Moreno, even sending Teresa to find the woman who had once been a nurse. But it was too late—the old priest died in the dusty alleyway behind a whorehouse in Nuevo Laredo.

"Did Primo know him?" Lucia asked as they watched the undertaker load his body onto a cart and take it away.

"*Si*," Pedro said. "The priest was his only connection to the woman."

Pedro waited, sitting outside the cantina, watching the street for days. Primo had promised him he would not go back to Texas, but all the same, Pedro shouldn't have let him go off by himself. The man deserved some time alone once in awhile, but Pedro knew he was prone to drinking too much.

Primo drifted into the cantina several days later, from where no one knew. Pedro took him aside and told him about Father Moreno's death and that he had come to deliver a message. When he told him the old man's dying words, Primo quickly put it together. Senora Carlton could only be Meg. No one else knew the connection between him and the priest.

The two outlaws arrived in San Antonio on a Sunday after riding almost without stopping. It didn't take long for Pedro to learn where to find Maggie. He simply asked one of the stable boys, who asked his cousin, a delivery boy for one of the local groceries. Pedro paid her driver, who was lounging outside by the back door on Windsor Street, to give her a message.

CHAPTER 6

Primo stepped out of the shadows in the *establo* dressed in black, his pistol still strapped on his chest, the famous silver spurs on his boots, dirty and dusty from days of riding. He had not shaved since—he couldn't remember when.

He heard the quiet sound of a woman's footsteps, then Maggie came into view. She had a pink scarf tied around her red hair. Her eyes looked huge and deep. She was pregnant again. So this was the message from Father Moreno, then? A pregnancy?

"*Buenos tardes*, *senora*," he said, removing his hat and bowing his head slightly, as if that would compensate for his ungentlemanly appearance.

Maggie had never seen him in the guise of an outlaw. She was stunned, even fearful. It changed his demeanor, and there was no missing the pistol.

"Father Moreno?" she asked in a timid voice.

"He has died, *senora*. A heart attack, I think."

"He died in Mexico?"

"Yes, he was there. You sent him there, did you not?"

"I asked him to find you—to give you a message."

Primo stepped closer to her, but she recoiled. She seemed awfully skittish, and he couldn't tell why.

"What is your message, *senora*?"

"I wanted to warn you about the book … the novel about Primo."

"This is your message to me? About some book? You stand there so pregnant and you want to talk about books?"

She grabbed her side as if to stop a sharp pain. He reached out his hand to her.

"Let go of me." Her voice was shrill.

He jumped back. She had never spoken to him that sharply.

"*Senora*, are we not going to discuss the obvious?"

She looked at him, offended.

"What is so obvious? That I am pregnant again? It's none of your concern."

"What do you mean? Of course it is my concern."

"I mean it's not yours."

"*Senora*, it is my child," he emphasized, louder than he would have liked. "I know the moment it happened. I know the truth, *senor*a."

"No," she interrupted. "No, it is not. It is only your large ego that makes you think it is so."

"My ego had nothing to do with it, *senora*. It happened like it always happens … with one thrust."

"Ooh … you are so conceited. The big outlaw—the one

who takes what he wants. That's you, isn't it?"

She lowered her voice and stepped back. "Well, this time you can't have everything you want. If I say it's not yours, it's not yours."

Primo stepped forward to try to touch her, but she jerked away.

"Please, *senora*, I don't blame you for being angry, but please don't do this. Don't deny what we both know is true."

Maggie turned her back to him and started to walk away. Primo put his hand on her shoulder and tried to restrain her.

"It is better this way," she said. "The times we've had together were stolen. They weren't real."

He moved closer to her until their bodies were almost touching.

"For me, it is the only thing that is real. You are having my child—that is what is real."

She put her hand on his hand, and he tried to take hold of it, but she pulled it away.

"I will be back here tomorrow in the evening," he said. "If you are here, I will know the truth."

She walked out of the *establo* without looking at him.

Maggie started crying before she got outside the stable. She put her hand over her mouth to stifle it. By the time she reached her buggy, she could hardly breathe. She felt like she was convulsing, waves of nausea and pain rolling over her.

She struggled to get into the buggy, but the door wouldn't open, and the driver was nowhere to be seen. She took hold of the door handle and squatted beside the buggy.

Primo caught her just as she was about to fall backward into the mud. He put his arms under hers and pulled her up, then picked her up and carried her into the *establo*. He put her down on the hay in an empty stall. She was sobbing and screaming at the same time. He looked at her, not knowing what to do.

"*Senora*, is the baby coming? Tell me, is it coming now?"

She started to quiet down. She looked pathetic, he thought, sitting there with her large belly, her legs spread apart, her scarf falling off.

He squatted down beside her and put his hand on her abdomen to feel for any spasms or movement. But when he touched her, she started sobbing and screaming again.

She rolled to one side and tried to stand up but only landed on all fours. He pulled her back down and gently pushed her onto her side. He tried to put his arms around her to stop the flailing, but she squirmed free.

"*Senora*," he said, "what is happening? Please calm down so I can help you."

She lay down on her back, put her arm over her eyes, and struggled to calm down. She was heaving like a child who's been crying too long.

He sat beside her and waited, feeling sympathy but wary of trying to touch her again. He put down his hat and gently touched her hair, wet from crying and sweating.

She lowered her arm and looked at him.

"So? Are you ready to talk to me now?" he asked. "Go on, speak, Marguerite."

"I am pregnant," she whispered.

He nodded. He tried to fix the pink scarf, to contain the hair, which was now full of dirt and hay.

"And what else?"

"It is your baby."

He moved closer to her and put his hand on her abdomen again. He left it there a long time, then put his other hand on her abdomen, feeling the human form under her skin.

"I'm not in labor," she said.

"Are you sure?"

"I said I'm not in labor."

"Shhh ... *senora*. Be still."

He had his hand on her lower abdomen when he felt a contraction. Her body convulsed again. He pulled up her layers of skirts and pulled down her drawers.

He put one hand between her legs and his other hand on her lower belly.

"Now be still. Relax your legs."

He waited for another contraction, but nothing happened. He caressed her belly as he had seen the *vaqueros* caress the bellies of pregnant animals, which made her muscles relax. He lay down beside her until her breathing became normal.

She looked into his eyes for the first time since he'd gotten there, and she looked like a crazy person. Her face and hair were a mess. Her clothes were muddy and down around her ankles.

She started to speak, but he shook his head. She acquiesced. There seemed to be no quarreling with this man.

"Don't talk about going back to him," he said. "That is not going to happen."

———

Pedro and the two stable boys looked over a low wall into what they had thought was an empty stall. Primo and Maggie were asleep side by side on a shallow bed of hay in the corner.

Pedro motioned for the boys to follow him outside. He pulled out money from his vest pocket and gave each of them some.

"Let them sleep," he said.

He sat down near the stable door in the morning sun and waited. He could not imagine how this problem was going to be solved. A rich pregnant woman who is known to many people in San Antonio. An outlaw who is well-known to most Texans. On top of that, neither one of them is who they pretend to be.

Pedro shook his head. "*Ai-ai-ai,*" he said quietly. "*Es complicado.*"

Primo had finally fallen asleep just as the sun was coming up. He lay next to Maggie completely awake for most of the night. He had never felt so awake in his entire life. He could see every detail of the wood grain in the rafters above him. He could hear every small noise the horses made—the pungent smell of the animals almost overwhelmed him. He could feel his own heart pounding.

When Maggie moved, he put his hand out to calm her, but for the most part he tried not to touch her. He was afraid of starting another crying spell.

He woke up late in the morning, looked at her still sleeping, then went outside to wash.

Pedro watched his friend bathe in the old tub out back, shave off several weeks of beard, then put on the clothes he had stashed in the *establo*. It was clear it had become a routine for both him and the stable boys.

"They will give you away someday, *pistola*," he warned. "I'm sure they have figured it out by now."

"Don't worry, Pedro. It will not become a habit."

"Where will you keep the clothes, then?"

"I will not be needing those clothes for a while, *amigo*."

Pedro stood up and faced him.

"What are you saying? You aren't going to be Primo anymore?"

"No, you are going to be Primo for a while."

"No, no, no, Primo. I don't know how to be him."

"Sure you do," the younger man smiled. "It just takes the costume—that is all."

"And what about your stomach? What if you become ill again?"

"I know you think I cannot live without you, *amigo*, but I can—really."

"This is the worst idea you've had. Nobody will believe that I'm Primo."

"Everyone will believe it. They want to believe so badly that they will believe anything."

———————————

On the ride to the house on Windsor Street, Maggie was absolutely stone-faced. She had not spoken since she woke up in the *establo* earlier that day. Primo drove her buggy to the back of the house and stopped. There seemed to be no one there, but he checked the pistol in his inside pocket just to be safe.

Nathan was, at that very moment, meeting with another outlaw at a clandestine place down by the river. Pedro made the explanation and the negotiation simple, then backed it up with a rifle pointed straight at the gut of Nathan Carlton.

Maggie's eyes had a veiled expression, and her face and hands were bloated. He looked at her, but she didn't look back.

"Now go get your clothes, *senora*. I will wait for you."

She didn't move and didn't say anything.

"Fine. Then I will pack your bags myself. I have done it before, and I can do it again."

He opened the buggy door and took her by the hand, pulling her along, all the way through the kitchen, the parlor, up the staircase, and into the bedroom. He sat her down on the bed, found her bags, and started to put her clothes in them. He picked up the brush on top of her bureau and put it in her hand.

"Are you not going to brush your hair this morning, *senora*?"

She put the brush down on the bed. He picked it up again. He sat down next to her and started to brush. She jerked her head away.

"You are acting like a child, *senora*. Either you brush your hair and get dressed or I will do it for you."

He reached over and started to unbutton her clothing, hoping it would somehow make her snap out of the mood she was in. When it didn't work, he continued to undress her. She sat there in only her chemise and muddy drawers, turned her back to him and slowly started to take them off.

"Thank God," he said. "You can move."

She stood up and started to put on the clothes he had laid out for her. Then she looked in the mirror over the bureau and combed through her matted hair. He breathed a sigh of relief and finished the packing. He'd seen her be difficult before, but this was a whole new level of obstinacy.

When it appeared she was ready to go, he turned her toward him and looked her over. Her hair was down and the long waves were a bit unruly, but they were brushed. Her face was washed, the cheeks were pink.

"You look fine. Now you have to start acting fine. Are you listening to me, *senora*?"

She looked at him with tears brimming in her eyes.

He put his fingers to her cheek to wipe off a tear that had spilled.

"We will work on that later," he said. "We have to leave now before it is too late."

———————

He watched Maggie pace up and down in the small hotel room, visibly agitated and talking now about anything and everything. The woman who only a few hours ago would not speak to him was now prattling on and on about the dime novel, the danger, her husband, her clothing, and anything else she could think of.

"Why are you talking so much, *senora*?" he asked quietly.

"So now you don't want me to talk."

"No, talk all you want," he said, exasperated. "Just do not get upset again. I don't think I could stand that."

She screamed at him, "I'm not upset" so loudly that it made the hair on the back of his neck stand up. He jumped up off the bed and started to put his hand over her mouth, then pulled back. He put his hands up in a gesture of surrender.

"I give up. I don't know what to do with you, *senora*. You are out of control right now. Is it the pregnancy? Is it making you crazy?"

"Yes," she screamed at him. She doubled over for a few minutes, then straightened up.

The two stood there looking at each other for what

seemed like an eternity.

He nodded his head, resigned.

"Fine, then go ahead. Go crazy. I can be patient."

"That is the biggest lie you've ever told." She sat down on the bed. "You've never been patient."

"That is a beginning," he said. "At least we are getting somewhere. What else?"

"You swoop in ... you take over everything ... I completely lose control of my life. You make me pregnant. You make me put on the wrong clothes."

"Oh, come now, *senora*. You are reaching. You can wear whatever you want to wear."

For some reason, this made her smile.

He smiled back at her.

"Go on, spit it out, *senor*a. I can take it."

"I'm fat and ugly right now."

"All true."

"I'm in a bad mood and I don't foresee it getting any better."

"Go on."

"What about Nathan? He will be looking for me."

"That is not going to happen."

"How do you know it won't happen?"

"His silence has been paid for. He has accepted the money. The transaction is done."

Her eyes got wider. "So you have bought me, then?"

"*Senora*, if you choose to think of it that way, then do so."

He sat on the bed and started to take off his boots. He

was obviously angry.

"So if I own you, can I please ask you to stop quarreling with me?" he said as quietly as he could.

"How old are you now?" she asked, looking at him.

He stood up and raised his voice, which by this time had a hard edge.

"So now, we get down to the real issue, then."

"Yes, tell me the truth. How old are you?"

"I will be twenty-two in December. How old are you, *senora*?"

She looked away.

"Well ...?"

"I'm forty-one."

"Very well. Now that that is out in the open, can we please stop this? Are you going to quarrel with me like this forever?"

"Possibly."

He had a stern look. "*Senora*, I am not afraid of you."

"Oh, I forgot, the famous outlaw is not afraid of anything."

He leaned over with his face only a few inches from hers, and she could see she had pushed him too far.

"You would do well to remember that ... Marguerite."

Maggie's eyes popped open in the middle of the night. Rain fell steadily outside the open hotel window, and small drops ran down the window frame onto the floor. The stifling room smelled of wet clothing and boots. She tried to flex the muscles in her legs, but her body was aching all over. Her head was swimming.

She propped herself up on her elbows and looked around the shadowy, unfamiliar room. Next to her, his arms askew, the young man she loved lay on his back quietly snoring. He always looked vulnerable when he was asleep. When she put her hand out and rested it on his forehead, he opened his eyes groggily and looked at her. An open, unguarded expression crossed his face for a few seconds. It was a look she remembered from years ago.

"Close the window," she said faintly. "Everything is getting wet."

When that was done, they lay side by side not touching, looking up at the ceiling, trying to fall asleep.

"Please go back to sleep, Marguerite ... so that I can as well," he said finally.

At that moment, a clap of thunder shook the room. Maggie let out a low guttural noise and slapped her open palm down solidly on his chest. He took hold of her hand, raised his head, and looked at her just as she raised herself up on her elbows and bent her knees reflexively at the same time. The long wild waves of her red hair were falling over her face.

"I will get the doctor," he said, trying to put on his pants.

"No, no, there's no time," she yelled. "Don't leave."

"Fine, I won't leave," he said, sitting down on the bed, feeling helpless.

He took hold of her shoulders and tried to push her upper body onto the bed, but she resisted him and refused to lie down. Then she parted her knees, and he could see clearly the baby's head was already crowning.

"Lord have mercy," he said under his breath. The bed was now soaked with liquid. He spread Maggie's knees as far apart as far as he could, then got on his knees between her legs.

"What should we do?" she screamed in a tone that could've woken the dead.

He put both hands underneath the baby's head and looked at Maggie's contorted face. Her legs were shaking so violently, he had to put her hands on her own knees to steady them.

"Now, push, Marguerite," he screamed, trying to make himself heard over her hysterical yelling. Before he could even finish the sentence, the baby and a rush of liquid and blood came pouring out. He laid the squalling baby on the bed in a sea of body fluids. Finally, the loud knocking on the hotel room door penetrated his thoughts, and he opened the door to a small crowd of maids, the concierge, and other hotel guests.

Two of the maids came rushing into the room to assist, and the concierge hurried away to find the doctor. Primo, panting and red-faced, sat down on the wet clothes on the chair by the window, his own pants and hands soaked in blood and bits of afterbirth.

"*Salir, senor,*" one of the maids said, shooing him out of

the room. "You must go and let her recover."

After washing up as best he could, he made his way to the hotel bar. He had never needed a drink so much in his life.

———————

In the bar alone in the middle of the night, Primo was on his fifth or sixth drink—it was hard to keep track. His head was heavy, and he would've liked to put it down on the bar, but that would arouse too much suspicion, so he managed to hold it up.

The bartender stood cleaning some glasses, hoping the young man would decide he had had enough.

"You know, it is hard to decide," Primo said.

"What is, sir?"

"Hard to decide which is harder … stealing horses or dealing with her." He raised his hand and pointed toward the room upstairs.

"With her, sir?"

"Yes, with her … the woman … who has plagued my life since I was eighteen … or was it seventeen, I don't even remember now."

The bartender whistled. "Seventeen? That's young."

"Damn right."

"So, why don't you go upstairs and talk to her? She's probably waiting for you."

Primo shook his head a little too hard and just about

knocked himself off the barstool.

"No, I cannot go back right now. She is recovering from giving birth."

"So, do you wish to walk away from it all then, sir?"

"Walk away? I cannot walk away. I run into her arms every time like an idiot."

Primo took another drink and ran his fingers through his hair.

"From the first moment I saw her, it was an invitation to fall ... to break the rules, to forget about everything else and believe only in her."

The bartender nodded, sensing the young man was going to go on no matter what he said.

"That is funny ..." Primo went on, "breaking the rules. I don't even remember the rules anymore. They have been turned upside down."

Primo put his head in his hands and rested his elbows on the bar in an effort to keep his head up.

"You would not believe me if I told you," Primo said, trying to get the bartender's attention again.

"Told me what, sir?"

"I have done everything I know to do. Everything ... from a prison cell ... to a whorehouse ... to sleeping in an *establo*. You would not believe."

"So, she must be very beautiful to inspire all that," the bartender said.

"She is like a melody, *senor*, a very complicated melody. So complicated that every time you hear it, it is different. But so simple that the first time you hear it, it is completely fa-miliar—every note."

The young man really has a bad case, the bartender thought, maybe the worst case I've ever heard—and I've heard a few.

"So go back upstairs, son. You know you're going to. It might as well be now."

In the back of the bar another young man, who had also been drinking, sat listening. He stood up and looked around a low partition to try and get a look at the man at the bar. The voice was familiar, and he thought he knew where he'd heard it, but he was having a hard time imagining the outlaw Primo sitting in a downtown bar drinking in the middle of the night.

Matthew Piper caught a glimpse of his face as Primo stood up and turned around to leave.

Sometimes it pays to sit around in a bar, Matthew thought. You never can tell what you might encounter.

———————————

Maggie had a picture in her mind of the young Juan Miguel—the way he was when they first met. He was beyond beautiful to look at. He had an aura of light and ease around him. Even the angels would sing for him.

And, in truth, he was still all of those things. Now he was bound to her like your hand is to your arm. To say that he was part of her was not to say enough. To be so intimate with someone that you are literally the same person did not seem possible to her, and yet that was how she felt about him, lying in his bed, holding his child.

She pulled back the blanket and looked at the baby. She had his features but her own light vanilla skin, and there was a wisp of reddish blonde hair on top. Maggie kissed her on the forehead and lay back to rest. The last few days had been exhausting, and she had not been herself. She had taken his patience to the very limit.

She had no idea where they would go from here, but she needed him. Whether he was Juan Miguel or Primo, he was who he was—the one like no other one.

He opened the door with a somewhat guilty look on his face. He stood at the door, waiting to see what kind of mood was in store for him. She smiled a genuine smile for the first time in days and stretched out her hand.

"Come see," she said.

He looked with wonder at the small human being in her arms. He knelt down beside the bed and pulled back the blankets to get a good look.

"She is like you—perfect," he said.

He climbed up next to Maggie and put his arm across her and the baby. It was morning, but they slept.

———

When Martin Zamora walked into the lobby of the Marshall Hotel, the other guests gaped openly at him. He was a strikingly handsome man with a strong, well-defined jawline and short, light brown hair. The eyes behind his spectacles were piercing. He was dressed in a dark blue three-piece suit of wool flannel. At his neck he had a blue silk tie. Under one arm he carried several packages from fancy emporiums. He walked up to the hotel desk and took a gold watch out of his pocket to check the time.

"I am expecting a visitor at five," the man said to the clerk, "a Mr. Piper."

"He is waiting for you, sir, in the lobby."

Matthew Piper stood and looked with eyes wide at the man who walked in. It was him, but it wasn't him. He extended his hand to the gentleman.

"Mr. Zamora?"

"Senor Piper, thank you for coming. Shall we sit and talk?"

"Thank you, sir, for inviting me, but why are we here? If I may be so bold, I tried to talk to you before and you refused."

"Yes, *senor*, but now I accept."

The two men sat beside each other in two stuffed leather chairs. Martin Zamora was obviously in a different class than Matthew Piper. He had the highly refined mannerisms and relaxed demeanor only the privileged can afford to have. He had an expressive face that he knew how to use to his own advantage. He gave away only what he intended—nothing more.

Matthew, on the other hand, was a study in carelessness.

His body and eye movements were easy to read. He was pure venality, the easiest of all qualities to trump.

Martin looked at Matthew out of the corner of his eyes and sat with his arm around the back of his chair.

"So, *senor*, I am willing to help you tell Primo's next story. I will give you full access to all the information you want—even to the point of letting you ride along. But I have two conditions."

"Conditions? Are you really in a position to demand conditions? I could turn you in at any point."

"That will not happen," Martin said. "And we both know that, because that would end your career as a famous author. Is that not true?"

Matthew looked trapped. "What are the conditions?" he asked.

"The first condition is this: You will write the story as I tell it to you. You will rewrite the legend of Primo to suit a different purpose."

"What is the purpose?"

"That will be obvious to you at some point. But the story will be a good one, I assure you."

"And the other condition? What is that?"

"I will tell you the second condition later ... when the time is appropriate. But I guarantee your safety. You will never be in danger. I also guarantee the story will sell and make you a great deal of money. So, Senor Piper, do we have a deal?"

"I've already told my publishers the title of my next book

will be *Primo's Hidden Treasure*."

"And have you written it yet, *senor*?"

"No, I haven't started it."

"Good, then we will write it together. Do you agree?"

———————

Maggie stood in the middle of the hotel room with her hands on her hips. Turning slowly around, she surveyed the situation she was in, as if looking at the details of everyday life could give her the clues she needed.

The baby, Annabelle, was asleep in a bassinet. The new clothing and other gifts from Juan Miguel were strewn around the room and piled on every available surface. His gifts had been generous and lavish, as if he were trying to make up for the lack of order and structure in her life.

When he walked in, he could see immediately that she was frustrated.

"What is it, Marguerite?" he asked, approaching with caution. The events of the last few days—when she alternately turned sullen and magpie—were still making him wary.

"I can't care for a baby properly in a hotel room. We have to find a permanent home."

"I have a home for you. I have just been waiting to tell you."

"Waiting? Why would you wait to tell me something like that?"

"Because it is not in San Antonio, and it will require some sacrifice on your part."

"Are you sending me away?"

"I am sending you and Annabelle away, yes."

Maggie was angry, but she was trying to think fast—something that was required when you were dealing with Juan Miguel. She asked herself, which would be more persuasive to him: anger or seduction? She decided on the latter.

She smiled and walked closer to where he was standing by the bed. She put her hand on his forearm and, with the other hand, reached up to touch his now-short brown curls. He grabbed her hand before she could touch his hair.

"*Senora*, you will not get your way with that behavior," he said, smiling.

She pulled her hand back with anger, then changed her mood and looked at him in the eyes. "Will we ever make love again? It has been so long," she said softly.

"I want to as much as you do, *senora*, but I cannot be swayed by you this time. It is for your protection and the baby's. Pack your clothing and get ready to go."

"And if I refuse?"

"Then I will pack for you, Marguerite. I have done it before, and I can do it again."

"Is it because I was difficult?"

"No, *senor*a, you have always been difficult, and I have always loved you."

Maggie sat down on the bed with her hands in her lap.

Tears came streaming down her face. He sat beside her and put his hand on hers.

"This fight is over now …" he said. "This fight we have been having since the night in the *establo*."

He took her in his arms and buried his face in her unruly hair. She shuddered, probably from fear and uncertainty. He wanted to soothe her—as he had always done. He ran his hands over her hair, trying to contain the corkscrew waves.

"Everything I do is for you, *senora*, you know that. Even if it is challenging for both of us, I have to protect Annabelle."

She stood up and started to unbutton her dress. She pulled it down and stepped out of it, then took off her chemise and other undergarments. Her breasts were swollen and red from having just given birth. Her turquoise eyes were shining.

"Are you sure, Marguerite, you want to make love now?"

She reached out her arms.

He pulled her down onto the bed and caressed her swollen body, but he was afraid to make love to her, and he didn't change his mind. Afterward, she fell asleep. He got out of bed to quiet Annabelle, then packed Meg's clothing.

PART THREE

MEXICO AND TEXAS 1880

CHAPTER 1

He had a way of completely owning the space he occupied, which was part of his ability to make others believe. That and his pale brown eyes were the only things Pedro recognized when Martin Zamora walked up to him outside the hotel.

Pedro nodded and said, "*Senor* ..." Then they walked side by side toward the market square.

"We will be taking someone with us this time," Martin said, as if stating an absolute.

"Someone? What do you mean someone?"

"I mean Matthew Piper, the writer."

Pedro's eyes almost bulged out of their sockets. He shook

his head slowly.

"Have you gone mad, *pistola*? Has the woman made you as crazy as she is?"

Martin looked at him with a stern look meant to intimidate.

Pedro backed down. "What is the purpose of this?"

"So he will write what we want him to write."

"And what is that?"

"Something more flattering to Primo, to be sure."

"And Senor Piper will do this because?"

"The best of all reasons—because he has much to gain, not because we force him to."

Once more, Primo had a well-thought-out plan. He went over it in detail. Pedro listened, impressed as usual with the amount of detail and forethought. Had he not been an outlaw, Primo would have made a fine lawyer.

"There is something I want you to understand. The *senora* acts crazy at times because I have made her crazy. It is my fault, not hers." Martin said before they parted.

Pedro smiled at his old friend. But he didn't know whether she was crazy because she loved Primo or she loved him so much because she was crazy.

"I am sending them away—Marguerite and the baby," Martin said. "They will be in Bastrop with Beatriz and Jose, but you are not to tell anyone, do you understand?"

Pedro nodded. "*Si, claro.*"

"If something should happen to me, you are to care for them, *comprende*?"

Pedro nodded. "*Si, claro, senor.*"

"Fine," Martin said, betraying his feelings only for an instant. "It is dangerous for you here. We should go."

They started to walk in opposite directions. Pedro saw Martin put his hand over his stomach when he didn't think Pedro was looking.

Pedro stopped and turned to follow. "Is it your stomach again, *pistola*?"

"I am fine. I will be fine," Martin said, waving him away.

Parting from Maggie had been the most difficult thing he had done so far—more than prison, more than robbing, more than hiding. What made it so difficult this time? It was the baby, yes, but it was also Maggie's ability to take him into her upside-down world of emotion and sweetness. It crushed his heart. And now, she was more off-balance than she had ever been—and that was saying something. She needed him now more than ever.

Much of it was a game for her—the physical manifestation of her manipulating mind. He had always known that. Did that mean she didn't love him? No, it meant she loved him beyond her capacity to cope with it. If he could go back and do it again, would he? Would he follow her? Would he love her? It had been his destiny then and would be his destiny at any other point in time. As Father Moreno had once told him, in love, the conqueror and the vanquished are one and the same.

When Maggie and Juan Miguel arrived at the house in Bastrop, they both looked at it in wonder. The architectural style was antebellum. It was a simple clapboard facade, painted yellow with white columns framing lower and upper porches. The house was surrounded by oaks, crape myrtles, and a few stray pine trees. A magnolia stood close to the front door.

Maggie had questions on her face. "How will I care for this?" she asked.

At that moment, Beatriz walked out the front door and started toward their buggy.

"Beatriz and Jose are here," he said. "You remember them from the villa? You will share the house with them … and with Roberto."

He stepped outside the buggy and motioned for Beatriz to go back inside. He sat down next to Maggie. She had a wild, untamed look in her eyes that he had seen many times before.

"Marguerite, get out of the buggy," he said.

She shook her head.

"Do not resist. You know it has to be so."

She looked away and made no move to get out.

"What promise can I make to get you to do this?" he asked.

"That you will stop what you are doing and come back."

"Very well. I promise I will come back … very soon. How could I stay away?"

By this time, she had started to cry. The baby in her arms started to cry also.

He coaxed her into the house. But when it came time for him to leave, she couldn't be comforted. Beatriz, Jose, and Roberto went upstairs with the baby while he parted from her.

"Don't anticipate how difficult it will be, Marguerite," he said. "That only will make it worse."

She didn't say anything. She took off the wooden rosary from around her neck. He held out his hand, and she placed it in his palm.

In the end, he was able to pull himself away only by telling himself that staying would put their lives at risk. That was the only thing that could have torn him away from her this time. He had to promise her he would not die—a promise he wanted to keep, to be sure, but was doubtful about.

By the time he got back to San Antonio, he had a stomach pain that doubled him over. He went to his hotel room and went straight to bed.

———

Juan Miguel rode his horse down a caliche road that cut like a saber straight through an expansive golden meadow. A double row of dark green *abaso* trees lined the road for miles. It ended at an open wrought-iron gate, the front boundary of an inner courtyard surrounded on the other three sides by a red brick manor house trimmed with ecru adobe and forest green framing.

He tied his horse to one of the steel rings on the brick wall, walked across the stone courtyard past a marble fountain noisily gushing water, and knocked at one of two thick carved mahogany doors. He was visiting the Monterrey estate manor of his great-uncle, Juan Ignacio Castaliano—his mother's relative.

He had never met the Castalianos — he had only been told about them by his aunt. His father had never mentioned them.

An imperious butler answered the door and led him into a tall entryway, large enough to be a Texas ballroom. Juan Miguel took off his hat and sat on a dark red stuffed chair in the great hall, waiting for whom he did not know. Heavy purple curtains made the room quite dark for midday.

He had sent a letter to the Castalianos, introducing himself and recounting what he knew about his mother's life and her death when he was only twelve. To his surprise, he received a reply. It was a letter from Renalta Castaliano, the old uncle's spinster daughter.

Presently, the butler returned and ushered him into an even larger room, with the most ornate furnishings he had ever seen. There were at least three groupings of dark heavy furniture and, at the end of the room, a fireplace so enormous that he could have ridden his horse into it without ducking. A small fire burned in the middle—even though the weather was mild—as if it were only a formality.

Juan Miguel stood close to the fireplace, trying not to

sweat, and waited. After almost an hour, Renalta Castaliano entered the room. He was so shocked at her appearance that even he—who was so good at controlling his own reactions—had trouble not staring. She had on a high curly black wig, heavy eye shadow, and dark red lipstick. But what made her look so odd was the white chalky face powder laid heavily on her entire face, neck and *decollete*.

He bowed, then extended his hand to take hers. She had a ring on almost every finger.

"Senor del Valle?" She put her hand up to hide a row of yellow teeth and giggled slightly.

Juan Miguel thought, surely she is not flirting with me, her kinsman. He nodded and answered, "*Si, senora*, thank you for seeing me."

"It is *senorita*," she said, giggling again.

"I have a question for your father, *senorita*. Would it be possible for me to see him?"

"I have arranged a dinner for you this evening. You can talk to him then."

She walked over to him and looped her arm in his, then led him out of the room and down a hallway to a sitting room. She motioned for him to sit on a long, overstuffed divan.

Senorita Renalta then proceeded to flirt shamelessly with the nervous Juan Miguel for another couple of hours. Her hands seemed to be all over him. She ordered the maid to bring a small meal of wine with bread and pears, which she cut and fed to him. He kept telling himself he was there for a reason, and he needed to see it through.

Finally, the time came for dinner. She introduced Juan Miguel to three people whose names he promptly forgot. At last, the old uncle was ushered to the head of the table by one of his chattels. Juan Miguel ate and waited for a polite length of time, then broached the subject he came to talk about.

"Uncle," he began, "I have heard from my aunt that you own property north of the border. Is that so?"

"*Si* ..." the uncle said.

"And that property is in the vicinity of the Texas capital, west of there?"

"*Si* ..."

"And there was a silver mine on that property at one time?"

"*Si* ..."

"They say a pack train carrying forty jack loads of silver was pursued by a band of Indians, and the men in charge of the train had to bury the silver to hide it. Is that correct?"

The old uncle nodded.

"Do you know where it might be?" Juan Miguel said as politely as he possibly could. "Because if you were to tell me how to find it and I did find it, I would, of course, share the silver with you."

Juan Ignacio chuckled softly and took a long drag from his fat cigar.

"You resemble your mother," he said. "She, too, had light eyes and light hair. She was very beautiful, but she decided to marry your father and move to Texas. She could have married well and had a good life."

It was difficult, but Juan Miguel ignored the insult to his father's family. He would have liked to put the old man's head in a strangle hold.

"All I know is that the silver was hidden in a cave west of the city," Juan Ignacio continued. "I sent an expedition to find it, but they were unable to."

"Please, uncle, do you know anything else?"

"I know something more, but I ask a favor in return."

"And what is that, uncle?"

"Escort Renalta to the fiesta on Sunday."

Juan Miguel swallowed hard, hoping nobody noticed.

"It would be my great pleasure," he said.

A cold chill ran up his spine when Senorita Renalta smiled at him through her cracking face powder.

"I will tell you the rest after the fiesta."

After dinner, the old uncle summoned him to a private conversation in his study. They drank bourbon and water from tall glasses that sat on gold filigreed bases.

"And how is Pedro, *senor*?" Juan Ignacio asked.

Juan Miguel was not often surprised, but this time he was.

"How do you know Pedro?"

"He came here asking for help ... to fund the solution to your problem with the Mexican authorities."

Then it dawned on Juan Miguel that it was his uncle, Juan Ignacio, who had bribed the prison warden to release him.

How could he have thought Pedro could raise that much money? It had to be expensive—very expensive.

"Thank you, uncle. I am in your debt," he said.

"I did it for your mother's sake. It is the least I could do for the poor woman. What a shame she ended up in that hellhole … Texas."

Juan Miguel had a strong impulse to pull the pistol out of his inside pocket, point it at the old man's head, then discharge all six rounds that were in it. Instead, he smiled.

When Sunday came, he was exhausted from trying to keep his distance from his spinster cousin. He would have liked to say he escaped from her with his virtue intact, and that it was a narrow escape, but that wasn't what happened.

"I have heard the cave is near tall waterfalls that cascade over blue marble rocks," Juan Ignacio said, walking him out to the courtyard.

"And may I have your permission, *senor*, to look for this silver?" Juan Miguel said, barely able to mask his contempt.

"You may look for it, but I no longer own the land by the river. And, of course we will share it if you should find it."

He mounted his horse and rode as fast as he could back to Texas, where he belonged.

When Juan Miguel returned to San Antonio, he felt dirty, not just from the long ride, but from what he had to do in Monterrey. For the first time, he felt he had prostituted himself. He did it for the information, and then he learned the true extent of his prostitution.

He had been bought and paid for. In return, Juan Ignacio received the privilege of denigrating his mother and his father. There was probably some reason this was satisfying to him, but Juan Miguel didn't want to guess what it was. As far as he was concerned, his debt to Juan Ignacio was paid. If he found the silver, Juan Ignacio would never see even one ounce of it.

Now he understood the *senora's* feelings about being bought, and he felt deep remorse over taking her from the architect without her consent. He wanted her so much that he had become ruthless in his pursuit of her.

He walked down Main Street to the San Fernando Cathedral. Inside, he knelt and crossed himself. For a long time, he could not remember how to pray. The words didn't come easily.

He tried to pray: "God, do you not see how it is for me? My heart is pounding, my hands are shaking, my stomach is aching. Father, if you love me, please forgive me. I beseech you, don't count my sins against Marguerite or Annabelle. Father, please don't turn away from them—or me."

As he knelt with his head bowed, Father O' Rourke walked up behind him. When he looked up, he saw recognition on the young priest's face.

"You are Father Moreno's friend, are you not?" the priest said.

"Yes, father, that is true."

"I have a favor to ask. Would you come with me and we will discuss it?"

Juan Miguel rose. He was reluctant, but he followed Father O' Rourke to the rooms behind the altar.

The priest spoke quietly.

"In Nuevo Laredo, a very bad gang has taken over the streets. They are cruel to the inhabitants—even the women and children. The priest there has been driven away."

"Father Ybarra?"

"*Si*, he and the other priest have fled."

"Father, I don't see what I can do."

"I know you are the outlaw, Primo. I remember you, and I have been praying to see you again. Only you can do something. You are the only one who can stop these men."

Juan Miguel sympathized with the Nuevo Laredo residents, but he had no desire to be sidetracked from his plans.

"Surely, there is someone else who can help. What about the *federales*?" he said.

"I am afraid you are in no position to say no, Primo," the priest countered. "You are not recognizable dressed like that. But you fit the description, and your identity could be revealed."

"Are you threatening me, father?" Juan Miguel asked with a harsh tone.

"No, *senor*, never. But perhaps it would be to your advantage to take a trip to Nuevo Laredo."

That is how it continued—Juan Miguel's mission to Nuevo Laredo. It was a mission of mercy, but the method would be without mercy.

Primo and Pedro balanced on a narrow ledge, next to a sheer ten-foot cliff checkered with jagged outcroppings of multicolored limestone. Above was a stand of cedars and some brushy undergrowth—below, the Colorado River bending toward the south.

Primo pushed his black hat back and scratched his ragged beard. He turned the hand-drawn map given to them by an old woman in a nearby bar. It was supposed to lead them to the marble falls, but so far they had not been able to match the map to the landscape.

"I am afraid we will have to go back to the bar and get better directions, *amigo*," Pedro said.

"Let's just start looking and try to find them. How hard is it to find falls? We should be able to hear them," Primo said.

"We could be looking forever. Come on, my friend, let's go back. We can have some supper and a drink. How can we look for the silver and save the people of Nuevo Laredo at the same time?"

"Calm down, Pedro. We will do one thing at a time. First the silver, then the townspeople. Perhaps one will help with the other, eh? You walk up river and I will walk down. Meet back here by the time the sun sets. Agreed?"

Pedro shook his head. It was useless to argue with him.

"And if we find them?"

"Shoot off your gun three times in succession, and I will do the same."

Primo had been walking—and climbing—down the riverbank for about an hour when he heard the roar. When he got to the falls, he marveled at the beauty of the place— the rocks beneath the water really did look blue. He pulled out his pistol and shot it three times.

A cave behind the falls would be the logical hiding place, Primo surmised. The two men searched and found a way to walk behind the falls. The sun was setting by the time they found a narrow opening, too narrow for the average adult man.

Pedro leaned against one side of the opening, and his sheer bulk seemed to dislodge the rock somewhat. They looked at each other, then began to push. It was heavy—very heavy—but after several minutes, it budged. They moved it just enough to squirm through the opening and into a small cave.

Primo pulled out a match and lit it. There was not much to see in the cave, but the floor in the back had been disturbed.

"The floor is too hard to dig and bury something," he said, sounding discouraged.

When they turned to exit the cave, they saw them—three wooden cases hidden behind the boulder they had moved. They struggled to open them, finally using Pedro's knife to pry off the top wooden slats. Inside were three jack loads of silver. It was not the forty jack loads of legend, but it was enough.

It took the rest of the night and part of the morning to move the boulder aside and remove the boxes of silver, then carry them up the river to where they had left their wagon. Juan Miguel thought about the indignities he had endured to find the silver. He still had the scratches from Senorita Renalta's gold rings on the backs of his thighs.

"What is the danger point for this?" Pedro asked as the two men rode in the wagon to the capital. "When will you not be lucky anymore?"

"What are you asking me?" Primo said, so weary he could barely converse. "How did I find the silver? How did it happen that the name of Matthew Piper's novel came first? I don't know, Pedro. Perhaps God is winking at me. Perhaps he is laughing at me."

"What if it all comes down around your ears, *pistola*? How long can you carry this?"

"Until the end, I suppose." He winced and rubbed his stomach with his left hand.

"Lie down in the back, *amigo*. I can take the reins."

Toward evening, Pedro pulled the wagon to the side of what passed for a road on the way back to Austin. The two sat in the back and ate the tortillas they had brought with them.

"Pedro, I have to ask you something," Primo said.

"*Si?*"

"How did you know Juan Ignacio was my uncle?"

"You told me, *senor*. You asked me to go to him for the money to bribe the jailer."

Juan Miguel had a vague memory of it, but only vague.

"What else do I not remember from that time?"

"You were desperate, *pistola*, to get out of the prison. Because you were sick …"

Pedro knew if he told Primo everything, it might break him. He would take that secret to his grave.

Chapter 2

When Maggie had been in Bastrop for a month, she received a letter with the name Martin Zamora on the return address, postmarked Monterrey, Mexico. It came in a blue envelope and was written on paper of the highest quality she later learned was stolen from the manor home of Juan Ignacio Castaliano. She had never received a letter from Juan Miguel, and she didn't remember ever seeing his handwriting before. It was as graceful and vivid as he was.

Jose had given her the letter after a trip to town and she sat alone on the second-story veranda looking at the envelope for almost the entire day. Toward evening, she had the courage to open it with shaking hands. It said:

My Love,
You are the reason I live. You are everything to me.
Please forgive me.
I love you.
Juan Miguel
She broke down. The tears rolled down her cheeks onto

the letter, smudging the ink until it was almost unreadable. She held it to her face and rubbed the tears with it, then kissed it. She had no illusions; she knew what it meant. He had been taken by someone else.

The image of Juan Miguel's beautiful face came to her. The memory of his love for her and all he had endured for her should have sustained her, but the thought of someone else's hands on his body and touching his face flashed through her mind unbidden. She had always counted on his faithfulness—his innocence—even in the face of her own faithlessness. She felt locked inside herself.

Jose and Beatriz worried about the *senora's* silence. They decided to send for Juan Miguel.

––––––––––––––

Juan Miguel was dressed simply, only as himself, when he went to visit Maggie. He didn't wear Primo's black clothing and silver spurs or Martin Zamora's suits and ties. He had shaved, and his hair was growing out, falling across his forehead as it had when he was seventeen. His eyes were as they had always been—soft, knowing.

He crept into the upstairs room. Maggie was sitting in a rocking chair, staring out the window. He walked up to her and stood in front of her, but she showed no signs of recognizing him. He knelt down in front of her and put his hands on her hands, but still there was no reaction. He took her hand in his and sat on the floor by the chair.

Then he began the story.

"I was very young and you were very beautiful ... We met in the lobby of the hotel ... The spirits were spooking your dog ..."

He continued the story, including as many details as he could remember. At first, she only stared, unblinking. After some time, he saw a glimmer of awareness in her eyes. She blinked and lowered her eyelids. Her chin quivered slightly.

He had an overwhelming desire to take her in his arms and cure whatever was making her sick, but instead, he went on with the story. She turned her head and looked at him. Her eyes were dull and veiled, but he could see her in them. He breathed a sigh of relief.

"Tell me what happened in Monterrey," she said, with little kindness in her tone.

"*Senora*, I had to give myself to someone else in return for information," he said, looking her straight in the eyes. "She was quite unattractive and undesirable, and it was something I did not want. Please forgive me for this. Only with your forgiveness can I forgive myself."

He made no excuses, even though there were many: Matthew Piper, Father O' Rourke, the women and children of Nuevo Laredo, his debt to Juan Ignacio, the prison sentences that might be hung around his neck. Father Moreno had taught him well. The confessional is a place to cleanse the soul, not unburden the mind.

When she heard the confession, she put her hand over her mouth to stifle a scream. She thought it would help to hear the words, but it made things worse.

"*Senora*, can you forgive me?"

She nodded her head.

"Never speak of it again," she said.

"I will never speak of it and I will never think of it—if you still love me. I am yours, *senora*; nothing else is true."

She pulled on his hand, which was still holding hers, and he bowed his head and laid it on her lap. She put her hand into his curly hair. It felt like satin. When he eventually raised his head, her eyes were shiny, and she smiled slightly.

"Come here, Marguerite, take off your clothes," he said. "It has been so long …"

Juan Miguel's touch cured Maggie's illness. Her madness gave him purpose. That was the crux of their relationship. He put his hands on her spiraling red hair and smoothed it down. He put his palms on her cheeks and touched her lips with his thumbs. He kissed her eyelids, then her cheek, her neck, her breast. He put his hands on her back and ran them down to her thighs. He put his hand between her legs and pulled her up to him. Her madness melted into his magic.

———————

He stayed for only one night and one day. He dared not stay longer and risk being seen there. Juan Miguel and Maggie sat on a quilt spread behind the house, in a grassy field between a live oak tree and a patch of purple thistles. He sat behind her with his legs around her, and she sat with the baby between her legs. He caressed Maggie's arms and kissed her cheeks. They watched Annabelle sleeping. A soft, damp breeze blew up from the gulf, bringing with it a faint smell of the ocean.

On the grass next to the blanket was his saddlebag, and in it, within arm's length, was his pistol. He reached into the saddlebag and took out a book bound in cherry-red Spanish leather, its pages gilt-edged, that he had bought for her in Monterrey. He handed it to her.

"It is a new journal for you to fill. Please write something for me. When I return, I want to read it."

She was delirious with happiness that day, except for the nagging thought that he would leave soon.

"We are together now and will be again," he said.

As soon as he left, her spirit careened downward again. Jose and Beatriz saw she was not really well, but they decided they could not call him back again so soon. They also knew her behavior would worry him so much that he couldn't cope with his other problems. They, like Pedro, continued to protect him.

At the cathedral in San Antonio, he knelt and begged the angels on the ledges to keep her and the baby safe. He took out the rosary and kissed it.

"Father, do not abandon me," he pleaded. "Help me go through it all."

He walked out the door, crossed the street to the Silver Elephant, threw his money on the bar, took a full bottle of tequila, and walked to the *establo*.

He was sitting in the corner of a horse stall, opening the bottle, when Pedro walked in. He looked at Pedro, then took three long drinks.

"What are you doing, *pistola*?" Pedro asked with a disapproving look.

"I just want to kill the pain for a little while."

"Your stomach again?"

Primo shook his head.

"The *senora*?"

Primo nodded, took several more drinks, and leaned his head back against the wall, pushing his hat down over his eyes.

Pedro squatted, balancing himself with his rifle. He watched as Primo made himself drunk in record time. Soon, his friend's head lolled to one side. Pedro walked over, took the bottle, and lowered him to the ground. He sat down next to him with the rifle on his lap and leaned back to sleep.

During the night, Pedro awoke when he heard Primo yell. He shook him awake, and Primo sat up, startled.

"What was it?" Pedro said.

"The devil, I think ... he was watching me with those eyes."

"What did he look like?"

"Fat and oily with black hair, yellow eyes ... fetid breath."

Pedro wondered, is he starting to remember?

———————————

Underneath the light blue canopy of the western sky, Primo and Pedro rode side by side, heading south. Behind them, having trouble keeping pace, was Matthew Piper, but they had no intention of slowing down for that prick.

They decided to take the western route to Mexico, avoiding some of the ranches near San Antonio they had targeted in the past. It would take longer, but it would be safer. Hidden in Primo's saddlebag was the fat roll of money they had received for the silver. It was a treasure they could not afford to lose.

The sun beat down onto the rust-red landscape from a sky so close they felt they could almost touch it. When they reached a high ridge that looked out over a vast treeless valley, Primo signaled for them to stop.

He dismounted and wiped his brow with his blue kerchief. Looking south, he could see nothing but emptiness and sky for a hundred miles. It had a freeing effect on the mind. Primo felt unsheltered but safe at the same time. It was a void across which he could write his own future. Just as Matthew caught up and started to dismount, they jumped on their horses and rode on.

After riding for three days, the men arrived in Nuevo Laredo early one morning. At the back door of the cantina, Primo nodded toward Pedro to go in and see who was there.

Pedro found the place mostly empty, so he motioned for Primo and Matthew to step inside. When Teresa and Lucia saw Primo, they ran up and gave him a hug. Teresa patted his face. They sat down at a table by the window.

Primo sensed that something was wrong. "What has happened here?"

"The men from Texas have been sent to make us unhappy," Lucia said.

"Who are they?"

"They are *mestizos*. They were sent to find out about the raiders. But we have not told them anything."

"So they came to find out about the raiding parties and then decided to stay?"

"I don't know why they stay, *senor*. They exact money from us and threaten us."

"Who leads them?"

"A man called Paulo Valdez. They are at *La Herradura* most of the time."

"Have they killed anyone?"

"*Si* ... they have shot two men who refused to help them. They threaten everyone. Valdez raped a cousin of Maria's who is only thirteen years old."

"How many men?"

"About ten, maybe twelve."

"Who sent them?"

"They say the ranchers ... but I don't know."

Lucia pointed at Matthew, who was writing something on a pad, but looked at Primo.

"Why have you brought him?" She didn't look at Matthew, as if that would be giving him too much credibility.

"He is writing a book," Pedro said with disgust.

Primo smiled. "Everybody calm down. He won't write anything we don't want him to write."

Matthew had been unusually silent the whole trip. He did not want to ruin his chance to get a good story—the chance of a lifetime. Besides, he had not forgotten the feel of Primo's gun barrel on his chest.

———————

Primo took Pedro out back, leaving the others inside. He took off his hat and squatted; Pedro did the same.

"If they have ten or twelve men, and we have, basically two, then we need more men," Primo said. "Go find some of the ones who have ridden with us before and meet back here tonight."

"They won't want to do this, *senor.*"

"I know, but all they have to do is ride with us to *La Herradura.* I can handle the rest."

"What do you intend, *pistola*?"

"To shame Senor Valdez."

"This is sounding dangerous. Wouldn't a surprise be better?"

"No, it has to be in front of everybody, or it won't work."

Primo took out his pistol and cleaned it with a soft cloth. He carefully checked the cylinder and the cylinder action, then loaded it. He set up bottles on the dusty alley and stepped back a good distance. He shot one of the bottles six times without blinking, until there were only shards left to aim at. Then he holstered the pistol, drew, and shot another bottle with five shots, but he missed with one. He kept trying until he could draw and shoot with absolute accuracy. He went through the whole exercise again, from a greater distance, then a greater one, until every shot hit its mark from one end of the alley to the other.

Pedro watched from the doorway. "It's been a while since you practiced, eh, *pistola*?"

"It has been a while, but it is coming back."

Primo had begun practicing with a six-shooter right after prison, as soon as he started to recover. He stole a revolver and holster from a drunk *vaquero* before they arrived in Nuevo Laredo. He held such anger that only shooting at something would relieve it. He had been imprisoned unjustly, yes, but the anger arose from his treatment in prison. Now, he remembered only the anger; he didn't remember much about how he was treated.

By evening, Primo was satisfied that his skills with a pistol were what they once were. He had Pedro load up his saddlebags with the money from the silver. With Pedro and the men he had rounded up, he set off for *La Herradura*.

Before he left, he handed Lucia a blue envelope.

"If I die, please make sure this gets to Father O' Rourke at the cathedral in San Antonio." It was a letter saying goodbye to Maggie and Annabelle.

———————————

Many people thought the outlaw Primo was fearless; however, in truth, he was often quite afraid. A man can become accustomed to fear just as easily as he can become accustomed to other things. The only thing that made him hesitate—as always—was his attachment to Maggie. His death would hurt her, even make it impossible for her to be well again. And then Annabelle would have no father or mother. This was the biggest risk—the important risk he was taking. He understood it, and he also understood that only by taking this risk could he get back to them. The route was circuitous but certain in his mind. Also, he knew he could count on greed and stupidity—two constants of humankind.

Primo and Pedro dismounted. As they walked up to *La Herradura,* the others stayed on their horses, forming a semicircle behind them. Primo signaled for Pedro to hand him the money.

"Paulo Valdez," he yelled. "I have a proposition for you."

There was no response, so he yelled the same thing again.

In a few minutes, Senor Valdez and his cohorts straggled out of the cantina. They were laughing at something, but no one could see what.

When they were all out the door, Primo said, "Senor Valdez, I understand you like little girls. Is that true?"

Valdez only smiled nervously, fingering the holstered pistol on his hip. His friends looked embarrassed.

"Come now, *senor*, you can tell us. Women are too difficult, eh? Maybe too large for the size of your manhood. Maybe only a little girl will work for you. Is that right?"

Valdez's eyes burned. He stepped into the street, away from the others.

"Who are you?"

"My name is Primo, the outlaw Primo. Put down your gun and ride away—leave Nuevo Laredo."

Valdez stood there, looking as if he was considering the idea, for some time. Swaying from too much whiskey, he stumbled backward several paces. His hand fumbled for his gun. He drew it, shot, and missed.

"I did not say draw, *senor*," Primo said. "I said leave."

Valdez aimed and missed again. Primo, on the other hand, was deliberate, patient, and accurate. Valdez lay dead and prone in the dust, and Primo's gun was back in the holster on his chest as the others stood looking at each other.

Primo's men drew their guns, and Pedro raised his rifle, aiming them at Valdez's men. Primo held up the money and fanned it out in his hands.

"We will give you $1,000 for every gun or knife you put down on the ground," Primo said. "You can either do that, or you can risk being shot dead right now by these fine men you see behind me. So what will it be, *senores*? All you have to do is put down your weapons, walk over and get your cash, then stand aside. Or is your loyalty to Senor Valdez so great that you will get killed for it?"

Slowly, they started to follow his instructions. Pedro and the other men collected the guns and a few knives and piled them into the wagon they had parked behind their horses.

Primo waved his pistol at Valdez's men, stopping it at the boot heel of the one on the left.

"Who sent you to Nuevo Laredo?" he said.

No one spoke.

Primo shot off the boot heel.

"Who sent you to Nuevo Laredo?"

"It was Ben Barone, *senor*, and his group … Der Kreis."

"Good, now each of you will lay down the money on the dirt, start riding, and don't stop until you get back to Texas, *comprende?*"

Two of the men considered making a move for their discarded guns, but with Primo's pistol and Pedro's rifle, they knew they would have no chance.

"You have cheated us, *senor*," one of them said.

"*Si*," Primo said, smiling, "and it was so easy."

As Valdez's men walked away grumbling, Primo and Pedro prepared to ride back to the cantina.

"They will be angry," Pedro said. "You should have let them keep the money."

"No, no," he responded. "Then we would have been the fools, and they would know we were fools. Now, they are the fools, and they know they are the fools. Knowing you are a fool does not promote self-confidence. And because they have no self-confidence, no money, and no guns, there is not much they can do."

Pedro laughed.

Matthew Piper eased his horse alongside Primo's. For

the first time that evening, he spoke. "Your shooting is already legendary," he said. "Once I write about it, it will become your shield. No one will dare cross you. You'll never even need to draw your gun."

Increasingly, Primo had a feeling of being dogged. An invisible string pulled him forward making it seem that every time he traveled to a new place, there were signs someone had been there before him, that his feet were walking in the tracks and grooves carved there before he even contemplated taking a step. It was an eerie feeling—like a redundant story, a repetitious sound, a legend written before the hero was born.

The horse called Umberto was living, breathing evidence. He looked like a thoroughbred—a rich dark brown color, a well-shaped head on a long neck, a lean body, and long legs. He had intelligent, knowing eyes and responded with sensitivity to commands. Primo loved the horse the moment he saw it, and he wanted it—no, coveted it. He recognized him, but from where?

He had been lying down in the upstairs room of the cantina, the one where he'd spent the winter being ill. The room was so stifling, he had taken off his shirt and boots. He could hear Pedro and some of the others celebrating downstairs. It sounded like they were getting tipsy and trying to sing the latest popular song, *Cielito Lindo*, but it was a poor attempt.

He was considering getting a bottle of tequila for himself when Lucia peeked in the door.

"*Senor*, the people have come to talk to you," she said. "They are outside."

Primo picked up his hat, strapped his pistol across his bare chest, and walked downstairs in his bare feet. What could they want now? he asked himself.

The scene outside was something he didn't expect— hundreds of Nuevo Laredo residents had gathered. Maria's uncle, Luis Nuncio, stood at the front of the crowd holding the reins of the large, brown horse. Several women held baskets of food covered with their best linens. One old woman held a white baby dress embroidered with blue and green flowers and edged with blue crochet.

"For your baby, *senor*," she said in a voice so tentative he could barely hear it.

"These gifts are for you," Luis Nuncio said. "They are to thank you for what you have done for us."

Primo smiled and blushed. No one in the crowd could remember seeing him smile. He walked up to the horse and stroked its neck and head.

"He is beautiful, but I cannot accept him from you. He is too valuable."

"That is why you must take him ... for our sake ... to seal our friendship," Luis said.

Primo took the reins and said only "*gracias*." Lucia took the food baskets and the baby dress.

Primo patted the nose of his new steed while the people

dispersed. Several of the women smiled shyly at him as they walked away.

"This is a great honor for you," Lucia said. "They are very poor. They have almost nothing."

"And, of course, they want me to leave the money," he said.

"No, *senor*, I have never heard them say anything about that."

"But that is what they want, and that is what they need. How can I do that without binding myself to them forever?"

"You can't, *senor*. You are bound to them now because of the horse. You are no longer free to roam around—that is all it means."

Pedro walked up behind him and put his hand gently on the horse's neck.

"Do you remember this horse, *pistola*?"

"No, I only know I have seen him before."

"You knew this horse in prison."

Primo gave him a questioning glance.

"We decided it would be well for you to remember the horse."

"But not the rest of it?"

"Just the horse, my friend. The rest is not worth remembering."

The people of Nuevo Laredo were without guile. They had been waiting for the right time to return the horse to Primo. It was not for the money, but for their love of him.

He left the money and Umberto with Lucia. He put the

saddlebag of currency on the bar with a note that said, "Divide it equally, and take care of the horse for me. I will return." It was signed "Juan Miguel del Valle."

Lucia read it out loud for Teresa. They looked at each other with tears in their eyes. They were moved by his generosity—not so much by the gift of money, but by his signature, his real name. They already knew it, but they would never have uttered it without his permission.

CHAPTER 3

"What are the people of Nuevo Laredo trying to do to me?" Primo asked Pedro. They held their horses' reins while they stood under a scraggly madrone tree for shade, the only shade within miles, waiting for Matthew to catch up with them. The tree leaned northward from the constant south wind, which they could feel at their backs.

"What are they trying to force me into?"

"They are not forcing, *senor*. They are trying to lure you."

"Lure me to what? I don't understand."

"They are luring you back—to your past. They want to help you get back to it without hurting you."

Primo looked at Pedro with sincere openness, something Pedro had not seen in a while.

"I am not afraid of the past—I just cannot remember much of it."

"I know and they know, and they do not want to hurt you, but they want you to be yourself again."

"But why? What difference does it make?"

"Your true heart—for the sake of your true heart. They knew you well, *senor*."

"Let's sit. That fool is probably an hour behind."

They rested their backs against the tree trunk, taking a few swigs from their canteens.

"This is dangerous for you, *pistola*," Pedro said, looking down at the ground between his legs. "The Primo disguise has been effective. It has kept you safe. But it has also been a burden."

For someone who was highly intelligent and often ahead of everyone else mentally, Primo was behind in this one thing—his identity and why he discarded it.

Primo took off his hat and shook his head. He ruffled his own hair and rubbed his eyes.

"If I allow myself to remember, will I regret it? Is it that bad?"

"So far, I have made that choice for you, hoping you would never remember. But lately, I think it should be your choice. Perhaps you will never heal or be whole again without it. That is for you to decide."

"I gave them the money to square things with us, so they will stop hovering over me like a host of earthly angels."

"That is not why you gave it. You gave it because they love you. And they will never stop loving or hovering, *senor*. It is all part of the same story—their loyalty, your pain and betrayal."

"Were they part of the betrayal?"

"*Si* ... they carry that guilt."

Primo suddenly sat up and looked into the distance.

"They were part of it ... they betrayed me, but they didn't know what would happen. Is that right?"

"My friend, to them, you are the anointed one."

"But I remember my past with the *senora*, right?"

"Not all of it, *senor*."

Primo shook his head. He choked back an emotion he couldn't quite identify—maybe hurt, maybe shame. That was as far as the conversation went, because Primo would sometimes walk up to the brink of the truth but never step off into the abyss. Pedro continued to wait for him.

They could see Matthew riding his old black horse up the rise, still miles away, but close enough for their satisfaction. They got on their horses and rode on.

The chicken and rice *poblano* at the Casa del Sol, just off the square in San Antonio, was some of the best Martin Zamora had ever tasted. It was not like his aunt's, but he liked the large chunks of *poblano* peppers, cooked until tender, throughout the rice. He was relishing the last bites with a glass of Spanish wine, waiting for Matthew Piper. The wine was an extravagance he felt he deserved after a steady diet of beans, tortillas, and tequila for the last two weeks. There was not a lot of variety in the cuisine in Nuevo Laredo cafes or on the trail.

He drank the last of his wine, put down the glass, and

signaled to the waiter to bring him another.

Senor Zamora was back in full costume. His soft gray Stetson sat on the table next to his plate. He wore spectacles, and his short brown hair was slicked back. His pistol was tucked safely into his inside jacket pocket. He carried a lot of money.

People were attracted to Martin Zamora—an obviously wealthy, educated, and calculating man. Several women—and at least one man—tried to catch his eye while he sat by the window eating his lunch. The midday sun shone on his tanned face and light hair. He ignored the attention, but he was certainly aware of it, as he was aware of everything.

Senor Zamora had a mysterious aura. Nobody could figure out where his money came from. There were rumors that it came from prostitution, that he inherited it, that he won it gambling, that he took it from a rich widow in Denver, that he made it from silver prospecting, that he got it in a legal settlement, and that he stole it.

Matthew Piper always kept silent when people asked him what he thought about Martin Zamora's fortune. He knew full well where it came from, but could not divulge that—yet.

Matthew had arrived back in San Antonio tired and stunned. He had a good story for his novel, that was true, but there was still so much he didn't understand. He asked for an interview with Primo to fill in the holes.

When Matthew walked into the restaurant and spotted Martin Zamora at the table by the window, he shook his head in amazement. How does he do it? he asked himself. That transformation would make a great story—maybe for the next book.

Martin had an irritated yet amused expression on his face talking to Matthew, as if he knew what an idiot he was dealing with. Matthew was too dense to realize it. Like most people, he was taken in by the impeccable manners and alluring image of Martin Zamora. It certainly cast a spell. But he was experienced enough as a journalist that he finally got around to asking questions.

Primo had told him a carefully edited version of where he got the money he gave to the people of Nuevo Laredo. He explained finding the jack loads of silver in a cave on his uncle's property. Matthew had witnessed the pistol duel and the fleecing of the gang members. His questions, though, were based on his own research into Juan Miguel del Valle, which he knew was Primo's real identity.

"*Senor*, may I ask you about the people of Nuevo Laredo?" Matthew began.

"Certainly."

"It's obvious they are attached to you ... that there is affection there."

"*Si* ... I suppose there is."

"But they were the ones who testified against you ... who sent you to prison, were they not?"

Martin Zamora betrayed nothing in his expression, but his thoughts were spinning, trying to catch up.

"*Si* ... that is true, but that was a long time ago ... in the past."

"But how did you go from that to giving them the treasure? Something must have happened to make you forgive them."

"Primo's past is not part of this book, *senor*. Remember, I told you there would be a second condition for the book, and this is it. You must not divulge that Primo and Juan Miguel are one and the same."

Matthew had a disagreeable look on his face. He picked up his beer glass and drained it.

"I agree, I suppose," Matthew said. "What about Primo's prison term? What about the Monterrey prison? Can we talk about that?"

"No, *senor*, that is part of Primo's past as well. You must not go into that, do you understand?"

Martin managed to maintain his cool emphatic demeanor, but Juan Miguel del Valle felt less confident. This pest of a writer was starting to unravel things before he could bring them into his conscious mind.

After Matthew left the table, Martin gazed out the window for hours. He ordered several more glasses of Spanish wine. He was searching, searching his mind for the lost memories, trying to summon them into the story line. He had been piecing things together now since the memory of Marguerite Barone came back to him over a year ago. It was raiding the ranches near San Antonio that jogged his memory. Then he remembered Father Moreno and his kidnapping and all that had happened between himself and the Barones. But so much after that was blurry.

Juan Miguel waited for Pedro by a group of maple trees near the market square. He was in Martin Zamora's disguise, but it was definitely Juan Miguel del Valle who was anxious to talk to his old friend.

"We should go to the *establo* so we can talk," Pedro suggested.

"No, it is better here, where no one will listen to us."

"What is so important, *amigo*?"

"Matthew has researched my past and is asking questions—some of which I cannot answer. The time has come to tell me, even things I don't want to know."

"*Si* … I agree."

"Tell me about the people of Nuevo Laredo. What happened?"

"I was not there, my friend, but only know what they have told me."

The two men sat down on a low wall.

"Juan Miguel was brought to Nuevo Laredo because he had confessed to being a raider. The Mexican authorities did not believe him, so he asked the people of Nuevo Laredo to lie to them and convince them he had been raiding and hiding there for the previous year. They testified to that at the trial, and Juan Miguel was convicted and sentenced to 20 years in prison in Monterrey."

"Why? Why did he want them to testify to that? It wasn't true, was it?"

"No, *senor*. It most definitely was not true. As you now remember, you had run your family's rancho for the past year. They were framing you, *amigo*. They wanted to be rid of you."

"Why did I want to be sent to prison?"

"This is the question I cannot answer. I was not there, but the people of Nuevo Laredo were convinced you were protecting someone else."

"Who?"

"My guess is Marguerite Barone, *senor*."

"How did you find me?"

"Jose and I went to Nuevo Laredo—and many other places—searching for you. The people told us you were in prison."

"About my time in prison—what do you know?"

Pedro hesitated. He knew about Juan Miguel's treatment in prison but could not bring himself to discuss it—for his friend's sake.

"*Senor*, it was bad. You were treated like an animal by the prison warden. That is all I can tell you."

Maybe Pedro should have divulged more, but he thought about Primo's bouts of stomach illness, about the three times in the Monterrey hospital and how near death he had been. He had feared for his friend's health and his life.

"What else?" Juan Miguel said, searching his memory for the truth.

"As I said, that is all I can tell you."

"You are afraid to tell me, is that not so?"

"*Si* … I am afraid of what you will do."

"And the *senora* … what is her part in this?"

"I fear that is the heart of it, my friend—your desire to protect her, your love for her. Even now, you risk everything for it."

Juan Miguel knew this was the truest thing he had heard. He nodded.

"Are you not going to ask whether Senora Marguerite betrayed you?"

Juan Miguel looked at him evenly, with no expression. He nodded again.

"As far as I know—she did not. But perhaps you should ask her."

Juan Miguel looked away to hide any hint of emotion.

"One more thing. I know Ben Barone's men were not just looking for information—they were looking for me. Somehow, Barone found out I was out of prison. The people wanted to keep that from me because they didn't want me to feel responsible for them, right?"

"*Si* … that is probably true."

"Will he be looking for Marguerite also? That is what I must find out."

———————

When Maggie started to write about Juan Miguel in her journal, she thought about his most striking characteristic. Not his beautifully proportioned face, not his light brown eyes and hair, not his muscular torso and arms, not his kind expression. The first thing she noticed about him was his hands. They said everything she needed to know—how he felt, how much confidence he had, how he would touch her.

She wrote this:

Your hands take the pain, the fear, the meaningless hours
Your hands sing lullabies, summon angels, paint colors
Your hands keep evil at bay
Your hands reach in my mind and straighten the bent
Your hands cast out demons, conjure the moon, ride the waves of madness
Your hands make me whole

She took out her pen and drew a sketch of his hands next to the words. Then she drew another one and another. Underneath it all, she wrote in large letters: Touch My Soul With Your Hands.

On the next page, she began the story he told her. She wanted it to be in his words, not hers. She wanted to write it down as quickly as she could before it slipped from her mind.

She started it exactly the way he started it: "I was very young and you were very beautiful … ," then she started over. It had to be just right so that Annabelle would know the story—the complete story—when she and Juan Miguel were gone. The story might be their only legacy.

Her hands shook as she tried to begin again. It was not working.

Perhaps it should be a song, she thought, a ballad. Perhaps the angels would sing it. The music played in her head, the familiar refrain. She drifted off into a fog of uncertainty again. If only he were there to touch her with his hands.

When Juan Miguel came to visit her, he came after dark so no one would see him. He found the journal under her bed with other personal articles—cast off as if she no longer valued them. He picked up the journal, the clothing, the other small items and held them in his lap as he sat on her bed.

He opened the journal. He read the poem and looked at the drawings; then he turned the page, and there was a jumble of words—not arranged in sentences, but written at random over the page. One of the words was "*luna,*" the word for moon; another was "*laguna,*" the word for lagoon. These were words from the lullaby he had sung to her. He looked down at the items in his lap. The seashell dish was among them.

"You think you are so clever, my love," he whispered, "but I know what you are doing."

Matthew Piper's dime novel, *Primo's Hidden Treasure*, was a runaway bestseller. No one could have anticipated the number of printings the publishing firm of Baer and Jacobs would go through to satisfy the demand.

The author amplified the character of Primo, building on the qualities he had outlined in his first book. The story line meshed well with popular lore—the man of integrity forced against his nature and against his will to be an outlaw. The treasure, the gun duel, the people, the horse—the story was tailor-made for the genre. It not only made Primo more of a hero than he already was, it also made him more of a target.

The unintended consequence of Primo's plan was that every jackal in Texas and Mexico wanted to challenge him. He thought the fast-gun part of the story would be unimportant. That turned out not to be the case. Already, only two months after the book appeared in stores, he had faced down two men who wanted to test themselves against his pistol. Another could not be persuaded to ride on, so he shot him in the hand before a duel could occur.

The intended consequence, however, was going well. There was less scrutiny of Primo and more of the ranchers and their secret organizations. The time was ripe, Juan Miguel concluded, to go on to the second part of the plan.

———————————

The late November evening air was chilly and damp in Bastrop. The smoke from burning mesquite hung in the air, mingling with the faint fragrance of wet pines. Juan Miguel watched Maggie intently as she entered the half-lit bedroom and stood in front of him.

Her red waves were partially pinned up, the rest falling down her back. She wore a low-cut white lace camisole and short pantaloons with a long gray flannel jacket thrown over them unbuttoned. On her feet were a pair of burgundy tooled leather boots he had bought her in San Antonio. In her hair was the ice-blue ribbon he had put on the wrapped package. He had never seen anyone look more attractive or alluring in such an eccentric way. One of the cherry-red waves was hanging rebelliously over her flaming blue-green eyes. The way she looked, coupled with the things she had written and casually left under the bed for him to discover, made him wary. What was she up to this time?

She tilted her head to one side, put her hand on his forearm, and caressed it. Then she took his hand. She put it to her lips and kissed it, then put it on her breast. He shivered and moved closer.

"What is this about, Marguerite?" he said, then kissed her.

"I want something."

"*Si* ... that is obvious. What is it?"

"Take me back to the ocean before I die ... please."

He slowly shook his head, then kissed her again.

"No, Marguerite, it would be too dangerous, but what is this talk of death?"

She kissed him and pushed him back onto the bed. He took off her gray jacket and pulled down her camisole strap. His resolve dissipated, then disappeared. He nodded.

"But only for a little while, *comprende*?"

"Soon," she said, "before I die."

"Shh ... stop it, Marguerite. Don't threaten like that. Don't tempt God."

She smiled to herself. She was the one thing he could not control and, therefore, loved above all else. God knows he tried. He had been trying since the day he first saw her. He tried—with his touch, his kisses, his caresses, his gift of love—to master the feral core of her being.

He woke in the middle of the night in an empty bed. After searching the house, he found Maggie wrapped in a quilt, propped against a white column on the front porch with her knees tucked under her chin and her arms wrapped around them.

The water droplets on the foliage were hard and engorged with the intense moonlight. The blue light cast a shadow on her features, turning her hair an eerie purple. He had an impulse to snatch the quilt from her and expose her nakedness to the moonlight.

"What are you doing, *senora*?" he asked.

She looked up at him with sly eyes, eyes that were not entirely warm.

"I have something to ask you, *senora*, but I don't want to offend you."

She looked away. He recognized this illusive tactic.

He sat down next to her.

"The time after my kidnapping and before my trial is hazy to me. Will you help me remember?" he said.

She nodded, almost imperceptibly.

"They gave you a choice. Is that right?"

He could see he was getting into dangerous territory by the vulnerable movement of her hands. Her fingers looked like the fluttering of angel wings.

"What did you choose, *senora*?"

Her mouth opened and she started to speak, then decided against it. He waited for her. By this time, he was used to waiting.

"They told me I would go back to the Barone Ranch unless I ..." She hesitated.

"What did you do, *senora*? Whatever it was, I will forgive you if I have to. But you have to tell me now."

" ... unless I told them where you were."

"So, they found me from your directions?"

"I couldn't go back and be beaten again. I didn't know what they would do to you."

She was absurdly calm, considering the admission she had just spoken.

"So, they let you go free, then?"

"No. They accused me of being a whore, of living with you in sin. I had to admit it, because everyone knew it was true."

"Go on, *senora*. We cannot turn back now."

"You traded for my freedom with your confession."

She wrapped the quilt tighter around herself. She rested her head against the pillar and allowed the tears to come once again.

He didn't have to ask any more questions. The memories

came flooding back like water rushing through a broken dam. He was consumed with compassion for her. He took her in his arms and kissed the wild, damp waves.

"Do you forgive me?" she whispered.

"*Si* … I forgive you, Marguerite. Now, please, no more talk of death. We cannot live with your guilt anymore."

"They took you away … we didn't know where. Later, we heard you were dead."

"So you left the rancho."

"Yes, I went to Austin to live with my sister, then to Galveston."

"To be near the ocean?"

"To be near you," she shot back with such vehemence that she startled him.

The conversation had veered off track into some uncharted territory in her mind. She looked tired, so he rubbed the tears from her face. He unwrapped the quilt and cast it onto the wet bushes, picked her up, carried her back inside and put her on the bed. The blue ribbon was hanging loosely in her tangled hair. The burgundy boots were under the window where he had thrown them earlier.

The rest of the night he spent in the rocking chair by the bed. When he was sure Maggie was asleep, he allowed himself to think about the past. He unraveled his guilt all the way back through every thought and action, to his own desire. None of the sins could be laid at her feet. All of them would be laid at his. He was to blame for almost every turn in the narrative. The threats, the accusations, the beatings would not have happened if not for him. He found it easier to deal with his guilt than to accept hers.

His chest began to heave. The leaden night air would not enter his lungs. All he could do now was carry the weight, a weight so heavy it could bury them if he let down his guard.

He did reserve one sin to count against someone else, and that sin was Ben Barone's. He stayed awake for a long time, considering the appropriate punishment.

Out loud, he said, "Barone is the devil."

Juan Miguel left Bastrop before dawn, having promised Maggie he would take her back to the ocean in the summer, and returned to San Antonio.

Juan Miguel wasted no time in finding Matthew Piper at the Silver Elephant. He didn't bother to change clothes or worry about his identity. No one recognized him when he walked in—not even Matthew. Juan Miguel walked up behind the writer and stuck his pistol to his neck, then lifted him up with the other hand.

"How does it feel, *senor*, to have a pistol constantly aimed at you?" he asked after several minutes had gone by.

Matthew recognized the voice.

"Can we talk outside?" Matthew managed to spit out.

"*Si*, I suppose that would be prudent, although I am not in the mood to be prudent."

He uncocked and holstered the pistol, then pulled

Matthew out the door with both hands gripping the back of his collar.

"You did not tell the truth in your novel, *senor*, and now you have caused me a great deal of trouble," Primo said.

"I only told the truth … and I didn't reveal anything you didn't want me to."

"You embellished … shall we say … the gun duel. I never intended to fight a gun duel. I simply shot him before he shot me."

"From my point of view, and everyone else's, it looked like a duel. You cannot deny, can you, it has made you a hero?"

"A hero, *si*, but now every idiot within riding distance is seeking me out."

"Really? You mean they want to duel with you?" Matthew was thinking this would make a good story.

"Were you born stupid, or did you acquire that characteristic?" Primo was so tempted to take a poke at Matthew that he could barely restrain himself.

"You and your stories are worthless. They have nothing to do with reality," he said through clenched teeth.

"But I only wrote what I saw."

Primo unleashed his anger and took a good jab at the foul-smelling fool. It landed on the jaw, and Matthew went down, falling backward onto the steps.

"Get out of my sight before I lose my temper even more."

Primo walked down the street to the *establo* with one thought consuming him—it was extremely satisfying to hit

Matthew Piper.

He was in his room at the Marshall Hotel when Pedro knocked. He was still steaming about his argument with Matthew, his strange encounter with Maggie, and the load of responsibilities on his shoulders. Grudgingly, he admitted Pedro to the room.

"What's on your mind, *pistola*?" Pedro tried to mollify his old friend.

"I cannot wait any longer, Pedro," he began. "You have to tell me everything that happened to me in prison, even if it is difficult for you to talk about. I cannot allow Ben Barone to be armed with knowledge I don't have. Sit down. Tell me … and don't hold back."

Pedro was surprised by Primo's tone. It was urgent and immediate … he was not kidding this time.

"It's not so easy to tell you, *amigo;* otherwise I would have done it by now."

"Get into it somehow … just begin."

Pedro sat down on the bed and wiped his sweating palms on his pants.

"The warden was an evil man," he said, "He tied you up and kept you in the stable."

"For what purpose?"

"To humiliate, my friend … to humiliate you and to unman you."

Juan Miguel's memory got a foothold on the word "unman," and he started to remember.

He looked out the hotel-room window and saw not the

city scenery, but scenes from the past.

"Stop ..." He held up his hand.

"*Senor?*"

"I remember now. I know what happened. He raped me."

Pedro put his hand on his mustache and started to stroke it. He hid his face by looking the other way.

"*Si* ... that is true ... but there were others as well."

Juan Miguel nodded.

"I know now. I remember it," he said. "Look at me, Pedro."

Pedro reluctantly looked his friend in the eye.

"You saved me. I knew you did, but now I know what it cost. *Gracias*, my friend."

Pedro nodded. He looked down.

"And the stomach ailment was from having to eat food meant for horses, right?"

Pedro nodded again. It was obvious his pain was even more intense than Juan Miguel's whose whole body ached from the tension.

"And this was done on Ben Barone's instructions?"

"*Si* ... I have surmised."

"And what happened to this warden?"

"I killed him, *pistola*, with my bare hands."

"*Si,* I remember. You beat the fat bastard in the stable. That is a scene worth remembering, *amigo*."

"We took Umberto with us. That poor horse—he also was mistreated."

"You went back for the horse later after you pulled me

out."

Juan Miguel smiled.

"We have done it, my friend. We have conquered the past."

"One more thing," Pedro said. "The money your uncle gave for bribing your way out. I could not retrieve it."

Juan Miguel shook his head as if to say, that is a small matter. Acquiring more money was the least of his problems. He let out a long, deep sigh, then slapped his friend on the back.

"I need a drink," he said.

———————————

He walked out to the spot by the river early in the morning. The night of drinking with Pedro did not get the better of him. He had shown some restraint for the first time in years.

He sat down on the bench where last year he had talked to Father Moreno about finding Maggie. How he wished the old priest were there now.

It was so early, the sun was not up—only its ambient light suffused the backs of buildings and treetops. It was cold but still, and the water lapped gently against the tall reeds on the bank. Juan Miguel was defenseless—without Pedro, without his pistol, unguarded in every way.

He laced his fingers, held his hands at his chest, and began.

"Father, my body was broken and abused and almost done."

He stopped when he felt the tears dropping on his hands. He wiped his face and upper lip with the back of his hand. He tried to hold back the self-pity.

"My mind was so clouded, I could not see. My heart was so sick, I could no longer be afraid. I was taken down to the depths. You were there, I remember. Wipe the scenes in the stable from your memory and don't look on me the way I was then. See me as I am now. Don't abandon me, Father."

He continued to sit and watch the lapping water as the sun started to rise over the treetops. The leaves of the dark red Spanish oaks popped out in relief. The russet-gold cottonwoods swayed, smooth and languid. The mockingbirds sang medleys, mimicking each other. The air smelled of decaying leaves and fried dough.

The sun's rays hit him in the face like a slap.

He took a deep breath and let go of the details: from the present, from the past. He no longer saw the individual features of the landscape before him, the individual acts, the individual people. He saw only the mystery. He released himself from one viewpoint and embraced the other.

He surrendered.

294

Part Four

Mexico and Texas 1881-1882

Chapter 1

On a cool February day in 1881, Martin Zamora walked into the Menger Hotel for the first time in four years. He relished the look and feel of it—the memories. He only glanced at the tall windows and marble floors. He could not allow himself the luxury of appearing to remember it.

Time and motion seemed to stop when he walked into the lobby and approached the hotel desk. All eyes were on Senor Zamora, as they usually were. He was well-dressed and beautiful and cock-sure of his own charisma.

As Martin took out his black leather money pouch, you could almost hear a collective swoon. It was stuffed with U.S. currency, which he made an elaborate show of trying to hide.

He had gold cuff links on his French tailored shirt sleeves and a diamond stud pin on his burgundy silk tie. His hands were well-formed like the hands of a British lord, his skin smooth and radiant.

Martin smiled engagingly. It was a smile that held a secret—all the more intriguing for those who were present that day. It didn't take long for rumors to swirl—Senor Zamora was back in town and staying at the Menger this time.

"Will you be staying long, *senor*?" the desk clerk asked, his manner fawning.

"*Si* ... indefinitely ... if that meets with your approval."

"What else can we do for you while you are here?"

"A good, healthy game of cards would be nice," Martin said, removing his spectacles and putting them in an inside pocket. "Also, have a bottle of Spanish wine sent to my room."

"I will take care of it, sir. Any particular time for the card game?"

"Tomorrow. It should be tomorrow."

One of the people in the Menger Hotel lobby that day was Ben Barone. He was visiting—as he often did—with his new wife, Isela. They were standing near the stairway, Martin observed, trying not to be interested in the commotion he caused. But he caught Barone's eye, and that was what he wanted.

Was there a danger Barone would recognize him? Of course—a small danger, although, Martin Zamora was so unlike anyone Barone had ever known, the chances were slim.

He looked different, his voice was different, his tastes were different, his mannerisms were different. Only the pale brown eyes were the same, but the expression was considerably harder and more conniving than Barone would recall. Martin never once doubted his ability to act freely and convincingly, because you could never overestimate greed, stupidity, and the willingness to believe.

"There is something I need to know, and I will pay you handsomely to find out," Martin said. Sitting in a cushioned yellow armchair by the window in his Menger Hotel room, he took an appreciative drink of the fine Spanish wine and ran his fingers through his hair.

Matthew Piper sat looking at him with some trepidation. After all, it was the same man who had socked him in the jaw a few months ago.

Martin handed him a deed, which Pedro had found through a little detective work of his own. It was a copy of the Spanish land grant to the del Valle ranch lands. It was granted to Juan Miguel's ancestor, Cameron Fernando Miguel del Valle, by the Spanish royal commission, dated 1768, and signed by commissioners Juan Armando de Palacio and José de Ossorio y Llamas. It included three separate tracts, totaling 230,000 acres of land.

Matthew looked at the aged paper, then at Martin.

"This is too complicated. I can't track this," he said.

"Sure you can," Martin said, smiling. "Just ask those fucking questions."

Matthew bridled.

"How much?"

"If you succeed, $5,000."

Matthew was by this time a best-selling author, but his royalties for the two novels did not even approach the amount Martin Zamora was offering. Matthew nodded in acceptance.

"I know Ben Barone is occupying the land now," Martin said. "Find out where it stands legally, and, if it is in his name, how he accomplished that. Who did he pay off? Whose approval did he get? Everyone involved, *comprende*?"

"It will take some time, *senor*."

"You have only until April. No longer."

"And if I don't succeed?"

"Then you get no money, and you will have proven yourself to be unreliable and, perhaps, not needed any longer. Do you understand, *senor*?"

Martin took another drink of the wine. "There is something else. I will pay you $200 to write an article for the newspaper and get it published."

"Something specific?"

"*Si* ... a story about the gun duel between Primo and Juan Miguel del Valle."

Matthew looked stumped.

"They had a duel in Nuevo Laredo. Primo won, of course, and he won a fine horse from Juan Miguel. I will tell you the rest later."

Matthew nodded again and got up to leave. Martin took back the legal document and handed him $100 for expenses.

"Keep in touch. I want updates," Martin said to the departing opportunist.

Martin took off the spectacles, put down the wine glass, and leaned his head back on the soft chair cushion. He stopped the act. Juan Miguel del Valle had turned twenty-two the previous December. Starting when he was seventeen, his life had been a maze of identities and lifestyles. In his life, he had been many things. He longed for the day when he could be only himself and live with his family, Marguerite and Annabelle, on his father's land. For a few minutes, he let himself dream.

It had all seemed so simple once. If he loved Marguerite and she loved him, then everything else would not matter. Now he knew it was much more complicated than that. Perhaps that's what she had meant years ago when she told him there was still much in life he didn't understand. There were so many other things to consider now—Annabelle, the rancho, his family's good name, and the future of all of this. It was all bound up together but he still believed he could make it all right. He still believed.

He could not stop thinking about the last time he was in Bastrop with Maggie. He had lingered longer than he planned, watching Maggie bathe, then helping her brush through the entangled mass of hair.

Before he left, she sat on his lap and wrapped her legs around him. She put her head on his shoulder and kissed it. He picked up the long waves of her hair and put them to his face. Her hair smelled like cinnamon. Her mouth tasted like the chocolate-covered cherries he brought her from San Antonio. He wiped some stray chocolate that still stuck to her upper lip with his thumb. Her body was soft, so soft it melted into his.

"Whatever it is you are planning, you have to hurry," she said. "I have less time than you do. I am older."

"While I am gone, Marguerite, please do not descend into acting like a child. And no more talk of death. Understand?"

He had no idea how to interpret the petulant look on her face.

"Is there something you want to say?" he asked, holding the long waves back from her face with both hands.

"Don't come here acting like someone else," she said. Angry sparks shot out of her eyes.

"I would never do that. I have always been myself with you."

"Never," she said emphatically. "Never try to do your playacting with me."

"Marguerite … why are you bringing this up?"

"Because without you, I can't go on."

"I know. I know how you feel. You don't have to tell me."

"I am frightened of those other people you pretend to be."

"Marguerite … they are all me. I don't change. Only the clothing changes."

"That's not true, Juan Miguel."

He had waited for years to hear her say his name again. She had not called him by his Christian name since that day in San Antonio when they went for a walk and she seduced him with her talk of sending him away, with her hand on his forearm, and with her calculating denial. He was shocked that this time, she said his name in anger.

All that he had done … all his coaxing … all his sacrifice … and she still drifted far away from him, wandering aimlessly, pulling him along, like the moon constantly teasing the ocean's tidal waves.

He reached up with one hand and put her head back down on his shoulder. He put his other hand on the small of her back as if he were trying to hold her down. The only way he could feel closer to her was if he became her.

The scene left him worried. She swung back and forth like a pendulum. Would she swing so far out, he could not bring her back?

If she was trying to make it more and more difficult to leave her, she was succeeding.

CHAPTER 2

Martin Zamora knew a thing or two about cards, that was obvious. Perhaps he was a card shark. Perhaps that is where his money came from. This is what all five men who sat at the table with Martin were thinking.

The real truth they would never have guessed—he learned to play poker as a child, sneaking out to the bunkhouse when he was home from school. By the time he was thirteen, he was playing poker with his father's *vaqueros* until all hours of the night.

When he got reckless, they cautioned him. "Never tip your hand, *pistola* ... to anyone," they would say. When he was too timid, they goaded him. "Don't hold back, *pistola* ... you can't win if you're not in the game."

They were three hours into the game, and Senor Zamora had amassed quite a pile of money. He had taken off his dark grey suit coat and hung it on a hook by the door. His manicured hands and French cuffs were refined compared to the rough hands and relatively plain sleeves of the ranchers with whom he played. No doubt, they looked on him as somewhat of a dandy—someone to admire but not to trust. Several of their wives proffered the theory he was from Spain—the son of a Spanish duke.

One of the men at the table was Ben Barone. Not once did Martin Zamora betray that he had known Barone before and hated him like no other man. Not once did he betray that every hand he played was for the benefit of Barone, to give him a certain impression.

Martin held a fairly good hand, three of a kind, three jacks. It was time for him to overplay his hand. He bet too much. The others squirmed uncomfortably. He was bluffing, they surmised.

Two of them took the bait and saw his bet, and one of them raised it. Martin saw that bet and raised again. It went on, back and forth until Martin Zamora was betting most of his money. He called. The man who was still in the hand laid down his three eights.

Martin sniffed, tamped his cards on the table, then tossed them, face down. "It is yours, *senor*," he said.

He picked up the cards and started to shuffle them, then decided against it.

"What can I do? One hand and I am wiped out," he said, sounding only mildly disappointed. No one doubted he had plenty of money where that came from.

He smiled, stood, put on his coat, and left. He wanted them to have time to talk about what just happened.

"He is a good poker player, but he is greedy, and he

bluffs," one of the men said.

That was exactly what he wanted them to think.

———————

Isela Barone was in the market square with two friends when the outlaw Primo made an appearance. He came riding up the main street on a beautiful dark brown thoroughbred, stopped at a strategic spot by the most crowded part of the market, and dismounted. He took out a cigarette and lit it, then smoked it for several minutes. By the time the police deputy came around, he was gone.

The town was soon abuzz with the news—the brown horse was the one he won in the Nuevo Laredo gun duel—the one in the newspaper article.

The pertinent lines from the article said this:

The outlaw Primo shot the gun out of the hand of Juan Miguel del Valle in a Nuevo Laredo gun duel last week in a dispute over a thoroughbred horse. Both men are wanted for stealing horses from ranchers in Texas and Mexico.

Primo, the subject of recent popular dime novels, is known for his fast gun. Juan Miguel del Valle is the son of a prominent Texas Spanish landowner. He was incarcerated in Mexico for a year after being convicted of horse thievery. He was later released on parole.

Primo reportedly took possession of the horse, which del Valle acquired from the Monterrey Prison warden. It *is said to be a thoroughbred race horse from Mexico City, worth upwards of $5,000.*

Del Valle sustained only superficial injuries in the duel.

Isela rushed back to the Menger to tell her husband she saw Primo—the subject of dime novels—in person at the market square. She was titillated, as were most of the San Antonio residents who saw him.

"He had his huge pistol strapped across his chest," she said. "He had on a snakeskin tie and silver spurs shaped like stars."

Ben Barone stroked his beard and thought, if I know Juan Miguel, he will want that horse back. If I could somehow acquire the horse, I'll bet I could smoke him out.

Barone put the word out he would like to meet with Primo. He guaranteed the safety of the famous fugitive outlaw—he was only interested in the horse. Pedro, Primo's sidekick, sent a message through the concierge at the Menger Hotel, "Primo meets with no one."

"What about the man who sent the message? Will he meet with me ... alone ... if I'm willing to come alone?"

The concierge passed the message, and Pedro accepted; they arranged to meet at the Silver Elephant. Pedro's English was not the best, but he was the only person Primo trusted to meet with Barone. He knew he could be tough, and he knew he could handle himself if danger arose.

Late at night on Sunday when the bar was mostly empty, Pedro and Barone sat at a table in the back. They managed to converse, partly in English and partly in Spanish. Pedro—

who was not as adept as Primo at hiding his contempt—could not wipe the condescending sneer off his face. Barone, however, was not attuned to other people's opinions, so he didn't notice.

Barone, in truth, was not attuned to anything around him. If he had been, he might have remembered that Juan Miguel also had silver spurs shaped like stars. But thinking only of his own purposes made him blind and deaf.

"*Senor*, I am afraid you are too late," Pedro said. "The horse has already been sold."

"Sold? Already? Who to?"

"Senor Martin Zamora bought the horse. That is why it was brought to town yesterday."

"What does he plan to do with it, do you know?"

"Why, he plans to race it, of course, in Mexico City, I think."

"How much was the sale price?"

"Oh, *senor*, that I cannot say. Perhaps you can ask Senor Zamora. I understand you know him. As for this meeting, it would be well for you to forget you saw me or spoke to me."

Pedro rose and picked up his rifle, which he, seemingly inadvertently, aimed at Barone, leaving the overstuffed arrogant son of a bitch to stew in his own putrid juices. At least, those were Pedro's thoughts as he left.

When Pedro got outside, he spat to get the horrid taste out of his mouth. "I curse you," he said. "The devil take you."

Barone started to make a new plan, a plan that would involve a game of cards and Martin Zamora.

Maggie found the first bluebonnets of the season in the south pasture where the sun was direct most of the day. The violet-blue and white petals were like small pockets, holding tiny dew droplets, clustered precariously on tall delicate stems.

She sat amongst the thick grasses and weeds, her quilt spread out and covered with pens, paper, and paintbrushes. Her hair was tied up in a vain attempt to keep the stiff south breeze from blowing the waves into her face. She was wearing a long blue apron she had borrowed from Beatriz and her burgundy boots. The sunshine was raising a few stray freckles on her forehead and tingeing pink the end of her nose and the tops of her cheekbones.

Twenty paces behind her slept the young Roberto with his pistol strapped on his hip and saliva rolling down his face onto the limestone rocks. Maggie was greatly relieved that he was finally asleep. She found it hard to work with his eyes boring into her back. They were impatient, frustrated eyes, revealing Roberto's real feelings—he would rather be anyplace else than guarding Senora Marguerite. She sat for hours staring at the same plant, carefully drawing the lines. He couldn't think of anything more boring. He would much rather be out looking for adventure, putting the pistol to good use like a real *desperado*.

Juan Miguel wanted to give Maggie her freedom within the confines of his protection, so he had told Roberto to accompany her when she went out to look for new plants. Roberto was almost seventeen and beginning to be a man, although he was certainly nothing like Juan Miguel had been when he was seventeen. He was skilled with a pistol, but he lacked Juan Miguel's judgment and character.

"Never leave her alone," Juan Miguel said. "And make sure you are armed."

Roberto nodded, but his attitude was less than agreeable. Guarding a woman out in the fields was not his idea of a suitable activity.

Juan Miguel's intense love for Maggie radiated from him like a spring day. He gave her everything and did everything for her. He indulged her like a doting parent indulges a beautiful, gifted child. From the beginning, even when he was only seventeen, he had been the parent in the relationship, not her.

She had come to accept him as he was—precocious, creative, able to master any situation. What she could not accept was his absence. She wondered why he could not see the hole he was leaving in her life when he left, why he continued to pursue his own goals—goals she barely understood. She had given up two husbands to be with him. Was that not enough for him? Was that not enough to keep him?

He sensed her feelings and tried to fill up her days while he was gone. He asked only one thing of her: to write in the journal. When he found that she was slacking off on this responsibility, he started giving her assignments to keep her mind busy and connected to the real world.

He started by asking her to copy recipes, keep track of Annabelle's development, and write about day-to-day activities. She did the assignments dutifully, but none of that inspired her. Then on a visit in early March, he asked her to do something that struck a deep chord. He remembered that she loved the natural world and was a keen observer of the things around her. He asked her to catalog, draw, and describe all the wildflowers and wild plants and grasses she could find. He brought her new pens and watercolors for the task.

It was a natural fit for Maggie, taking her back to the most pleasant memories from her childhood and later when she loved wandering the countryside looking for plants and identifying them.

What started out as a resonating idea became an obsession for Maggie. In the early spring, she started the work. She sat in the grasses and weeds doing her sketching. She tramped through the nearby woods and fields looking for new flowers and plants. She took her sketches back to the house and spent hours painting them. She wrote long descriptions of the plants' habitats and habits.

She cataloged the yellow Mexican hats, the pure-white snow lilies that bloomed underneath the tall grass after a spring shower, and the cross-shaped, four-petaled mustards. She wandered the sandy fields looking for the red corn poppy with the deep black center. She found the white frothy redroots in the rocky soil along the river. She drew the patches of buffalo grass and the lacy lime-green new leaves on the mesquite trees.

Studying the wild plants cleared the haze in her mind and put her in harmony with the things around her. It made the crooked straight. She thought she could do it forever.

When Juan Miguel returned in late March, she showed him what she had done. He looked at her as if she were a precious treasure, newly redeemed.

"They are beautiful," he said. "They are beautiful and re-markable. I am so proud of you. I have never been so proud."

He grabbed her and hugged her like the prodigal child returning from a long journey.

"You must continue with this," he said, looking at the drawings again.

"Do you think anyone else would like to see them?" she asked timidly.

"*Si*, what are you thinking, Marguerite?"

"Maybe someone at the new university."

"When you are further along, I will have someone take you there," he said.

She wanted to tell him everything she had bottled up. He was the only person who would understand what she was seeing and experiencing. She could not tell him fast enough.

He listened as long as his patience would allow. Then he unpinned her hair, which looked as if it had not been brushed for days. He took off the paint-smeared, food-smeared apron and the mud-caked boots.

Her eyes were sharp daggers when he asked, "*Senora*, do you not brush your hair anymore?"

Neither her anger nor her unseemly appearance made him want her less. They had the opposite effect.

While they were making love, she would not stop talking about the shape of petals, the color of shadows on dark red, the way the light plays at midday. He used his fingers, then his tongue to stop the incessant talking.

Every time he visited Maggie, he arrived earlier, left later, and stayed longer. But he feared that the odds were becoming stacked against him—that sooner or later his luck would run out and he would be recognized.

CHAPTER 3

The ownership of ranch lands in south Texas had been disputed since the 1840s, when the Treaty of Guadalupe Hidalgo confirmed all Mexican land ownership—in theory. However, since then there had been an erosion of the lands held by the Spanish aristocracy, which had been in the hands of the Spanish families for many decades. Anglos arrived with warrants, titles, and veterans' land certificates, claiming parts or all of the ranchos.

The Mexican landowners did their best to defend their ancient claims in court but often lost under American laws. An angry, aggrieved Mexican aristocrat had been single-handedly responsible for starting a border uprising in 1859.

It was just such a veteran land certificate Ben Barone used to claim what he called "unoccupied" lands once owned by the del Valle family. The court upheld his claim after local constables researched and found only poor Mexican families holding small herds of cattle on parts of the land. There seemed to be no one in charge, and the herders said the last member of the del Valle family was incarcerated in Mexico for horse stealing.

The court proceeding took place in the Atascosa County Court at Law. Witnesses for Barone included the two constables, John Maloney and Evert Copeland, who were members of the secret society Der Kreis. No member of the del Valle family was informed of the proceeding, and no evidence was presented on their behalf.

Out of court, Judge Liam McAllister was well aware that the constables and Barone were business associates, but he ignored that evidence and ruled in Barone's favor. Thus, on the word of two questionable witnesses, the del Valle Rancho lands, ceded to the family under the auspices of the king of Spain, were stolen.

Matthew delivered the bad news to Senor Zamora in his room at the Menger.

"The court ruling seems to be final," Matthew said.

"Only death is final, *senor*," Martin said.

"So, have I fulfilled what you asked me to do, then?"

"You have done well, but only so far as it goes. I must know where to find this judge and these constables. That is next."

"What will you do to them?"

"*Senor*, it is not what I will do to them, it is what I will do for them—save them from the angry Juan Miguel del Valle."

Matthew could not keep up with this kind of scheming, so he didn't even try.

"And," Martin said. "There is one more thing. I want you

to find my brother, Carlos del Valle. For that, I will pay extra."

"Where should I start?"

"He loved to gamble. Perhaps you could start there."

"These things will take time."

"Go find them," Martin said. "And return by May."

Just as Matthew was leaving, a written message arrived for *Senor* Zamora. It said:

Easter Celebration

April 30, 1881, 8:00 p.m., Menger Hotel Ballroom

Dinner, dancing, and gaming

Ben and Isela Barone would be honored to receive you as their guest

Response respectfully requested

Martin Zamora could not have been more pleased to accept the invitation.

When Primo and Pedro visited the del Valle Rancho for the first time in many years, they arrived in secret to reconnoiter. They knocked on the doors of the humble adobe shacks late at night. Divulging their true identities to the few who did not recognize them, they asked questions. Not only did they receive earfuls but also quite a few good meals, including one really fine supper of mutton and yams.

They wanted to know how profitable the rancho was, how many head of cattle the owner was running, how the people were treated, who represented the owner as an overseer, whether the owner ever visited, and, if so, how often and on what schedule.

The herders told them that the right to part ownership of the cattle had been taken away from the people. They were now only serfs on the land they had worked even before the del Valles owned it, when it had been a mission rancho owned by the Catholic Church. The new owner, Ben Barone, visited the overseer, Richard Lincoln, at the end of every month. He would be due for a visit in about a week, they said. Barone had made the rancho somewhat profitable, although he continued to fight low market beef prices. The overseer was aided by four armed *Anglos* who kept watch over the *vaqueros* and their families.

One evening, Primo and Pedro took advantage of the absence of Senor Lincoln and his men to call all the people together at the chapel. Several hundred *vaqueros*, their wives, and children crowded into the small chapel, now neglected and run down.

Primo stood in front of them. The people were silent, waiting for him to speak. He took off his black hat and his holster and laid them on the small table next to the altar.

"As most of you already know, I am not only Primo, the outlaw," he began. "I am also Juan Miguel del Valle."

They nodded. Several of the older women crossed themselves. There was no one they loved or trusted more. That he was among them once again was no less than a miracle to them.

"It has been my intention and my hope to take back my

family's land and also restore all of you to a higher status. Please believe that is what I am working for."

They looked at him with wide eyes and open souls.

"So here is how you can help me. First, do not tell Senor Lincoln or his men that I was here and we had this meeting."

They nodded in agreement.

"Second, tell him Primo and Juan Miguel del Valle are one and the same."

They looked at each other with questions.

"I know it sounds like a bad idea, but believe me, it is not. Just tell him—casually as if it is common knowledge. We are just planting a seed, that is all. Can you do it?"

One man on the front row said, "*Si*, we will do it, but will it not endanger you?"

Primo smiled, a broad, open, generous smile.

"*Si*, but I have been in so much danger for so long, it will not make much of a difference. Believe me, *amigos*, I will be fine."

The next day, Primo and Pedro were gone. Coincidentally, it was discovered that Barone's two prize bulls had broken out of their pen during the night and were lost.

A week later, two longhorn bulls brought extremely high prices when they were sold to two Mexican ranchers at a cattle auction in Monterrey. The ranchers were only too happy to look the other way when they saw the double B brand on the bulls' hindquarters.

———————

Lucia and Teresa were dressed in their best clothing—the first new dresses they had bought in years. Lucia's was a pale green and Teresa's a pale yellow. They had swept the cantina and washed down the tables and bar. Teresa brought in some scraggly wild daisies she found down the road and put them in a tall glass. Lucia had spent most of the day cooking the rice and beans. Luis Nuncio smoked the goat meat in an open pit in back of his house, cooking it slowly for an entire day, basting it with a pungent sauce made from his grandmother's recipe.

Lucia and Teresa were like small children waiting for Christmas, counting every minute until Primo and Pedro arrived. The two men had stopped by on their way to Monterrey to say hello and said they would be back in three days to spend the night. The women invited hundreds to the party, which was to be a surprise, to show their gratitude for the money they had given the townspeople. They only hoped Primo—who was known to be reclusive—would not mind the fuss.

Finally, toward late afternoon, the two men walked in. The people clapped and yelled, then ushered them to the table of honor—the one with the daisies. Teresa brought them two bottles of tequila, and everybody drank a toast. Primo tried to stifle a smile but could not. They sat and ate their smoked meats and beans, drank their tequila, and listened to Luis' daughter sing and play the guitar.

For dessert, Lucia brought Primo some apple-filled enchiladas served with goat's milk. He kissed her hand, and she blushed a bright red.

"Speech, speech," they yelled after dinner. Primo only shook his head. He bowed deeply and whispered *gracias* but declined to speak.

The women and children left at sundown, leaving the men to drink. Primo was not shy about asking for another bottle of tequila. He sat looking out the window, thinking of Maggie and his baby daughter. He ached from missing them.

"I wish you were here to see all this," he said out loud. "I wish you were here."

They all knew who he was talking to. No amount of kindness and fellowship could make up for her absence. Nothing and no one could make him happy when he was away from her.

Fairly early in the evening, Primo picked up the bottle and went to bed in the room upstairs. He had been asleep for several hours when he awoke to loud yelling coming from the bar. It sounded like Pedro was trying to calm someone who was being belligerent, but the yelling got louder and more serious. Primo put on his boots and strapped on his gun and went downstairs to see what was happening.

When he appeared on the stairway, everything got quiet.

"*¿Que paso?*" he asked, easing down the stairs with his hand on his pistol.

A young sandy-haired man, drunk and angry, looked at him with an evil grin.

"And you would be Primo, huh?"

"*Si* ... that I am," he said quietly.

"The Primo with the fast gun?"

"*Si* ... that is who I am," he repeated.

"But it's only a story, right? You're not really that fast, are you?"

"*Si* ... it is only a story," he said, even more quietly.

"*Senor*, do not test him," Pedro said to the young man. "It is more than a story."

The man stepped back and waved the others away.

"Let's see how fast you are, then."

"No, *senor*, I have no desire to draw against you."

"Because you are afraid?"

"I have no reason to draw against you. I don't draw for no reason."

The blond man sneered and his fingers fidgeted. He moved his hand only a fraction, and a bullet grazed his jaw.

"Do you wish to lose an earlobe next, *senor*?" Primo asked, popping the pistol back into the holster.

The man put his hand to his face and felt the blood flowing from the bullet wound. He picked up his hat, and he and his friends left the cantina.

Primo climbed the stairs. He hung his head as he sat on the edge of the bed. He asked himself, is there no end to the idiots who want to get themselves killed?

Suddenly, he was overcome with doubt—doubt so acute it was like a lance in his side. He could see his own arrival and departure getting closer and closer together, until only a sliver of time remained.

All the pain, the sorrow, the loneliness, the abuse fell on

him. They weighed so much, they flattened him. He was without dimension or form, only a description, a hollow man with a fake identity.

The memory of being raped—which had been only sketchy—became vivid. He could feel it. He could see the others watching. He felt the humiliation as if it were happening to him all over again. The thing he had strived to keep at bay came pounding at his door. It didn't matter that he outsmarted them in the end. It happened, and he remembered it. He felt he would never be free of his fear, his weakness, his willingness to do anything to make it stop.

He lay back on the bed and clutched his stomach. The pain shot through him. He bit his own hand to keep from screaming.

Lucia woke Pedro early the next morning, only hours after he had fallen asleep in the back room.

"He is sick again," she said. "He was awake all night. I heard him get up many times."

Pedro climbed the stairs two at a time and opened the door to Primo's room. He took one look, then called down to Lucia.

"Find the woman who used to be a nurse," he yelled. "And bring some cool water."

Primo was more ill than Pedro had ever seen him. He appeared to be dehydrated and delirious. His body was weak and sweating and hot to the touch. Pedro dipped a cloth in the cool water and tried to get him to suck on the cloth.

"*Jesucristo*," he said. "*Dios nos ayude.*"

Primo squirmed and moaned, then lay quietly, then squirmed and moaned more. Lucia sat by his side to give Pedro some rest. Every few minutes, she wiped the tears falling down his cheeks with her handkerchief. She wiped her own tears as well. She dipped a rag in the water and wiped it over his skin to cool him.

Hearing he was sick, people came to see how he was, but Pedro sent them away.

"The noise will bother him," he said.

He lay near death for three days. On the third day, Pedro sent for the priest, who said the prayers for the dying over him. Pedro lost faith he would recover, but slowly, as in the past, he got better.

"Does the woman, the *senora*, know how ill he is?" Lucia asked Pedro on the fourth day.

She scrubbed the same spot on the bar over and over again, obviously upset.

"He doesn't want her to know," Pedro said.

"You should tell her so that he won't die without her."

"*Si* ... you are right."

"Something else, Pedro, the next time someone wants to draw on him, you should just kill them."

She threw down the wash cloth on the bar and stomped off.

It took a week for Primo to be well enough to get out of

bed. It took ten days for him to be well enough to start back to San Antonio. He and Pedro rode back at a slow pace, stopping frequently to rest. Primo was thin and pale. Pedro was watchful.

The story about Primo shooting the foolish young sandy-haired man in the jaw spread like wildfire throughout the southwestern United States and Mexico. The stories in the dime novel were one thing, but the true story of what Primo did in Nuevo Laredo was even more fascinating. He was obviously a dangerous man—someone to fear—not someone to challenge lightly.

Another story spread in the area around San Antonio, that Primo and Juan Miguel del Valle might be the same man. Eventually, the story reached the ears it was meant to reach—Ben Barone and the constables and judge who were responsible for taking the del Valle Rancho. If it were true, this man—Senor del Valle or Primo—might one day want some answers. Maybe at the point of a gun.

Beatriz met Maggie at the door one morning when she returned from drawing plants.

"There is someone to see you, *senora*," Beatriz said. "It is Pedro Garcia, a good friend of Senor Juan Miguel's."

"Are you sure it's safe?"

"*Si* ... he is a friend of ours, too."

Maggie put down her paint box and quilt and walked

into the parlor. A large man with long black hair and a black mustache stood by the window. He had worn clothing and leathery skin. There was a week's worth of trail dust on his chaps and boots.

"Sir?" she said. "What can I do for you?"

"May we sit, *senora*? I have something to tell you."

Pedro was surprised at the appearance of Senora Marguerite. She was so unlike what he expected that he stared. He would not describe her as beautiful; he would describe her as peculiar. She had skin the color of cream and startling eyes, but she managed to look both old and young at the same time. She looked like no one he had ever seen—like someone who had thrown convention to the wind and was totally unaware of how a woman should dress, wear her hair, or even sit.

She sat on the settee with one leg tucked under her and fidgeted with her fingers. She was genteel and graceful, but she also had a nervousness that conveyed itself to people around her like waves of energy.

He cleared his throat and began.

"*Senora*, I am a good friend of Juan Miguel. We have been close friends for many years."

She looked surprised. Evidently, Juan Miguel had not told her this.

"We were in Nuevo Laredo two weeks ago on our way from Monterrey, where we did some business, back to San Antonio. While we were there, Juan Miguel became ill."

She jumped as if she had been struck.

"Ill? What kind of illness? Is he well now? Where is he?"

"He is fine now, *senora*. He is back at the Menger and has almost recovered. He has a stomach ailment—a very serious one. He has not wanted you to know about it."

"That's not true. He would've told me. I would've known about it."

"No, *senora*, it is true. He has attacks, and when he does, it is very serious. This time, he almost died."

Maggie put her hand over her mouth and gasped. She looked frightened and grew wan.

"*Senor*a, are you not well? Shall I get Beatriz?" he asked, getting up from his chair to find someone to help.

"Why did he not tell me?" she said in a high thin voice. Tears came into her panic-stricken eyes.

"Senora, I am going against his instructions by telling you this. But those of us who love him think you should know about it."

Maggie turned her head away and began to sob quietly.

After several minutes, she said, "Thank you for telling me. Now, I want you to take me back with you, so I can see for myself whether he is well."

"That I cannot do. It would put you both in danger. But I promise you I will take care of him."

In an uncharacteristic gesture, he put his hand on hers—for only a moment—long enough to offer some reassurance.

After he left, Maggie went to her room and retreated into herself. Beatriz stood outside her door and listened, but she could not hear any sounds.

CHAPTER 4

The week before Easter, Juan Miguel brought Annabelle a light pink bonnet embroidered with tiny white roses. He brought Maggie a ring with a square blue lapis stone in the center and two cream-colored pearls on either side. He also brought her an emerald-green silk blouse with black piping and a black velvet ribbon for her hair. He brought each of them new brushes and combs. The brushes were backed with gold plates engraved with their names and had soft bristles made from horsehair.

Maggie held Annabelle in her arms as she opened the gifts. She smiled at him with love and adoration. After the gifts were unwrapped, she looked into his eyes and tears welled up in hers.

She reached out her arm and said, "Hold us."

He scooted closer to her and took them both in his arms. They sat like that for the entire evening. He stroked Maggie's hair and kissed Annabelle on the top of her light red, wispy hair. Maggie would not let him go.

When Annabelle was fed and asleep, they sat on the bed embracing. Maggie looked at him and said, "Juan Miguel, there is something I have to tell you."

The use of his name signaled she was serious.

"What is it?"

"I never told you ..." She hesitated.

"Tell me," he said. "You can tell me anything."

"I never said how much I love you."

This shocked him to his very core. Not the fact, but the words.

"I know that, Marguerite. You don't have to say it."

"Do you love me?" she asked shyly.

"I love you," he said. "But these are things we already knew, so what is this about?"

She put her hand on his cheek, then his chin. His face was as beautiful as ever: the long black lashes framing the soft brown eyes, the strong jaw, the sensuous mouth. If everything else in the world turned imperfect, his face would remain perfect. The stubble on his chin was thicker than it used to be, perhaps, but his skin was still soft.

"I know you have been ill. Pedro came here and told me," she said.

He looked down and took hold of her hand.

"I wanted to spare you," he said. "That's why I never told you."

"What else have you not told me?"

"There is much in my life I am ashamed of, *senora*. I cannot talk about it. Please don't force me to."

"I know you, Juan Miguel. I know whatever you are ashamed of was not your fault."

He smiled slightly and looked at her guardedly.

"Please," he said. "Can we not talk about this?"

"You will tell me someday?"

"No, I will never tell you."

"Because you don't trust me." She felt the distance between them.

"It is not a matter of trust, Marguerite. It is a matter of pain."

The two of them lay back on the bed. He sought to bridge the distance by reaching for her hand. He succeeded and they made love.

Later that night, he insisted that she put on the green silk blouse so he could see her in it. She put it on over the white lace petticoat edged with yellow satin. He pulled back her hair and tied it with the black velvet ribbon.

He got up from the bed and took her hand.

"May I have this dance?" he said.

"Do they allow gentlemen to dance naked here, *senor*?"

"*Si* ... they are very tolerant."

"But they require hats, do they not?" she teased, picking up his light gray hat, placing it on his head, and pulling it down over the beautiful eyes.

"There's no music," she said.

"I will sing. You have always admired my singing."

He started humming a song called "Beautiful Dreamer" that he'd heard in a San Antonio bar.

He sang some of the words softly in her ear,

Sounds of the rude world, heard in the day,

Lulled by the moonlight have all passed away

She put her hands on his bare shoulders as they swayed. He held her close, and they danced for hours. A warm breeze blew through the open window. It carried with it the fragrant aroma of the magnolia blossoms and married it with the heavenly bittersweet aroma emanating from the two lovers.

At one point she looked at him and said, "There is so much I don't know about you. You keep secrets from me."

"You don't need to know everything, Marguerite. We are the same person when we are together—that is all you need to know."

————————

After he left, Maggie knelt by her bed and tried to pray, remembering how she had seen Juan Miguel do it. She had never tried to pray before and had never addressed God directly.

She wanted to pray for Juan Miguel's health and safety, but she found herself thinking something else.

God, if you love him—and I know you must—why do you torture him this way? Why do you make him sick? Why do you make his life so complicated and full of fear? Can you not ease some of his burdens?

She stopped, because she knew she would get no answers.

She remembered the conversation she had about Juan Miguel with Father Moreno years ago. She remembered something he had said—something about blessings and curses being one and the same. Maybe Father Moreno knew what he was talking about. Maybe that was part of the answer.

She realized that the love he inspired in some people was coupled with the hatred and jealousy he inspired in others. His great beauty was coupled with the desire to own him—to ravish him. His intelligence was coupled with his inability to stop out-thinking, out-scheming everyone else.

His compassion, turned on its head, became his devotion and commitment, just as it had for her. She had always known that pity was the first emotion he felt for her. He sensed her terrible, gnawing hunger for love before she was willing to acknowledge it.

She had not realized until that moment what grave danger he was in and had always been in. He is like a delicate, valuable flower petal about to be blown away, she thought. Then she stopped herself again. No, he has an uncanny way of winning the day in any situation.

Isela Barone was all she was expected to be—agreeable, malleable, shallow. She looked in the mirror and saw only her hairdo.

She thought about things like finding the best curtains for the dining room, what her lady friend said her other lady friend said, how she looked on the arm of her husband, and how to make a good light cornbread.

She made sure she performed her wifely duties well—nodding in agreement, keeping things from Ben Barone he didn't need to know, and meeting his needs when the occasion arose. In return, she got status and money, which were not small things.

Isela was widowed when her first husband, Nathan Manchester, was felled by a Confederate sharpshooter in the battle of Vicksburg. He was a colonel in the Union cavalry who was not known for bravery or enthusiasm for battle. That served him well and allowed him to survive for several years, but time and circumstances caught up with him. After the war, Isela, quite an opportunist, came to San Antonio with her two daughters, Julia and Emma, both of whom were now of marriageable age. She had inherited enough money to fund a nice lifestyle for a number of years, during which time she had to find herself a husband to fund the rest of her years.

The new Mrs. Barone was what you might call "a handsome woman," with dark brown hair and blue eyes. She had not allowed herself to grow overly fat. She had bulbous breasts, which she stuffed into a corset and pushed up to make an astounding cleavage. She wore expensive dresses and hats with fine jewelry. She often carried a satin parasol as an affectation—a sort of badge of wealth. She had convinced herself she was important.

But, all in all, she was not a bad person. She could be quite interesting to talk to, if the conversation stayed on the subject of her and her immediate concerns. Anything out of that sphere was beyond her.

The Easter celebration at the Menger—which her husband had suggested—was just her cup of tea. She could plan it down to the last detail and make it a showcase for her wealth and position. It was also a good opportunity for her daughters to meet eligible men who might one day make suitable husbands.

It had crossed her mind that Senor Zamora might be one of these men, although she knew the odds were against it. He was the best-looking and most charming man in San Antonio, perhaps in Texas. He was rolling in money. A man like that was obviously well-traveled. He had been to Europe, to South America, to the East Coast. He could have his choice of anyone, and Julia and Emma were not exactly stand-outs. They both inherited bad skin from their father.

The Easter celebration was to open with a lavish dinner. Isela had ordered shellfish, packed in ice from one of the new steam-powered refrigeration machines and brought by train from the Texas coast at great expense. She planned to serve turkey as the main dish, with a number of freshly grown vegetables on the side, including corn and collard greens with bacon. For dessert, both chocolate and pecan pies.

After dinner would be dancing to music provided by pianist Gerald Seismore. Then the men would retire to the back rooms and play cards, smoke, and drink. The women could either go to bed or visit with Isela in her suite, where she planned to serve tea and show them her new dresses from Europe.

Martin Zamora also looked forward to the Easter celebration, and he also had planned what he would wear, how he would present himself, and what he wanted the result to be. But for him, it was a job. It had nothing to do with him—the real him. Unlike Isela, he knew who he was.

———————

Senor Zamora had one hand in his suit pocket and the other on a railing in the Menger ballroom. Overhead were white paper streamers draped from the candlelit chandeliers to the walls and back again. Yellow roses were bunched in pottery vases at strategic points around the room. The dark wood floors were newly polished and shining.

He smiled his refined smile and nodded agreeably to the women standing against the far wall. He should pick one and ask her to dance—just for appearance's sake, but he couldn't make his feet move. It was one thing to act like Martin Zamora, the man of the world who had known and danced with many women. It was quite another thing to pretend he was interested in dancing with anyone except the woman he loved. Although many hands had touched him, both in lust and in love, Maggie was the only woman he had ever touched. Just this once, he would not give in to the needs of Senor Zamora. He knew if another woman was in his arms, he would look awkward.

Isela Barnoe roused him from his reverie by introducing her daughters.

He bowed and nodded.

"They would be so thrilled, *senor*, if you would dance with them," she said in her flighty voice.

"Regrettably, I will not be dancing tonight," he said. "I have hurt my foot."

"Oh, what a shame," she said, looking dubious. "Will you join us for some punch, then?"

He accompanied them to the punch bowl and took a glass, but he didn't drink it. He had not had alcohol since he was sick. He talked amiably, but he felt himself sweating in his clothes, something that had never happened to him before. He felt light-headed, and the thought occurred to him that he might be getting sick again. Or maybe it was how tired he was growing of the pretense.

Martin deliberately started his card playing at a different table from Barone. He wanted to make Barone approach him and propose a game.

He sat through the hands, basically unchallenged, and won a good amount of cash. As the evening wore on, he could see Barone glancing repeatedly in his direction. Finally, Barone walked over to his table.

"Mr. Zamora, we invite you to join us. We've lost one of our players," Barone said. Then he chuckled. "Maybe you want a chance to win back the money you lost when we played before."

Martin nodded and smiled. "Senor, it would be my pleasure," he said.

Barone introduced Senor Zamora to the four other men at his table. "You remember Will Harper and Zachariah Schmitt?"

"*Senores ...*"

"This here's Ned Bailey ... runs a import business in New Orleans. And that's Matthew Piper ... writes dime novels ... wrote the one about Primo, the outlaw. You likely heard of it."

"I have heard of it ... my congratulations, *senor* ... your book is very successful, I understand."

No one asked Senor Zamora about his profession. No one dared.

Matthew nodded once and tried to look unself-conscious, but he felt his face burning, and he didn't know what to do with his hands. Senor Zamora looked anything but self-conscious. His face and hands were perfectly relaxed.

After an hour or so, Senor Zamora had won more hands than the others. He was skilled at the game—that was evident. Then he and Matthew Piper began to bet against each other, raising each other and squinting from under hooded brows. Piper was getting the edge and won a considerable sum with an evident bluff. Senor Zamora seemed to fume, although he was smiling.

"Have you two fellas met before?" Bailey asked as he dealt a new hand.

"Matter of fact, we've met and we've played," Matthew said. He kept his eyes fixed on his hand.

Barone sat back and stole a glance at Harper. Both men had the same thought—when two players are intent on beating each other, it opens up all sorts of opportunities. They often make suckers out of each other, and themselves.

"Well then, that does make things interesting," Barone said. He put his cigar in his mouth and began to chew it.

Several hands later, Senor Zamora shocked the ranchers by betting more than half his money in a reckless attempt to get back at Piper. They didn't look at each other, but their thoughts were on the time several weeks ago when he had overplayed his hand. But this time he won the hand by drawing to an inside straight—an obvious bit of luck he didn't deserve after his brazen bluffing.

The next five hands, Senor Zamora continued to try to ride that wave of luck, but it wasn't working. Piper won back his money and then some. Barone sat by and watched in amusement, then snapped to attention when Senor Zamora dealt him a full house—three threes and two queens. He was stupefied. It was the best hand so far that evening. He didn't see how Senor Zamora or Matthew Piper could have a better hand, but he tried his best to "slow play" and keep them from throwing down their cards too early.

He upped the bet, and Senor Zamora saw it. He upped it again, and Senor Zamora smiled. "*Senor*, you have me at a disadvantage," he said. "I have run out of cash."

"Do you have other collateral?" Barone asked.

"Much of my cash is tied up right now, but I do have the race horse I just bought."

"The one you bought from the outlaw?"

"*Si* ... that is the one. Would you accept it?"

Barone was jubilant. It was all falling into place just as he had planned.

Senor Zamora threw in the horse—figuratively speaking. He called. Barone laid down his full house and won the hand.

"Are you out, then?" Barone asked.

"I have just remembered," Martin said. "I do have some cash in my room. Will you allow me to get it and continue to play?"

They all looked surprised, but they nodded.

When Senor Zamora returned, he took out a roll of cash the likes of which they had never seen. He put it on the table and smiled.

"Shall we continue, *amigos*?" he said.

That's when the poker lesson began. As fast as Senor Zamora could bet and raise, he was matched by Matthew Piper. One could hardly get the words out of his mouth before the other would chime in. The two were resolved to do each other in, and the stakes went higher and higher. Staying in the game and matching them raise for raise now became a matter of pride for Ben Barone. The other three players fell by the wayside, leaving only Senor Zamora, Piper, and Barone as the evening turned into nighttime.

Sometime during the night, the race horse changed hands again when Senor Zamora took it back. Then whiskey, fatigue, and bad judgment took over. Barone was losing—hoping to catch Senor Zamora in another bluff—but this time there was no bluffing, only winning. Martin Zamora backed Barone up against a wall, and then the wall crumbled. Against his better judgment and everything he knew about poker, Barone persisted. He was determined to win back that horse.

Late into the humid May night, only an hour or so before sunup, the fatal blow finally came. Matthew Piper had taken off his jacket and rolled up his sleeves. Sweat soaked the front and back of his shirt and rolled down the sides of his face. Periodically, he would sit back in his chair and eye Senor Zamora with obvious contempt. Senor Zamora remained unfazed. It was not his temperament to show his feelings, but he could not help but be rattled by Piper's aggressive stance.

Once again, Senor Zamora dealt Barone a winning hand, a flush ... five diamonds, jack high. By this time, Barone's funds were depleted. But a flush ... how often was a man dealt a flush?

The thing Barone didn't realize, of course, was that while

he was carefully observing the two poker opponents, making sure he understood their weaknesses and their inclinations, Senor Zamora was carefully observing him. Barone had a "tell," one of the most telling "tells" Senor Zamora had ever seen. When Barone had a good hand, he held it close to his chest and cupped his right fingers around the edge of the cards. Senor Zamora could hardly keep a straight face when he saw it. It was like a signpost.

Even though Matthew Piper had learned to play poker just the previous week in four all-day sessions with Juan Miguel del Valle, he picked up on it, also. Juan Miguel noticed, and he prayed silently that Matthew would not give himself away.

The two had sat for hours in the Menger Hotel room, Juan Miguel trying to impart all the poker knowledge it took him years to learn. Matthew was not a quick study. His inclination was to be brutally honest. Finesse was not part of his nature.

"You must fill the space between you and the other players," Juan Miguel said, "because if you do not, they will fill it for you."

Matthew looked puzzled. "I'm lost," he said. "I don't understand."

"Someone must be the sucker, *senor*," Juan Miguel told him. "If it is not them, it will be you. This is a lesson I learned from Barone himself."

"Because he's the one who took everything from you?"

"He took everything because I let him."

"I thought in poker, it was just a matter of having a winning hand," Matthew protested.

Juan Miguel laughed and patted him on the shoulder. "Such a simple philosophy, *amigo*. I envy you."

Matthew felt himself being played once again.

Both Matthew and Senor Zamora had read Barone's "tell" and folded. The flush was wasted.

Barone was ecstatic at the next hand, when Piper dealt him two pair. It was the makings of another good hand. The betting began and went on and on. He hoped to draw a full house, and when he didn't, he didn't seem to care. He could hardly believe his good fortune as the betting continued. First Piper, then Senor Zamora, Barone, Piper, Senor Zamora. On and on until the pot was piled high. Barone asked them to accept credit, which, of course, they agreed to do. Barone threw in his marker, then another marker and another, until he had accumulated a large debt. When the card playing ended, Barone owed Senor Zamora $13,400 in cash—a fact that became legend as the most money ever taken as markers in a card game at the Menger.

"I have enjoyed the game," Senor Zamora said, preparing to leave. "As for the markers, you may take your time, *senor*. But I expect a full payment."

"You'll get your money," Barone said. "I've given my word."

"You have given?" Senor Zamora was smiling. He chuckled to himself, looking as fresh as he had at the beginning of the evening. "No, *senor*, you have not given ... I have taken.

And we shall see, *senor*, if your word is all I have taken."

Barone stood and watched Senor Zamora and Matthew Piper walk out of the room, seemingly together. The truth dawned slowly.

Chapter 5

Martin Zamora sat on his horse behind a stand of trees, looking at the house and outbuildings of the original Barone Ranch. What happened on this land had been his undoing. It seemed like decades ago. However unpleasant some of the memories were, others were pleasant.

In late spring, Martin had traveled to Bandera on business. He had recently purchased a small tract of land south of there on which to raise race horses, including Umberto, who had been saved from falling into the hands of the cattle baron, Ben Barone, by some skilled card playing.

Once in town, Senor Zamora ate a good lunch at a local cafe, then walked down the street to the law offices of O'Hare and Little. He was there by appointment to talk to William Little about a court case involving the del Valle Rancho. He was a friend of the family, he wrote Little in a letter, who had been empowered to look into the case.

Mr. Little confirmed, basically, what Matthew had told him about the history of the case, but he did say there was a chance to reopen it if Senor Zamora or the del Valle family could offer new evidence.

"It would have to be some compelling evidence—say, something in writing—in order to sway old "Mad Man McAllister," Little said.

"And if I find this evidence, will you represent the family?" Martin asked.

"I will, but only if I have a written request from one of them. So, have you talked to one of the del Valles?"

"I have. I have talked to Senor Juan Miguel del Valle."

"Was he not convicted of …"

"*Si* … convicted, incarcerated, then paroled," Martin said. "Give me some time. I think I can get such evidence."

The land Martin purchased was—not totally by coincidence—adjacent to the northernmost section of Ben Barone's original ranch near Bandera. He took a ride out to the land to inspect it and wandered onto the Barone land. He rode up to the ranch house where he had spent time as an employee and had given Ben Barone his due for what he had done to Maggie.

Martin avoided thinking too deeply about his long history with Barone. That would not be productive now, and he had other matters to think about. Barone had taken his family's rancho; he would take it back.

Inside the ranch house that evening, another scene played out.

"Not only did he insult your daughters, he also took your money," Isela yelled at her husband. "Are you going to let him get away with this?"

Ben Barone wanted to reply, "I have other problems right now, believe me. Juan Miguel del Valle is back in the guise of a ruthless outlaw, and he's probably out to take revenge."

Instead, he said, "Senor Zamora is a gentleman and much admired. I have to pay my debt to him. He has consented to wait for payment. That is all I can ask of him."

The fight had raged on in the Barone household for quite some time—since they had returned from San Antonio. The daughters were locked in their rooms sulking about the lack of suitors. The wife was angry about the lost opportunities and the lost money.

When Barone succeeded in getting rid of his wife, he sank into his chair in the parlor and contemplated his options. To raise the cash for payment on the debt, he would have to sell land. There would be no cash coming in from the sale of cattle until next fall. Could he get the cash fast enough? He had no idea.

The more pressing matter was the possibility that Juan Miguel would show up and confront him about the rancho lands. He remembered well Juan Miguel's anger, and he had heard the tales of Primo's anger. For the first time in years, he was frightened.

As Martin sat on his horse in the warm night air, observing the Barone home, scenes from the past tried to intrude. It was like the low hum of a barroom from a distance. He refused to acknowledge them. He called on the practical side of his nature. From Bandera, Senor Zamora rode south to

Pleasanton to look for the two constables whose lives were about to be turned upside down.

———————————

Pedro Garcia had known Carlos del Valle well, both as the son of his employer and as a friend to drink with on a Saturday night or play cards with in the bunkhouse. He remembered Carlos as a man who lived in the shadow of his younger brother—the favored one with all the natural gifts. Carlos' resentment was not well hidden.

When Juan Miguel asked Pedro to speak to Carlos, at first he refused. He felt it was not his place. But Juan Miguel convinced him that only he could make Carlos see reason, given their history.

He had been waiting at La Cucaracha, a bar across from the San Antonio train station, for almost an hour when the brother walked in with a couple of *amigos*. He had grown paunchy and soft, probably from drinking and idleness.

When Carlos spotted Pedro sitting at a back table, he approached cautiously and alone. He had come to the bar to meet "an old friend" after Matthew Piper promised it would be worth his while—meaning money would be involved.

"*Senor*," Pedro said, looking at him from under his broad-brimmed hat.

Carlos sat and put his hands on the table. Pedro looked more than a little dangerous.

"I have been asked to talk to you by Senor Martin

Zamora, who represents your family in a legal matter," Pedro said.

"I've never heard of him."

"He is well known to the del Valles. He wishes to get your signature on a legal document and, in return, will settle your outstanding debts."

Carlos laughed derisively. "My debts? What do you know about that?"

"I know you owe a great deal, as much as $1,000, and I am prepared to offer that much. For that, you will sign this legal document, which is a power of attorney, allowing Senor Zamora to proceed with a lawsuit on behalf of your family. Do you agree to this?"

Carlos picked up the document and looked at it.

"I need a drink first," he said.

After downing several shots of bourbon, Carlos sat back with the paper in his hand and considered how much more than $1,000 he could negotiate.

Pedro had been warned that this was coming, and he was prepared. He picked up the rifle from his lap and put it on the table, then pulled out a cigarette from his vest pocket and lit it. He put his hand back on the rifle handle and looked at Carlos with his well-known contempt.

"I would think this would be worth much more," Carlos said. "Maybe $3,000."

Pedro stuck his nose up in the air and looked down over his cheeks.

"*Senor*, the del Valles don't need your signature as much

as you might wish. It is strictly a formality. I have been told to offer $1,500—no more."

"They must need my signature—at least a little. How about $2,500?"

"As I said, it is a formality. I can go to $2,000, but that is the top."

Carlos walked over to the bartender to ask for a pen. He handed the signed document to Pedro. Pedro took the money out of his vest pocket and put it on the table.

"Juan Miguel sends this message. He wishes never to see you again," Pedro said. "You have betrayed your father and your entire family. Anyway, that is his message."

Pedro picked up his rifle and left Carlos sitting at the table, totally unaware of what he had signed away.

Before Martin Zamora had left on his trip to Bandera, Matthew caught up with him as he looked at French Napoleon style furniture through the plate-glass window of Reinhold Becker furniture emporium. Martin admired the black lacquered sideboard painted with gold filigree and a pale yellow and green floral design. The contrast between the black and the light colors had caught his eye but he also seemed interested in a plain highly polished cherrywood table.

"Are you an aficionado of European furniture, sir?" Matthew asked him as they strolled down the street together.

"*Si*, I am an aficionado of anything beautiful, *senor*."

When they came to a secluded part of the sidewalk by the side of a small cafe, Senor Zamora reached into his inside pocket and pulled out an envelope, which he handed to Matthew.

Matthew started to grab it, but Senor Zamora pulled it back. "Discreetly, *senor*, discreetly," he said. "You must learn some patience. All things are possible if you have patience."

Matthew had fulfilled his duties to Senor Zamora, and now he was collecting his payment. He felt satisfied he had done what was asked, although he knew nothing about the purpose of finding the information. Now, he thought, I can go back to writing about Primo. In order to do this, he knew he needed continued access to the man he had come to know as many different characters. He also felt a certain loy-alty.

Senor Zamora promised Matthew he would get the story of a lifetime if he waited to be summoned. Matthew had already decided his new dime novel would be called *The Ballad of Juan Miguel* and would tell the real story of the re-markable person he had come to know.

So he was willing to bide his time and hold his pen. Doing so had certainly paid off so far.

Before they finished their conversation, Matthew looked at the European dandy with the large bank roll and asked, "Sir, can I ask you something?"

"Certainly, *senor*, what is it?"

"How do you do this? How can you be so many different people?"

"The world is what you make it."

"It is true for you, but it is not true for all of us."

"*Si* … it is true for all of us."

"Which one is truly you?"

"You are a fiction writer. You know all the characters are merely the author in different moods. For me, it is the same."

"But, I am not a fiction writer. I write about the truth."

Martin Zamora laughed so heartily, he had to lean against a brick wall, take off his spectacles, and wipe his eyes with his silk handkerchief. He laughed for a good three or four minutes. When finally he could speak, he said, "*Senor*, you have deluded yourself. The truth is much too slippery to write about."

Matthew nodded, but he did not agree.

"Love and loyalty, *senor*. There is nothing else," Senor Zamora said, and he walked away.

———————

Before Martin Zamora could make it to Pleasanton, the Atascosa County seat, the outlaw Primo was spotted in the area.

One Thursday afternoon, Stephen Jackson, a local store owner and barber, had Constable John Maloney in his chair. He had given him a trim and was about to shave him when Maloney sat up, startled. He could see out the open doorway a man dressed all in black riding down the main street. Judging from descriptions he had read of Primo, it could very well be him.

Maloney pushed Jackson aside with his elbow and stood to get a better look. The man had a pistol strapped across his chest and silver star-shaped spurs, just as the dime novels described.

"That's enough," Maloney said, tossing some coins onto a nearby table. "I'll shave later."

As fast as he could put on his hat and wipe off his chin, Maloney was on his way to find Evert Copeland.

When he stepped outside the barber shop, he could see Primo entering the town bar. Primo had dismounted and had looked up and down the street, as if looking for someone.

Maloney found Copeland, and they discussed the possibilities.

"Why else would he be here?" Copeland asked. "T'ain't nothin' here to rob. He's looking for us ... it's gotta be."

Maloney shook his head. "Let's not jump to conclusions," he said, sounding less than convinced.

After they saw the notorious outlaw leave the bar, they high-tailed it down there and asked the bartender what he had said.

"He asked directions to the del Valle rancho," the barkeep said.

A cold feeling ran through both men.

Later that day, Judge Liam McAllister had a similar experience when a man fitting Primo's description entered his courtroom and sat on the back bench. He sat with his black hat pulled down, obscuring his face. He stared at the judge for almost an hour, then left.

There were a number of other sightings of Primo that day, including at a whorehouse several miles south of the town. The son of a prominent local family witnessed the whore, Gabriella, try to seduce him. She danced on the sawdust floor barefoot, raising her skirts high as she danced. He paid her, but all he asked her to do was rub the knotting cramps from his legs. When she tried to rub higher, he stopped her.

"He was so good-looking, all the whores wanted to touch him," the young man said.

That sealed it. Primo was definitely Juan Miguel del Valle.

An emergency meeting of Der Kreis was called that Sunday. Almost everyone had heard the rumors—Primo is actually Juan Miguel del Valle. He has returned to exact revenge, they said to each other. To a man, they denied ever having any part in Juan Miguel's kidnapping or subsequent arrest. There was, however, a written record of Maloney and Copeland's part in the scheme. Those two did not have plausible deniability, so they were hung out to dry by their cohorts. So much for loyalty.

By the time Martin Zamora got to town, Maloney and Copeland were beside themselves.

"The del Valle family wants to know if you might have been threatened to the point of intimidation when you gave your testimony?" Senor Zamora asked the two constables. "Because if that is true, then no one could blame you for coming forward now with facts that were overlooked the first time, eh?"

That was all that was needed for Maloney and Copeland to sign a letter to the judge confirming that they had been coerced. When they showed Senor Zamora their signed letters, he smiled, because the irony of the situation was apparently lost on them.

Senor Zamora assured them that this simple act would elicit the undying gratitude of Juan Miguel del Valle and the entire del Valle family. Judge McAllister considered the letters from the constables and the power of attorney signed by Carlos del Valle and agreed to reopen the case. He set a court date for October.

CHAPTER 6

When Juan Miguel was with Maggie, he couldn't afford to waste even a second. He was well aware he was living on borrowed time—walking the edge of the precipice. There was no time for boredom, for doubting, or for discord. He loved Maggie every second he was with her with all his heart and body.

They rode the train from San Antonio to Galveston like any other couple on a trip with their baby daughter. He held onto Annabelle's hand as she attempted to walk between them, swaying with the motion of the train. He put his arm around Maggie and touched her hair. He gazed out the window as the moon rose over the coastal plains behind a bank of thunderclouds. The feeling of normalcy brought tears to his eyes, it was so longed for.

On the beach, they watched Annabelle pour seawater into a hole, chase a hermit crab, and run on tippy-toes up to the wavelets, then run away. They sat with their legs uncovered in the sun and drank the lemonade they brought from the hotel. He and Annabelle fell asleep on the quilt while Maggie drew in her journal.

At the end of the day, the setting sun cast a pinky-peach glow over the landscape. The glow fell on the woman with the dark red wavy hair flowing down around her hips and the toddler with the curly strawberry wisps. It lit their freckled faces and contrasted with their sea-blue eyes. It was the most beautiful sight Juan Miguel had ever seen.

That evening, he held Maggie in his arms in the moonlight beaming through the open window.

She asked him, "Do you want other women sometimes? Do other, younger women tempt you sometimes?"

He said, "I love only you. You are perfect to me."

She knew exaggeration when she heard it, but she appreciated his desire to ease her fears.

"Don't others want you sometimes? They must see what I see."

"They want me, Marguerite, but that has nothing to do with us. Now, stop. Speak no more of this."

He put his hands on her cheeks and kissed her, then held her.

"Promise you won't leave ever again," she whispered.

This was the one thing he could not give, so he said nothing.

She sat up and looked at him.

"Juan Miguel, did you hear me? Promise you won't leave us."

"I will always come back if I can," he whispered.

She looked stricken. She put her face in her hands and started to cry softly.

He pulled her hands away and spoke to her sternly.

"If you don't enjoy the time we have, then what difference does it make if we are together?"

As soon as he said it, he regretted it. He knew she didn't see things the way he did. He had resisted marrying her. He could easily live with the freedom of choosing her over and over again. She, obviously, could not. He was frightened of putting a name to it, putting it in a box, and closing the lid.

"Please don't do this," he said, sounding exasperated. "Can we not just relax and be together?"

"Will you marry me, then?" she asked, looking out the window instead of at him, as she sometimes did when she was most intense. He could feel her slipping away.

"I want to marry you, Juan Miguel. No one else, not Primo or Senor Zamora. Do you understand?"

She lay down next to him, and he embraced her, but she felt like a leaden weight in his arms. Her body was stiff, her muscles tense. She had a wall around her—a wall built of fear and need.

"I will marry you if that will make you happier," he said finally, just to console her.

He gave her everything he could give her within the short time he had with her. He would do anything to hold back her madness.

That was how he came to sign his real name on the marriage certificate.

The Menger Hotel concierge approached Pedro first. He was afraid to talk directly to Primo, and, besides, he didn't know how to find him. Pedro met him in the hotel office behind the desk.

Joshua Nash was a former slave who had done well for himself. He learned to read and do simple math as soon as he was freed by his East Texas owner after the War Between the States. Because he was well-spoken, smart, reliable, and extremely well-mannered, the Mengers promoted him from porter to assistant concierge, then concierge in the space of nine years. He also was discreet, perhaps the most necessary quality for a hotel concierge.

"Sir, there is a man in town who would like to talk to your friend about appearing in his Wild West Show," Joshua said to Pedro, keeping his voice low. "He has asked me to contact him and arrange a meeting."

Pedro thought this sounded like a bad idea, but he could never predict what Primo would think.

"Primo meets with no one, as I have told you before," Pedro said.

"Will you at least pass the message and come back with his response?"

"*Si* ... I suppose that would be fine."

"The man's name is Ralph Butler. He told me he has secured the services of several other westerners for his touring show, including Eric 'The Wild' Porter. There would be remuneration offered, of course."

Pedro picked up his rifle, put on his hat, and left without saying anything. The whole idea of a Wild West show was laughable to him.

But, as he could never have predicted, Martin was receptive to the idea.

"This could fit into our plans very nicely," he said. "I will meet with him as Primo's representative. Go ahead and arrange the meeting."

As soon as Martin returned from Galveston, he met with Butler in the Menger Hotel bar. Joshua Nash was there to introduce the two men. When Nash shook hands with Senor Zamora, he chuckled. He had seen the man in a Nuevo Laredo cantina. It really is quite amusing, he thought, the way he pulls the wool over their eyes.

After introductions, Martin asked the bartender to bring him some pumpkin bread from the hotel restaurant with a cup of *cafe con leche*. Nash busied himself behind the bar, pretending to help the bartender but actually watching Butler and Senor Zamora. He could not pull himself away, it was such a fine performance.

Ralph Butler was struck by the man who represented the notorious outlaw. He was not the sort Butler usually encountered, even as a business manager. Judging from his tailored suits and unusual accent, Butler placed him as hailing from Havana. He talked knowledgeably about art and music. He even mentioned seeing the English actress, Adelaide Neilson, onstage in "Romeo and Juliet" before she died the previous year.

"She was very beautiful," Senor Zamora said. "They say she had a Spanish father."

"And did you get a chance to meet her?" Butler asked.

"Why, yes, I did. We had dinner on her veranda. She had recently learned to rumba and wanted me to dance with her."

"So, you danced with her?"

"No, I did not. It was quite dark that night. The moon was not up."

There was a discernible twinkle in Martin's eye when he said the word "moon."

Butler decided he was definitely from Cuba—the rumba originated in Cuba. Where else would he have been exposed to so much culture?

They agreed on a price without much haggling, but Martin did have an important question about exposing Primo to the public.

"The authorities will look the other way while he is performing," Butler said. "So far, that is what they have done with the other performers."

Martin was puzzled by this—they would not arrest him while he was pretending to be an outlaw onstage, but they would arrest him offstage?

"They can't afford to interfere in a profitable and popular enterprise," Butler explained. "Otherwise they would lose support."

"He will agree to this, but he must be here in Texas for a

previous engagement in October," Martin said.

Martin then asked for another concession.

"Primo wants Pedro Garcia, his partner, to be in the show as well. He is the real *vaquero*, the one who taught Primo everything he knows," Martin said.

The Wild West Show tour was to begin in San Antonio, then proceed to New Orleans and St. Louis, and move on to Chicago and six East Coast cities. A tour of West Coast cities was contemplated if the proper venues could be found.

Primo would be known simply as "Primo," since his name was so descriptive. Pedro would be called "Pedro the Vaquero." Primo would have a featured part in a gun duel re-enactment. He and Pedro would put on a sharpshooting exhibition. They were also expected to participate in the opening and closing parades. Primo would receive top billing, second only to Pawnee Bill.

Joshua Nash waited until Ralph Butler was gone to approach Senor Zamora.

He spoke cautiously. "Sir, I met you in Nuevo Laredo last year."

Martin looked at him with a half smile on his face.

"*Senor*, you are most gracious to remember," Martin said. "You have been most helpful. If there is ever anything I can do for you, please ask."

A three-room log building in the town of Pleasanton

doubled as the Atascosa County courthouse and local jail. The amenities were few in this dusty small-town government building in an out-of-the-way, sparsely populated area of ranch lands. Justice was dispensed in a practical, common-sense manner, with a passing nod to established legalities.

If the long arm of the law made mistakes, they could be corrected later, either in the courtroom or out, with some strong-arm tactics. So it was not unusual for the judge to allow lawsuits to be reopened and redressed as power shifted.

When Judge Liam McAllister reopened the legal case establishing the ownership of the del Valle ranch lands, there was surprisingly little interest by the general public. Almost no one cared about the case except the people involved.

What was unusual was the number of attorneys on both sides. Both Barone and the del Valle family were represented by local attorneys as well as "big city" attorneys from San Antonio. This particular power struggle may not have interested the public at large in the beginning, but it involved some important players. Eventually, with the help of some newspaper articles about the case by Matthew Piper, interest grew.

The original hearing reopening the case put both sides on notice that Judge McAllister would not allow shenanigans, but he was prepared to be quite lenient in hearing all the facts surrounding the case, including what had happened to Juan Miguel del Valle.

The surprise star witness had "hearsay" evidence, but the judge allowed his testimony based on the fact that another witness, Father Moreno, was now deceased.

Father Timothy O' Rourke sat on the rickety wooden witness chair in his dark brown cassock, prepared to do anything he could to help the man who had saved the people of Nuevo Laredo. It was that simple.

He told the story as it was told to him by Father Moreno. Juan Miguel del Valle was spirited away to Mexico and made to stand trial there on trumped-up charges. He was paroled and released from the Monterrey prison and was, therefore, still a legal heir of the del Valle family. The Spanish land grant, which had never been nullified, was still in his family's name.

Constables Maloney and Copeland testified that their research into the status of the land had been sketchy at best and had not involved a legal search for the owners.

Barone himself did not testify, although he allowed his attorneys to present legal arguments. Barone was shocked to find himself on opposite sides of the lawsuit from Senor Zamora, who represented the del Valle family.

After the proceedings, in an act of unprecedented magnanimity, Barone approached Senor Zamora and said, "I hope you know there are no hard feelings on my part."

Martin said in his silkiest voice, "*Gracias, senor*, but we have the small matter of your debt to discuss. When might that be possible?"

This put Barone on edge. Did he not have enough problems with losing more than half of the del Valle ranch lands? How could he be expected to repay a large debt when he had just lost a large chunk of his wealth?

What did not come up in the proceedings, but became well known through the newspaper articles, was the most fascinating fact of all—Juan Miguel del Valle was actually the outlaw Primo. No one could say exactly what his legal status was at the time, but the public was inclined to be forgiving. He had the best story to tell, and they loved it.

Juan Miguel had had the foresight to protect all his various identities by making sure his story was known to the public. If anything should happen to him, the finger pointed straight at Ben Barone.

Under the court's ruling, 56 percent of the ranch lands reverted to the del Valle family. This was the original land ceded to them by the Spanish crown and included the land on which the villa and the surrounding village stood. The remainder of the land, which had been added at various times over the years, would remain under the ownership of Barone. Barone offered another 9 percent of his land to Martin Zamora as payment on a gambling debt. Senor Zamora accepted it on one condition. He asked Barone to sign a legal document waiving any further claim to the del Valle lands.

The judge had, as they said, "split the baby" and allowed both parties to walk away with their heads up. It had the desired effect. Neither seemed to be in the mood to pursue further litigation.

When Matthew asked Juan Miguel later why he was willing to stop his pursuit, he thought for a moment, then said, "The time comes when besting someone no longer works."

____

The odors were familiar to him when he stepped inside the door of the bunkhouse—tobacco, human sweat, dirty boots. His steps were tentative as he faced the contingent of *vaqueros*, some of whom he had known as a child.

"Who have you chosen?" he asked.

One who looked somewhat younger than the others stepped forward.

"I am the one," he said. "My name is Frederico Garza. I can read and write, and I speak some English."

"Good, then let us sit and I will explain."

The *vaqueros* sat in chairs or squatted. He squatted as well.

"The first order of business is to rebrand the cattle with the del Valle circle and cross. Put the brand directly over the double B brand, so there is no question that we are not stealing."

They nodded.

"We will go back to the *caporale* system, but I will require no deposit this time," he said. "Divide evenly. Do not fight with each other."

He handed Frederico a satchel full of money.

"Start to fix the buildings," he said. "Begin with the outbuildings, then the chapel, then the villa. Fix up your own houses as well. Celita will oversee the villa renovation."

He took off his hat and laid it on the floor.

"I trust you," he said. They nodded. "I will be back in the spring, and we will work together at that time."

He stood. One of the older *vaqueros* stood and stepped forward.

"We are happy for you, *senor*," he said.

"I know," he said. "I am happy as well."

He put on his hat. He tried to hide the tears in his eyes, but they were quite evident.

He knew it was only a beginning. The rancho was in disrepair, and it would require time and effort to bring it back to its former status.

Meanwhile, he had to work on the status of Primo and Juan Miguel.

CHAPTER 7

He was a sensation. He really was.

His good looks. His regal bearing. His natural gift for playacting.

When he appeared before the crowds riding the sleek and shining Umberto, the crowd went wild. Before and after the shows, they swarmed him, reaching out to touch him, trying to take a piece of him.

He wore a white leather shirt with fringe across the chest and down the sleeves and bright blue and red embroidered stars across the front and back. A white hat, white pants, white chaps, and blue tooled boots were unlike anything Primo had ever worn, but they became his trademark look. Around his neck, he wore a red silk bandana and, on his hip, a pistol, so it wouldn't interfere with the costume.

He usually rode at the head of the opening parade with a rider carrying an enormous American flag right behind. He would stop and hold his hat high in the air, his long brown curls catching the light just right, as Umberto bent one leg in a low bow.

The show started with the "Star Spangled Banner," played by Butler's Cowboy Band, then moved to a presentation of Wild West Riders of the Plains with mounted police, bands of Indians, *vaqueros*, Europeans, regular Army, and even a few stragglers from South America. After a riding exhibition and race, a mock buffalo hunt followed. Then came the star attractions.

Pedro the Vaquero demonstrated the use of the lasso and performed other stunts of roping and riding. A group of horsemen on Arabians did a full-blown pageant. Primo performed "unique feats of sharp-shooting and horsemanship."

The show ended with a battle, sometimes between Indians and cowboys, sometimes between Americans and foreigners, sometimes just a jumble of fake fighting.

With every triumph, Primo's popularity grew, and the likelihood of his arrest diminished. In New York, the mayor and the chief of police not only came to his show, they invited him to join them for photos and a dinner at the famous men's club, Keens restaurant.

The show included hundreds of participants and more than a thousand horses and buffalos. It billed itself as "an immense array of Indians, scouts, cowboys, and early pioneers." There were two performances daily and seating for 10,000 people under waterproof canopies.

During his first tour, it was estimated that more than two million people attended Butler's Wild West Show. More than anything else, the show shaped their perception of the

American west. But the Wild West Show had almost nothing to do with the life of Primo—or any other character he knew. It was all show.

The poet Mason Willamett wrote a poem about Primo titled, "Primo's Death." Photos of the cowboy outlaw with the beautiful eyes—"*Ojos Bellos*" they called him—and his horse, Umberto, appeared in every major newspaper and magazine of the time. Children adored and worshipped him. Women swooned and offered him sexual favors. Men wanted to be him, or—that not being possible—wanted to be his friend. His cachet was unmatched. His celebrity reached the point of hysteria.

———————————

"Next, they will want to see me fail," Primo said matter-of-factly to Pedro one evening after a particularly successful show.

"No, *senor*, they love you," Pedro said.

"The seeds of my destruction are in my success. Failure is next—maybe death, unless I stop soon."

They sat on some stacked-up bales of hay, food for the horses. Primo pulled out a handful of the hay and looked at it.

"I remember having to eat this," he said. "It reminds me how near failure is, how near death and humiliation are. They are always just around the next corner."

"This is crazy, *amigo*. You are beloved. You worry too

much."

Primo threw down the hay and stood.

"This is crazy," he said, swiping his arm in a circle to encompass the whole of the Wild West Show circus. "It is unreal, and it will fail. There is no doubt."

"They say more people have seen this show and others like it than any other show in history," Pedro said.

"When they realize it is not the real Primo, they will turn on me. Then they will want to know the real me. There is no end to their appetite for devouring me."

Pedro looked puzzled. "What do you want to do, then?"

"Go home. Return, if that is possible. Take Marguerite and Annabelle back to the rancho."

"You are always talking of returning, and yet you are always going off on these wild schemes. You are too hard to keep track of."

Primo looked at his old friend as if he had been caught in a truism. He smiled and nodded. Pedro was hard to fool.

"If you miss the woman," Pedro said, "Why do you not just say so?"

Primo's smile got wider.

"I miss her," he said, looking resigned.

"*Bueno* ... then return. Will she be angry that you have been gone so long? Will she make you pay?"

"*Si* ... she will definitely be angry," Primo said, but he didn't look worried about it. Quite the contrary.

———

Juan Miguel remembered that Maggie's anger often opened the door to other strong feelings. He couldn't wait to see those blue-green eyes shooting sparks. She had reason to be mad. It was late in March, and he had been gone for four months. He had missed Christmas with her and Annabelle.

His father once told him when he returned home from an adventure, he would sometimes open the door and throw his hat inside. Then he would wait to gauge his mother's reaction. If the hat stayed, he could safely enter. If it came flying back out the door, he had best wait a while longer. That was probably a good tactic for his father, but it would not work with Marguerite. She was too smart for that.

He had a smile on his face when he slowly and carefully opened the front door of the Bastrop house. He peeked inside, and, seeing no one, walked in.

He looked in the parlor, but no one was there. He opened the kitchen door and saw no one. He walked as quietly as he could up the stairs and opened the bedroom door. When she saw him, she threw down the pottery pitcher, shattering it in several pieces and leaving a puddle of soapy water on the wood planks. She picked up a shoe and threw it at him. Then she threw the other shoe. He successfully ducked both shoes but got hit on the arm with the metal brush he had given her. When she ran out of objects to throw, she picked up the quilt and threw it over his head.

Her face was red, partly from sitting for hours in the sun drawing in her journal and partly from anger. She shook in her inner core, which usually means a truth is being faced.

"I hate you," she said, barely able to utter the words with her quavering voice. "You can't just walk in here like this."

He pulled the quilt off his head and threw it on the bed. He walked over to where she stood, put his hand on her chin, and tried to give her a small kiss on the mouth. She pushed him away with both hands. He took hold of her hands and pulled her closer.

"Shhh … stop this," he said. He put his arms around her and held her until the anger subsided. When he felt it was safe to let go of her, he walked over to the door and locked it.

"We have some things to discuss, Marguerite," he said, "And I don't want anyone to disturb us."

She crossed her arms and looked like a woman who was prepared to stand her ground.

"I have nothing to say to you," she said sharply.

He reached out his hand and took hers. "Then we will use body language," he said.

"You could at least warn me so that I can get prepared. My hair is a mess."

"*Si* … your hair … it has always been so reckless, so heedless of what is expected of it."

Her hair was an emblem of her inner rebellion. How many times had the hair continued to spiral out of control despite his efforts to corral it? How many times would he have to subdue her before she was truly vanquished?

Every time, he thought he had the answer, but he did not.

He had meant to ravish her. He had been thinking about it for weeks. Instead, he looked in her eyes and saw something else—closed doors and closed windows.

"I made my way back to you once again," he said, with a lump in his throat.

She demanded, "Which do you love more, your wife and daughter or your fame?"

He was taken aback. He had not been aware he would be required to choose.

"You are the one who brought Annabelle into the world, Juan Miguel. Do you remember that? Yours were the hands that lifted her up and made her take her first breath."

This was not the reaction he had expected. This was not the discussion he had planned.

He felt shame like he had never felt before. He sat on the bed, and tears came into his eyes.

"Choose now," she said, raising her voice. "Choose one. But if you choose fame, you will never see us again."

"I choose you and Annabelle," he said. Tears were rolling down his cheeks. "I will never leave you again. Will you allow me in?"

She walked over to him and embraced him with her arms around his head.

"You have always asked so much," he said.

"And one more thing," she said, softly stroking his face. "Shave."

He felt his real self fly into his body from far away on some solitary perch in the netherworld. He didn't realize until this moment the black void he had been living in.

He wiped the tears from his face and asked, "Will you think less of me for crying?"

"No" was all she said.

He saw the road back to her stretching out before him, and it was quite long. Perhaps it was she who had been taming him all these years.

———

Captain George Neel had a burr in his saddle—the outlaw Primo and his newfound celebrity. Neel knew the outlaw's real identity, which only made things worse. Juan Miguel del Valle had played them all for fools, and now he traveled all across the country, playing them for bigger fools.

The captain's cousin, Barrett Neel, who lived in Chicago now, sent him a front-page photo of Primo from the *Chicago Evening Journal*. It showed the notorious-outlaw-turned-performer getting the keys to the city. Unbelievable, Captain Neel thought. Do they not understand law enforcement up there?

What could he do? He couldn't travel all the way to Chicago and arrest Primo in another state's jurisdiction. Besides, the governor would never stand for that. He would have to catch him here, in the state where he was wanted. So he waited for the outlaw to return.

Meanwhile, Captain Neel was getting a big break, but he didn't know it yet.

Emma Hunnicutt, who had worked in the state marriage-license office for years, was old-fashioned enough to dutifully record every name and address on every marriage certificate in a marriage log. When she came to the name Juan Miguel del Valle, it struck a chord. She asked her husband where she had heard of him. Her husband was a friend of Gregory Dingle, a Texas Ranger working out of the Austin office.

It became common knowledge in the nearby town of Bastrop that Juan Miguel's wife, Margaret, owned a house there. Dingle asked the local sheriff to keep an eye out for the outlaw, and he did.

———

The day after Juan Miguel's arrival, he sat down to Sunday dinner with Maggie, Annabelle, Beatriz, and Jose. Roberto didn't arrive on time, so they started without him.

Roberto had become a problem in the previous year, although Beatriz and Jose were not comfortable talking about it. He had found Primo's old pistol, black hat, and chaps tucked away in a trunk. He took to wearing them around the town, acting like a *bandido* but not really robbing anyone. Beatriz and Jose thought at first it was harmless playacting, but lately they wondered whether Roberto was seeing a bad crowd. He was often gone for a long time, and they had no idea where he was or what he was doing.

Beatriz had started passing the fried chicken and potatoes when Roberto walked in, glanced at the gathering, and stomped upstairs.

Jose went up to talk to him, and the Sunday diners could hear a loud argument. Soon, Jose came down, and Roberto left again, dressed in Primo's clothing and wearing Primo's chest holster and pistol.

Juan Miguel stood up.

"I should go get him and talk to him," Juan Miguel said. "He should not be going about dressed like that."

"No," Beatriz said. "Let him go. He will cool off."

Then Roberto made a fatal mistake. He rode off on Umberto.

The sheriff saw Primo, the notorious outlaw and celebrity, riding toward Bastrop. He approached with his gun drawn.

"Drop your pistol," the sheriff said. "Throw it on the ground."

Roberto put his hand on the pistol, trying to draw it from the holster, but as he did, the pistol got caught on his jacket and he twisted the barrel in the direction of the sheriff. The sheriff saw the gun pointed straight at him and discharged his gun, hitting Roberto in the shoulder.

Roberto was so stunned that he forgot to drop his weapon. Instead, he continued to point it at the sheriff as he clutched his shoulder with the other arm. The sheriff fired again and hit Roberto in the chest just above the holster. Another inch lower and he would have been saved.

The sheriff put the body of the dead young man on his

horse and led it to the house. He knocked on the door, Beatriz opened it. The sheriff announced, "I have killed Primo."

Beatriz screamed. Jose looked confused. Juan Miguel stayed out of sight. When things calmed down, Beatriz went upstairs to talk to Juan Miguel.

"He thinks he has shot you, *senor*," she said with a tear-stained face. "We have let him believe this is true. This is our gift to you, for all you have done for us."

"No, I cannot let this stand," Juan Miguel said. "He is your son. I cannot let you do this."

"We know he is our son and we will mourn him, but this is the best way to honor him. Let him do this for you, please, *senor*."

And so Margaret, as well as Jose and Beatriz, identified the body of Juan Miguel, otherwise known as Primo the outlaw. The body was released to his family for burial. His death was the biggest news story in many a decade. The sheriff who killed him became reviled in Texas and had to move to California. Even there, no one would hire him.

Senor Martin Zamora accompanied the widow and her daughter to the del Valle Rancho for the funeral.

When the people of Nuevo Laredo and the people of the del Valle Rancho saw the body in the casket, those who knew him best knew the truth—it was not Juan Miguel del Valle. They immediately recognized their friend when they met Martin Zamora.

Why did some recognize him when others did not? Because they saw his soul.

Nonetheless, they attended his funeral, and they celebrated the greatest story of their lifetimes.

Martin Zamora disappeared, and Marguerite del Valle hired a friend of his, Juan Lopez, who was part dandy and part desperado, as overseer of the del Valle Rancho. He was handsome and intelligent. More than anything else, he was kind. He soon became the darling of the ranch owner and her daughter, accompanying them on trips to South America, Cuba, and Europe. In Switzerland, a doctor successfully treated him for a chronic stomach problem.

Juan Lopez was an efficient overseer, but he sometimes disappeared for long stretches of time, leaving the rancho management to his assistant, Joshua Nash. No one knew where Lopez went.

Marguerite del Valle continued with her plant drawings and descriptions, eventually contributing them to the Texas Agricultural and Mechanical College library. Having been married three times, she never married again. Those who knew her often remarked it was fortuitous that Juan Lopez came along when he did, because he was one of the few people in the world who could handle the temperamental Marguerite.

ABOUT THE AUTHOR

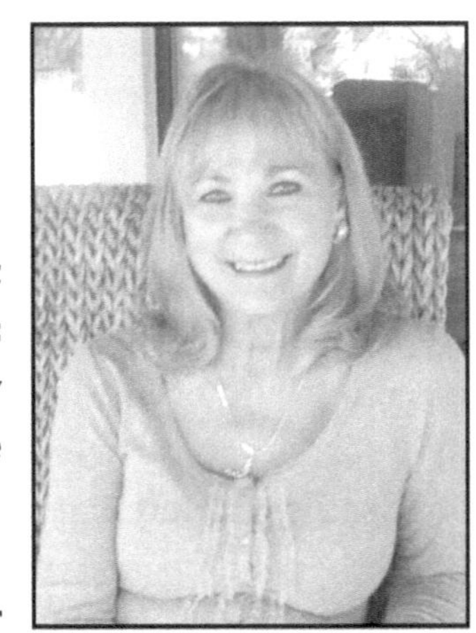

My books may be romantic historical fiction set in Texas's colorful past, but they are really about who we are and how we know who we are.

Some people discover their authentic selves through therapy, others through art and music. A fortunate few know who they are from the moment they take their first breath. I found myself through writing and studying the place where I live. Lucky for me, Texas has an amazing history, full of characters and adventure and extremes of weather and landscape. How people dealt with this place—and how they still deal with it—that's the interesting part. I am Texan through and through and part of every person, battle, tall tale, and twist of history that led us to where we are.

I grew up on the great high plains of Texas, far up on heaven's tableland, a place so flat and empty, you can see the curvature of the earth. For reasons only God knows, it's also a place that fosters an independent mindset and a creative spirit. Many great artists, writers, and musicians come from there. I aspire to be one of them. Sadly, few of them stayed.

It's just too hard. Most of us drifted south to softer, more lush climes. For me, it was Austin and that's where I've been.

I worked as a journalist for years. Then one day, life "threw a craving on me," as we say in Texas. I wanted to write fiction. I was done with reporting and editing and page layout. I had acquired useful skills, but my spirit wanted to do what my spirit wanted to do. I wanted to write historical fiction because I love history and I love stories and I love Texas.

— Anna K. Sargent

9 781938 749063